THE BURNING WOOD

David Williams

Anansi Toronto

Copyright © David Williams, 1975.

Cover design by Newton & Frank Associates Inc.

Printed by Triangle Graphic Services

Published and produced in Canada with the assistance of
   The Canada Council
   The Ontario Arts Council
   The Manitoba Arts Council
by
   The House of Anansi Press Limited
   35 Britain Street
   Toronto, Canada M5A 1R7

ISBN: 0-88784-435-9   AF 34

Canadian Shared Cataloguing in Publication Data

   Williams, David L
      The burning wood.   •

   (Anansi fiction series ; AF 34)
   ISBN 0-88784-435-9

   I. Title.

   PS8595.I4763B8   813'.5'4
   PR9199.3.W

CONTENTS

Portions of this novel have appeared in slightly altered form in *Queen's Quarterly* and *Journal of Canadian Fiction*. *The Burning Wood* is fiction, and any resemblance to actual persons living or dead is coincidental. The author would like to thank the following persons for their assistance and support:

Darlene Williams who typed and read
John Teunissen who taught
James Polk who edited.

in memory of a grandfather and a brother
and to a teacher who held *eadem, sed aliter*

1. Sun Dance

He left the barn door open the width of his hand, in case the men should talk of something besides the scours, and stepped out as quietly as he could onto the squeaking snow. It was dusky in the corridor between the balestacks, though sheltered, unexposed; he seemed to take comfort from the haybales themselves, tight-pressed in their walls above him and smelling, even to a nose scoured by the cold, remotely of summer. He let his feet search out their steps, the feet perhaps of David in the cave at Engedi, approaching now so carefully, carefully, to cut the skirt of the sleeping king's robe. Though he knew, really, that it was because he did not want to quit the cover of the hay. It was as if someone looked down and out at him, not like in a mirror though with a face quite as familiar, from inside the bristling stack. He did not want to go out yet into the open stackyard, thereupon to be set adrift and alone on a cold pond of light. Besides, he was still straining to hear the voices from the barn amidst the singing round of the milk. *David's voice followed the king from the cave, and Saul, when he knew the truth, wept.*

He had to look at once at the house around the corner, resting his cheek on the stubble of a bale-end.

Auntie Bee said A chip off the old block. It's too bad they couldn't have split the wood without chips, so long as they'd decided to chop. She said Why don't you go out and play and leave the little ones in peace. Why don't you go someplace where you don't spoil everything by us having to look at you. She said it on the stairway, with the rest of the women downstairs helping Grandma in the kitchen.

When she had first come upstairs she said, "Take the dish, Joel. Grandma wants you to pass around the candy."

"I don't want to," Joel said. He was building a castle drawbridge on the bedroom linoleum. It was with the Meccano

1

set Grandpa had given him. They were all helping him, Susan and Michael and Janie and Lizzie too. "Can't Joshua do it?"

"It's not his birthday," Auntie Bee said. "You're the only one here who has a birthday with Grandpa. Besides, Grandpa doesn't want him to touch his candy again. He's a thief."

He was left to say it then, first waiting for the others, on his own behalf. "I never stole Grandpa's candy. Grandma told me to pass it around. It wasn't stole — we all had some, didn't we."

His sister Janie was nodding.

Auntie Bee said, "You did so steal. Grandpa found the empty bag on the radio. You know how much Grandpa likes his humbugs. To do a thing like that to him on his birthday."

Joel said, "We didn't know. He told us Grandma sent them up."

"She did," he said, beginning to despair. "She told me they were in the radio cabinet."

"She did not," Auntie Bee said. "She never said a word when Grandpa asked who took them. So it was only you. And here's you, a ten-year-old, asking little ones to share your guilt. You shouldn't be allowed to play with them. Here Joel, take the dish. These ones are barley sugars." She held up an unwrapped orange egg, then put it in her mouth. "Mmmm, Joel, good. Take the dish and pass it around."

Joel was fastening the bridge to the castle wall.

"We're full," he said. "We had enough."

"I could pass them downstairs," Joshua said without hope. "I don't mind not helping to finish the bridge."

"You'll do no such thing," she said. "Spoiling Grandpa's and Joel's birthday party. You'll let worse enough alone."

As soon as she had gotten between him and the door, she set the candy dish down on a chair beside the bed.

"I'll leave it here, Joel," she said. "Don't any of the rest of you touch it unless Joel passes it."

A chip off the old block, she said. You're just like they say he was. Why don't you run away to the Indians too and leave us here in peace.

In the oven-warm kitchen, Joshua made his way round his mother's eyes. He said, "Grandma, you told me awhile ago to pass the candies, didn't you. When you were down cellar looking for pickles, you told me where they were when I asked and you said to pass them, didn't you."

Grandma was standing at the cupboard, grating cabbage for the salad. Her thin arm jittered from the elbow like a drive belt between the tractor and chopper. Her crinkled cheeks were drawn in with the effort; her hair whirled in dust devils about her face.

"What's that?" she said, the stone bowl now filled with cabbage shreds. She was reaching about distractedly for another bowl.

"Here, let me help," Auntie Bee said serenely, soothingly.

"The candies," he said. "Did Grandpa think I stole them?"

Auntie Carolyn looked in sympathy at him. She was peeling potatoes with his mother at the table. The slop pail stood between them, the cupboard door beneath the sink still open, exposing its darkness. Auntie Carolyn was as blond as his mother. They looked like sisters, though they were not. Both their families had emigrated from a town in Minnesota.

"I don't know," Grandma said. "I think he said so." She was changing hands to grate to the other side. "Why don't you ask your Auntie Bee? You talked to him, didn't you, Bee?"

"But you said to pass them. You said they were in the radio cabinet."

"Did I?" Grandma said, her frail arm jittering, intent over the bowl once more. "It must have slipped my mind. Why don't you ask your grandfather?" Her voice was panting with the motion. "He's out with the men doing chores."

"No one is saying he really stole it," Auntie Bee said. "He passed them around to the children. They all said they got. So it's really only Grandpa he has to make it up to."

"Joshua," his mother said, looking at him over the bowl of skinned potatoes with her eyes already red. "How could you? How could you do it?"

I couldn't have, he thought, *I'm sure I couldn't, not without some kind of help from Auntie Bee. Bee nothing, his father always said. It's foolhardy to call that bite a bee-sting — more like a cut from a battle-axe. Or has this whole fam-damily lost its sense? Bees are good for something, even if they do sting sometimes. Because there's more than a drop of honey somewhere for every sting, you can count on it. But that one give honey? On the day we can expect strawberry jam from a spider. Only spiders are skinny. Nope, I still say Auntie Battle-axe is the name should cut nearer to the bone. Though how you get to the bone through all that fat —*

3

"Richard," his mother would say, but with her voice helpless, only her eyes sending their mute appeal down the table, "please don't teach them to hate anyone, least of all their own aunt."

"Why not? She hates them. She says worse than that right to them, for crying out loud."

It looked for a moment as if his mother would cry out loud. Then she would say softly, "We never hear it, except from them. You know that. She hides her hate from everyone but them. And unless we teach them in private to be merciful, how will they be able in the last day to expect mercy for themselves?"

"Hah," his father would say, looking deliberately away at the stove, acting as if she had had to leave the room, only the heat of his vehemence spreading across the table, keeping supper warm. "What mercy can they expect from her? We know how she buzzes in my folk's ear the minute there's a bad word to be said about either of them. And we've heard too often how she treats Joshua when nobody's around. Don't you see how she acts as if she can prevent him yet from being the first grandchild? Disqualify him, maybe, because of how he looks?"

His mother's voice came, it seemed, from off the wall. " 'Blessed are the peacemakers,' " she would say, and Joshua could not keep his eyes down from the plaque above the stove, following the words in brown lettering though he knew them by heart, " 'for they shall be called the children of God.' Isn't it better, Richard, to remain as little children? Even if we do have to suffer for it sometimes? I know in my heart I'm a child of God. Maybe she is too. After all, we don't know her heart. Only God knows that."

His father would swing round, then, his face printed with bitterness.

"We know her heart well enough, Helga, or have you lost your sense? Nobody needs God to describe her heart after Joshua was born first, with them married more than two years already, and her running to my folks to try to stop us from using the name, like it was reserved for them. As if it was Owen's brother and no one else's who'd died, and she was going to shut us out from even that. 'Blessed are they that mourn,' you say? 'Blessed are the meek for they shall inherit the earth,' I'd say. Six whole feet of it."

"Richard," his mother would say in a voice that quavered with tears. "How can I bring them up right when you set an example

4

like that? Isn't it our Christian duty to be the light of the world?"

I'm going to let it shine, Auntie Bee said. That's the name of the chorus we're going to learn today. The words go like this: Hide it under a bushel, no! I'm going to let it shine! Hide it under a bushel, no! I'm going to let it shine, let it shine, let it shine, let it shine, let it shine. The next verse starts, Don't let Satan snuff it out, I'm going to let it shine, Don't let Satan snuff it out, and then you repeat it like before. The last verse begins, Let it shine till Jesus comes, and you go through it the same way, only with the new starting line. Now let's sing it, and you old folks at the back help these little children, because some of them are going to have to go home from Sunday School today with no one there to help them shine.

The light was on in the kitchen now, he could see Grandma at the window, though it was nearing sunset. Beyond the house, the sun was mixing like an egg yolk through the trees. It spread out slowly over the snow. At the last instant, before the yolk dripped away, the snow caught fire. Tongues of flame licked up the butter icing.

They could not see the flames from their lawn on the hilltop two miles away. But the black smoke billowed out above Grandpa's bush and stood like a column supporting the declining afternoon. They watched it, wondering at first, in the burning heat of the sun, how anyone could want to set fire to something today.

"Maybe he's burning out the underbrush between the maple trees," Joshua said.

"More likely he's honked the horn once too often waiting for Grandma," his mother said, "and she's set fire to the house."

"Aw, Mom, be serious," he said.

"Perhaps the cows were playing with matches in the barn?" she said. "Lighting cattails soaked in gasoline, like you and Joel were doing last Saturday? Is that serious enough?"

"Aw, you don't have to remind me. You didn't get a licking."

"I know," she said. "Have a strawberry."

"Mom," Janie said. "He had four."

"Have one yourself," she said, moving aside her hand in the bowl where strawberries and stems still floated together.

"How long is it," Joshua said, "till rodeo time?"

"Oh, a couple of hours, I guess."

"Tell us again," Janie said, stemming her strawberry. "Do men really ride cows?"

5

"Bulls, stupid," Joshua said. "Cows are for girls."

"Joshua, don't talk that way to your sister. I'm not sure, dear. This is just a little rodeo. Not like the one I saw with Daddy once in Medicine Hat."

"You were sure lucky," Joshua said. "To go so far as Alberta. Nothing exciting comes to dumb old Saskatchewan."

"There's not much money any more to go places, Joshua. Not with your doctor bills and so much medicine. But there's enough to take us to Nisooskan."

"Yeah, a whole eight miles." Though he had to admit to himself no matter how he yearned to go away, that he'd been thinking all day long of the rodeo. Horses came thundering down the rows of corn after little calves, sometimes so near he had to drop the hoe, and men burst out of chutes on bucking bulls that tore up the pasture.

"Be grateful, Joshua," his mother said. "Your father works so hard and gets so little for himself."

"I know," he said. "I just wish it all didn't fall on my head."

"Speaking of which, my beauty, me boy, we've got to rub you with some more of that new ointment when we've finished cleaning these strawberries."

"Uggh," Janie said. "Phewie. That stuff smells like the henhouse does."

"Don't you feel bad," Joshua said, "or I'll stick your head in the henhouse stuff."

"There's too much smoke over there," his mother said, looking away from the lake-end to the east. "I sure hope there's nothing wrong at Grandpa's or Uncle Glen's."

It's one of the houses or else the barn is on fire, his father said. He had left the tractor right beside the house. His face was black with dirt. We've got to get over there.

When they drove into the yard, the high barn roof was just collapsing. Through the windshield they could see the timbers fall soundlessly down, then inward, as the walls went. The barn-red flames whirled and danced higher than the sun. The sky rained sparks. A crowd of people fell back in the heat. Then they could hear the snapping tongues and hoarse breath of the fire.

"Oh, he's lost, he's lost!" Auntie Bee was shrieking. She was squatting down as if someone had kicked her in the stomach. "My baby, my poor little baby!"

6

Uncle Owen held her, as much as he could, from behind.

Grandpa's hair was singed, his shirt stubbed with burn-holes. His face looked baked, like it did the time he and Grandma wintered in Florida.

"He's not in there," he said clearly. "I'm sure he's not. Have faith, Bee. Trust God."

Grandma and Auntie Carolyn were crying.

"Don't bother bucketing the barn any more," Grandpa said to the chain of men reaching back to the well. "Help the ones wetting down the houses and the granaries."

"What is it?" Joshua's father said. "Dad, what's happened here?"

"Who knows for sure?" Grandpa was standing upright with the heap of fallen timbers behind him. His face was peaceful in the midst of tumult. "It's plain the barn caught on fire. Where have you been 'til now? Didn't you see it before?"

"I was working that field at the foot of the hill. I couldn't see 'til I got out from the slope."

"Then no matter. Glen got in from the field in time to wet down the shingles on the houses. We've had plenty of help since then. It's Joel, as you can see, that we've been worried about. We think he might have started the fire."

Auntie Bee, who had not stopped moaning, stood up and cried aloud, "My baby! My poor little baby!"

They found him that night, after the barn, the haystack, and chicken house were floating in a pool of embers, at home in the garage. He had run the mile through a field of barley, missing everyone on the road, and had hidden in the truck. On an impulse, Uncle Owen opened the truck door when he put the car away. Joel was asleep on the seat. The minute Grandpa heard the good news, he sent the Mountie from Nisooskan and the fire inspector from Melfort home who were waiting to dig through the coals.

There wasn't another rodeo in Nisooskan. Grandpa rebuilt the barn inside the old foundations. He did not build a gabled loft like the one that had rounded off his father's barn. So there was no room now to swing on a rope through the hay. Nor did the swallows return, save for four or five. Auntie Bee made it very clear to Grandpa where the torches had come from. She said Joshua had been switched for it right before Joel's eyes. Richard Cardiff said he knew another kid who could stand a licking for it, and that kid lived not more than a mile away. But Joel, who had been given up for dead and had suffered more than enough, was only scolded. Grandpa, who was a little stiff for a time over the loss of his barnyard, could not be stern too long with a boy for whom he had risked his life. He sometimes asked Joshua, though, if he were teaching the other kids to play with cattails.

And David cried out to Saul, saying, Wherefore does my lord pursue his servant? for what have I done? or what evil is in my hand?

Joshua squealed the barn door back on its frost-pinched track. The smell of cows and steaming manure washed onto his cold skin. Uncle Owen stood at the edge of the farthest stall, one hand on a harness post. The harness above him was dull with dust. Joshua's father leaned against the door opposite, looking into the stall where Owen stood. Across the runway, Uncle Glen sat milking, his cheek flanking the red hide of a cow. Several cats sat in a crescent watching him. When the door rolled shut, Uncle Glen looked back. They looked at one another for a moment, man and boy, and then Uncle Glen winked. He raised a teat from the cow and squirted milk at the row of cats. It was above their heads and a fluffy grey stood up, clawing at it. It grinned horribly, licking at the milk, and its whiskers dripped ivory. Joshua laughed and Grandpa's voice stopped. His father looked up; Uncle Owen looked back.

"Joshua?" Grandpa said. Both milk pails were silent.

"Yes Grandpa?" He got to where he could see in. Grandpa's face was eclipsed by the shadow from the stall.

"I'm glad you chose to face me. You ducked through here so quickly before, I wasn't sure if you were sneaking off by yourself again." Grandpa's voice was gentle but distant.

Saul, when he knew, wept.

"I wasn't sneaking, Grandpa. I never stole those candies. Grandma said to take them. She said where they were and she said to be sure and pass them. Only she doesn't remember now."

"If he took them without permission," his father said, "he'll get a licking." He stood up from leaning against the door. His black suit coat showed beneath his parka waist.

Grandpa did not speak for a moment. The milk was singing in both pails again.

"I'd rather you left him entirely to me, Richard."

8

The milk song rose and fell.

"Come here, Joshua. I can't see you out there."

Grandpa's eyes, so green and meadow-merry, were troubled now, filled with a strange regret, like they were so often when they happened to light on him.

"Those humbugs weren't yours to take," he said, "any more than they were Grandma's to give, if she did. They were part of a birthday present from your Auntie Bee."

Joshua watched the milk foam up in the pail.

"I didn't mean at all to take your birthday present. We all wanted candy and you were talking in the sun porch. Grandma was alone in the basement so I went to her. I didn't think they were only yours."

Saul wept.

For an instant Grandpa's face held back too much sorrow. The cow kicked slightly, touching the pail. She lifted her head out of the manger and looked around, munching. Bits of chop sifted from her side-working jaws.

"Well then," Grandpa said, "if you're going to argue, I'd like you to do something for me. When we come with the milk, I want you to go into our bedroom and I want you to take, without anybody noticing you, a bag of humbugs from the top right-hand dresser drawer. Hide them out in your Dad's car and when you get home tonight, I want you to eat them or share them as you like, only when you do, do it with the understanding that I said you could. I'd have you know that you must not take from another man what is rightfully his, unless he should first give it to you. You won't be too stubborn to do that for me, will you?"

"That's a funny way to skin a cat," Uncle Owen said. "Wouldn't it be better to take his pants down and snip his little water off?"

"Talk like a grownup, Owen," Grandpa said. "You got out of Flying School, didn't you?"

Uncle Owen looked like he would say something; then he decided against it.

"Tell Josh about the papers you signed, Dad," Uncle Glen said from across the way. "I'm sure he'd like to hear what else you're giving away on your birthday. It isn't all just humbug, you know," he said, grinning at Joshua. He winked, as if they, and not the men, shared a secret.

9

"I guess I really ought to," Grandpa said slowly. "Since he decided to face me. He'll find out soon enough anyway. But will you promise me a couple of things, Joshua? Will you take those candies and do like I asked? Will you remember that you've no right to another man's goods, unless he wants you to share them with him? That you can take them, but you'll never possess them without his permission?"

Joshua nodded, shame and expectancy now seeming to compose a wave, trough and crest, upon which his head bobbed helplessly.

"All right then," Grandpa said kindly, "you shall hear the rest, but you must promise not to say anything until I announce it in church. Is that a deal?"

The head was still tossing up and down.

"I bought a quarter-section at the far lake-end," Grandpa said. "We're going to build a Bible Camp in the woods along the shore."

A chip off the old block, she said. Why don't you run away to the Indians too?

It was all he could think of to say.

"Is it going to be near the Reservation? Will the Indians be there?"

He didn't necessarily want them to be.

Grandpa looked so strangely at him.

"What did I say to you?" he said to the men. "I knew I shouldn't buy there, I knew it was too near. That the first thing he should think of isn't Camp, but Indians, proves it. I knew we should go someplace else. But it was the only place on the lake for sale, so if not there, where?"

"It would have been all right sixteen years ago," Joshua's father said. His face looked like an abandoned house. "If we had had a Camp, even a tent Camp, on that Reservation sixteen years ago, we would have Josh still playing his horn today. If not with us, in India. But he'd be home sometimes on furlough."

"I didn't want him going out to those Indians," Grandpa said. "I didn't want him going to the ones at Ft. a la Corne, either. I only ever wanted him to go to India. How could I know God would call him home before he went out? You can't blame me for that, Richard. It's not fair to me. You've never learned to accept God's will in his death."

10

Grandpa's face was filled with the same sorrow and regret. But his eyes held Richard's steadily.

Joshua's father looked away, over Glen's cow to the wall opposite.

"If he'd just gone out here, like he wanted, like he said God was calling him to do. Instead of asking the C.S.S.M. into Ft. a la Corne. The river's no place for a camp. It's no place to swim in. We could have guessed what would happen."

Joshua knew, without having to remember, what had happened. Uncle Josh was drowned in the River. It happened on the last Saturday of Camp. There would have been no swimming on Sunday, the closing day. A Cree camper, in his 'teens already, who was old enough to know better, went deliberately beyond the roped-in swimming area. He was rushed away so quickly by the current that it was a miracle anyone could swim out to him. When Uncle Josh grabbed him, the boy climbed in terror all over him. They could see from the shore Uncle Josh trying to get out from under him, trying at the last to save himself as well as the boy. By the time a canoe got to where they struggled, Uncle Josh was gone beneath the water. That muddy water, his father once said, filling the throat which had always blown a trumpet so clean.

"I didn't want him going to any Cree," Grandpa said. "You know that. But he said it was of God. I had to honour that. I only asked him not to go where it was no use already. Those Indians on Lac Jardin were so corrupted. But you know that as well as I do, I shouldn't have to say it any more. We've had proof enough for a lifetime in this family."

"We might still have had him, that's all I know," Joshua's father said. He was looking away as dumbly as the cow in the stall.

"About as surely as we might still have had my father," Grandpa said. "I didn't — and I don't — ever want one of us going out there again. Joshua must not go running to them just because we happen to put the Bible Camp in the wrong place. You can't mean it about the Indians, can you, Joshua? You know there's only death out there. If not for your body, for your soul. You know that, don't you?"

Grandpa looked so strangely at him.

He stopped stock-still and looked at him, coming out of the doctor's office, as if he were seeing him for the first time, though Joshua knew he had been looking that way and not knowing it for

11

months now, probably longer. Early, very early that Remembrance Day, Grandpa had picked them up in the new Oldsmobile. It was blue, shiny blue, and smelled so new inside. They were all going along, even if the stores in Regina would be closed. Janie had said it wasn't fair that she couldn't stay and see the specialist too. It wasn't fair that Joshua was going to get to stay alone in a hotel for two nights with Grandpa in the city. Grandma and Mom and Janie sat in the back seat. They were sleeping now. Joshua sat between Grandpa and his father. Grandpa drove. His father had on his blue Air Force suit. The stars were bright above them, as much as they could see through the windshield. The car lights made a tunnel through the dark.

"I followed a star for half an hour one time," his father said. "I thought it was our Squadron Leader but it was a star. I couldn't figure out why he was keeping his wings so steady. Usually he would lead us quite a chase when we flew in formation. I told him after I got down and they all came in it was only because I thought he was such a steady pilot that I would fix my sights on a star."

Grandpa looked down at Joshua, both his hands firm and quiet on the steering wheel.

"You didn't know your Dad was so star-struck, did you?"

Joshua laughed. He was thinking of a joke somewhat similar, though he hadn't dared to say it. Once he had ridden in an airplane which his father flew at Melfort, and Uncle Glen, who was in the back seat, had made some crack or other, just in fun. Richard Cardiff didn't say anything, but even from behind, it was plain he didn't like it. Flying was a thing of beauty, he said later to Joshua, and one should never joke about something beautiful if it was true and good. Grandpa had paid for the plane that time in Melfort, and he had laughed at Glen's remark. Apparently he thought, even now, he could afford to joke.

Joshua felt guilty, though, about having laughed. He wanted to say something to make it up to his father.

"Are you going to march around the Cenotaph, Dad? They won't be making speeches all the time? I'd like it if you marched."

Richard Cardiff was quiet for a moment.

"I'm not going to fly around it, that's for sure," he said finally, looking out his window. "Those days are gone for good."

"I remember," Grandpa said, "how crazy you were to be gone after Owen joined up. You talked as if he were out in search of the

12

Holy Grail, and you were afraid he might find it."

"Don't forget," Richard Cardiff said, "that I stayed home two weeks longer that fall to overhaul the tractor for the spring. You never did get used to motors, though there wasn't a better man around for horses."

"It seems like a man remembers mostly what he wants to. Anyway, I was recalling what I thought would be a lesson to Joshua — that most boys want to run off too soon, and mostly, they are tempted to run off for the wrong —"

"What I did then was for the right reasons, unless you mean to say that Hitler was right."

"I wasn't talking about you; I said 'mostly,' if you'll remember. Mostly, I was going to say, young men are in a hurry to get into things that in the long-run will be to their det—"

"Well flying wasn't, and if he wants to do that, more power to him."

They were out on the wide plain before Watson. Headlights came like a spitfire up the road at them. Grandpa slowed so they wouldn't meet on the narrow wooden bridge. The sports car flashed past them, its low beams contending with the darkness.

"You know, Richard, I often had the feeling you were looking for an easy way to die, to be done with sorrow and remembering, only you knew it was wrong. I prayed that that would keep you, and maybe it did. But it's strange — your brother's death was hard, so hard to bear, because he knew it was right. He never deserved to die, he was so unlike your grandfather. That's what made it so hard, he wasn't in the wrong and still he had to die. Do you know, though, what he told me one time? It was the spring of the year he was to die, and I don't know if he had a premonition or what, and he said suddenly he might never return to us, not in this life at least, only it wouldn't matter because — I think these were the words — 'Only one life, 'twill soon be past/Only what's done for Christ will last.' He really meant it too. He was that way, wasn't he?"

Joshua heard the breathing from the back seat, deep and regular. He worried that they were all asleep.

"I know it was that kind of hope offered me, after my dad was killed, that kept me from madness, probably worse. I felt it so terribly, how he'd left me nothing to live by, and nothing to live for, not at all like Josh was going to do for you and Joshua here, for all of the family."

Grandma spoke from the back.

"My, isn't it true, though? I don't know how folks live without something like that to give them strength. I don't know what we'd have ever done. But it's Him we really need to give us the strength. Don't you think so, Helga? It's not works of righteousness that we have done, but according to His mercy He saved us?"

"Yes," Joshua's mother said. "Yes, it says so in the Bible, doesn't it? I know Richard thinks so too."

"Sure," Joshua's father said, looking out and up at the stars again, as if he wished he could go out to them. "There was never anything in this uniform as good as him. And I don't suppose there ever will be again."

No one said anything for a long time after that. Something in his voice forbade it.

The early fuss of the setting out had dwindled now into a steady unrolling of the road beneath their headlights. There was nothing to look at, nothing to do, and nothing any more to listen to, so Joshua settled down again into the letting-go of sleep. The blue worsted of his father's tunic did not look as inviting as Grandpa's woolly suit. He rested his cheek lightly against the brown material, feeling Grandpa turn a little to make them both more comfortable, and then the last he remembered was the hairy cloth, scratchy and warm, surrounding the side of his head.

The sun was rising when he woke up. They were driving right into it. Then the road fell away, the car with it, on its run into the valley. Grandpa pumped the brakes, easing them down and around the first turn. Away from the glare of the sun, Joshua could see the water. It was dark blue, there was no ice in it, and the snow was patchy on the side of the bare, far hills.

"Qu'Appelle?" he said, squinting into the whitening sun.

"Qu'Appelle, qu'appelle," his father said, "and back the waters answered."

Then they were running out along the valley floor, the hills tumbling right down above them, and ahead was the bridge across the little neck of water. At the bottom of the farther slope, a semi-trailer faced them from the opposite lane. It appeared to be stopped. A figure skipped in the road beside it. Grandpa was slowing the car to pass by.

"Dear Lord," he said. "Somebody's cut his head nearly off."

It was a woman by the body and dress. Her head dangled back, cut almost through the middle of the neck. Blood cascaded down her front.

"Stay in the car," Joshua's father said. He was out and running before they were stopped. Grandpa followed. Joshua got out and sidled toward the terrible thing. It danced like a puppet. Bits of blood spattered the air, the pavement. His father took the shoulders from behind. The body flapped and jerked like a chicken off the chopping block. The hole in the throat bubbled blood and air. Joshua couldn't look any more.

Between the truck wheels he could see the smashed front of the car, a little sports car. It went completely under the rear of the trailer, sliced off its top on a crossbrace. A body was mashed down over the steering wheel. The road up the hill was marked off with flares. Out across the valley, the road ran blindly past the sun.

"Get some blankets," his father said.

Grandpa went.

The woman lay in the road. Her legs twitched horribly beneath her coat.

Grandpa came back.

"Can we move her, put her in the car maybe, and take her to the hospital?"

Black clots vomited out of the slice across her neck.

"It's no use," his father said. "Joshua, I told you to stay in the car."

The legs stopped twitching, slowly relaxing. Joshua's father let go of the shoulders almost tenderly. There was blood bright red against the blue of his suit.

"How bloody awful," he said. "What a horrible way to die. What hell it must have been."

"So awful," Grandpa said. "So terribly awful. We've got to bring a doctor at least."

The doctor followed him into the ante-room.

There doesn't appear to be anything wrong, medically speaking, with your grandson, he said. Neurologically, he checks out fine. And the dermatologist says he can't find anything up top would seem at all out of the ordinary. It's very odd — he seems so fit in every other way. There's nothing else you might know from his history which could help us?

You were told of the fever he had with the mumps? Grandpa said.

15

The doctors in Melfort thought it had something to do with it.

It could. Mumps is a funny thing, you know. If you contract it after you've grown up, it can make you sterile. Of course, he's too young to have it affect him that way. But mumps . . . I don't know . . . it's hardly anything to go on. Not yet, at least, with what we know at present. What about his family history? Obviously he doesn't inherit it from you, unless recessively. Are there signs of it in his father, or on his mother's side of the family?

My father, Grandpa said, his eyes going from flat-warm-green to high and domed like the sky at night. Of course. My father.

He went bald as a boy? Were there mumps as well in his case?

It's a shame there weren't. He was grown up. It was Indian women, years of them. He went bald, as bald as a billiard ball, shortly before they killed him.

I see, the doctor said. Would you like to go in the other room to talk?

After their cold walk back to the hotel, Grandpa took him to the restaurant for some hot chocolate.

Have you read any good books lately? he said. He was looking yet with those high, distant eyes at him, though trying now to come near again, just the reverse of before when his eyes looked merry as a pasture, with the frozen stars only beginning to show through.

I read one of Dad's books about the war. And some Hardy Boy books. But the best was Huckleberry Finn, *I think. That was really good, Grandpa. Did you read it when you were a boy?*

Clemens wasn't a very good man, Grandpa said, stirring his hot chocolate as if the cup were all his care. He's fine to read about the injustices to slaves, but he never missed a chance to rail against God. Remember how he preferred to send Huck to hell than back to Sunday School? If he'd known your great-grandfather, he wouldn't have scoffed like that at hell.

At the Bible Society bookstore, there were other adventure stories. Grandpa bought him three titles for a dollar of the Andy Arliss series. Andy Arliss was the son of missionaries to Mexico. In each book he went to a different country to assist his missionary relatives and friends. The three books Grandpa and he picked out forwarded Andy from Nicaragua to Nigeria to Nepal. In each one, he helped to rescue somebody from loss of life or limb and then he stayed to help win souls to Jesus Christ.

Uncle Glen stood up from milking his cow. He hung his stool

on the post.

"Man, I find this a bit confusing," he said. He was smiling a little. "I've always heard we're supposed to preach the gospel in every land and to every nation. But you seem to say we're not. Is it because we're not a nation, nobody would think it of us yet, including us ourselves, that we shouldn't start at home?"

Grandpa's eyes came near and quiet, like the inside of the church.

"You know I don't think that, Glen. Of course the mission field starts at home." His voice was gentle, but with strength in it. "I know that Josh's going among the Cree brought some of them to Christ. It took his death to teach me that. That's why I've tried to give to home missions too, as much as I could. Richard, you've done my income tax every year since you've been back. Have I been giving a fair share at home or not?"

Joshua's father thought about it.

"Three hundred a year to the Northern Canada Evangelical Mission. A hundred to—"

"I've been doing that," Grandpa said, "every year that I had money since Josh died. I don't want his work to end, either, with his life."

"Our own Indians on Lac Jardin come closer to home, though, don't they? I mean, we could almost run them into the church on their way to the pub. You've heard about the way they used to run buffalo on a hunt? Put them into a converging alleyway and stampede them over a cliff. Or down a pit, maybe, onto sharp stakes. Except that we could have the church there at the end—"

Grandpa was standing up now too. His face looked like a woodcut of earnestness, the capital E weighty and serious.

"We must not go among them, Glen, for the same reason that Paul refused to go to the Corinthians. For exactly the same reason. Because a little leaven leaveneth the whole lump. Only the Cree refused, they absolutely refused, to purify their lump. Not even the Evangelical Mission could minister to them after my father died. They were blissfully heathen. So to us they are dangerous — eternally dangerous — like he always was. A mad Welsher and savage Indians, they make the worst possible sort of pagan. I maintain that no one with his blood had better go near them. We can't, we just can't, afford to lose any more of us."

Grandpa's face was rigid with earnestness, yet withal so easy and winning, so absolutely collected and logical. Only his body spoke differently, his trunk appearing to construe his head as a separate thing. The set of his knees like branches embracing the wind, the fitful clench-unclench of fingers rousing milk to slop in the pail, the rise of shoulders square against his jaw, all left his visage floating in an alien, even hostile, element, with, perhaps, just a hint of violence in it.

"Well, then," Uncle Glen said, "I guess there's only the cliffs left to us."

While the men were down cellar separating the milk, Joshua could feel Grandpa's eyes searching through the floor boards. He closed the bedroom door onto the kitchen, tiptoed to the dresser. The humbugs were where Grandpa said they would be. Through the cellophane package they gleamed like lumps of silver.

O Lord, if I have done this; if there be iniquity in my hands; if I have rewarded evil unto him that was at peace with me, let the enemy persecute my soul and take it.

When Grandpa came back from feeding the calves, Auntie Bee was waiting for him. Her hands were folded in front of her in the posture of prayer.

"Did the calfies enjoy their supper, Grandpa?" She was licking her lips like a mother coaxing a child to eat. "Did they drink it all up?" She laughed in short stutters at everything she said. The laugh never made you want to laugh with it.

"Did they ever," Grandpa said. "Even the roan cow's calf has a white face now."

"Grandma's got such a lovely supper prepared for us folks too." She laughed again, but with her lips pressed tight together. Her eyes looked always like they waited, or hunted, for something. "The turkey will soon be ready. But first could you give Joel a haircut? It's so long and curly — I want him to be just spruce for both your birthdays. Would you mind? I know you're tired. Maybe I shouldn't have said anything. You shouldn't have to work any more on your birthday."

"Why not, Bee? You know how young I feel as long as I'm working. It's these winters start to make a man feel old. Send Joel out to the sunporch. I'll get out of these coveralls and just spruce up a bit myself."

Auntie Bee's voice was high and crooning now.

"You're not getting any older, Grandpa. Not you. I don't know that winter has ever fazed you less. You look young enough to have a boy Joel's age. Everybody says he looks like you. He even has the same head of hair as you, when it's trimmed."

"Then we'll have to trim it, won't we?" Grandpa said, his eyes avoiding Joshua's.

Joel sat on a stool in the middle of the sun porch, crying and crying. He kept pulling his head away from the clippers, his face wet and red.

"Hold still, Joel," Grandpa said. "I'm not going to cut your head off."

Uncle Owen looked up from the chesterfield, over top of *The Saturday Evening Post.*

"Hey kid, why can't you be more like Joshua? He never cries over anything. Why can't you try it for a change?"

Everyone sat down finally at the big table set in the living room. Grandpa sat at one end, in the corner by the upstairs door. Grandma sat on a stacking stool by the kitchen door. At once the family sang, without any prompting. The room sounded as if the morning stars sang together, voices beginning to lose themselves, some more than others:

> *Praise God from whom all blessings flow*
> *Praise Him all creatures here below*
> *Praise Him above ye heavenly host*
> *Praise Father, Son, and Holy Ghost.*

The A-men swooped, then up and away, like a winged formation.

Then the congregation rose to sing 'A Mighty Fortress is Our God.'

After the service was over, Reverend Haagshed said, "Brother Bran Cardiff has requested that the men stay for some new church business. That's all the men, not just the deacons. Everyone else is dismissed."

Joshua did not go out into the porch, or downstairs where the kids were going. He stayed at the back of the church, pretending to scan the missionary board, but he was looking sidelong, as much as he dared, at the front where the men sat shoulder to shoulder. Grandpa was telling, hurriedly and a little embarrassedly, about the woodland along the lake. It was paid for, he said, and he hoped the members would see fit to found a camp upon it, in the name of the Lacjardin Gospel Assembly. He sat down quickly, between Richard and Owen.

"It's an answer to prayer," Reverend Haagshed said. "Do we even need to vote on it?"

Mr. Hosea Ely stood up. His manner was aloof and superior. He had more sons on his quarter section than other noticeable assets.

"I'll not address the question," he said in an accent so much more elegant than his cheap black Sunday suit. "I'll simply thank Mr. Cardiff, on my sons' behalf, for his generosity. Though I wonder, Bran, if you'll be financing as well hired help for those of us who need our children at home. Summer camps are wonderful for those whose circumstances will permit it, but advertising them in front of others, I think, creates a grave injustice."

"Oh come on, Hosea," Mr. McGillvary said. "You can afford to let your boys go for a change." Usually Mr. McGillvary spoke so slowly everyone forgot what he said. But this time he was excited. "Bran always did while his boys were growing up, and look how the Lord prospered him."

"The thing I'd like to know," a man who turned around grinning said, "is what makes Bran so generous with everybody. I can afford to send my kids to Camp, that's for sure, and yet here I am, worried that he'll help Hosea there and I won't be able to pass his means test. What makes you do it Bran? You'd almost think you were making up for a wicked youth."

"I am," Grandpa said. "My dad was a wicked youth. I give what I can, that's all."

Everyone must have thought how each year-end, Grandpa wrote the cheque to cover the Gospel Assembly's debt. Last year, Joshua's father said, it was in the neighborhood of seven hundred dollars.

"Well then," Reverend Haagshed said, "what we need now is an election of officers."

It turned out that Uncle Owen was elected, after Grandpa declined the nomination, Chairman, Joshua's father the Treasurer.

"Why is it," Richard Cardiff said, "that I always get elected Treasurer to these things?"

"Because," Reverend Haagshed said, "you're so close with your money, Brother Cardiff. We know you won't be wasting ours."

Everyone laughed a little. Joshua's father sat up straighter. The back of his neck turned red, dull red like a stovepipe.

Reverend Haagshed was graduated from the same Bible School as Uncle Josh. Grandpa had heard him, two years ago at the Bible School's Fall Missionary Conference, addressing young people. When the pastorate at Lacjardin opened up, he wrote in the name of the Assembly, offering personally to guarantee his salary.

At Lacjardin, Reverend Haagshed preached his first sermon from Ecclesiastes chapter twelve. In ringing tones, he admonished for forty minutes the congregation to remember their creator in the days of their youth, and that morning, almost every youth in church discovered the Song of Solomon. After service, Joshua listened to some of the girls giggle while Jimmy McGillvary touched them in turn with his eyes, saying in his cracked voice, "Thy two breasts are like two young roes that are twins, which feed among the lilies."

The following Sunday, Reverend Haagshed preached about the terrible realities of hell, reserved forever unto them who have transgressed against the Lord, for their worm shall not die, neither shall their fire be quenched. He read from Psalm 51, and by the time he was through emphasizing all the verbs — Wash, Purge me, Make me to hear joy, Create in me, Cast me not away, Restore unto me, Deliver me — there were many broken and contrite hearts in his audience. He followed up Sunday by Sunday with a host of sermons on the wanderings in the desert of the children of Israel. It was a continuous story of backsliding, suffering, and repentance.

When the voices of the men turned into menbusinessvoices, Joshua looked at the parade of faces around the missionary board. They stared, unblinking, at him out of photographs on printed cards. Always a father and mother were seated in the centre, with the mother holding a baby, and the children flanking them, the older ones standing behind. Underneath were printed the names of all the children, the initials of the mission, a plea, "Pray for us" or a verse, "The fields are white unto harvest." Joshua wondered if the missionaries had been raised, like Uncle Josh, on a farm and knew what it really meant. For he could see where they were, but not where they'd been, by following the bits of colored yarn harp-strung out to mysterious lands. The strings ended in pins on the map of the world. There was a heavy cluster of pins, all with red plastic heads, on the triangle of India. He yearned to go there too, but he wouldn't send back a picture.

The men were talking now about work-days and equipment. He stood with the smell of varnish coming stronger through the empty part of the church, hesitating; then he wandered out through the porch where the women were talking. They didn't seem to be saying much either. One mother snatched up a little girl scooting by in plastic pants, lifted her chubby legs still running in the air, and held her. The baby girl pushed at her mother's breast, trying to get away. She fretted a little. By the door, Mrs. McHarg stopped him. She was a tall big-boned woman who squinted a lot when she talked. She didn't have any children of her own.

"Say, but you're a handsome young man this morning," she said. She told him that every Sunday morning.

"Thank you, ma'am," he said, as he was taught to do. Then he said, "I guess I haven't any hair, though."

"Pshaw," she said. "You can't have hair and brains too." She looked down at him, squinting so fast he wondered if she could see at all.

"You're a fine-looking lady," he said. It was the first time he ever said it and he felt good the moment it came out. Mrs. McHarg stopped squinting and her eyes shone.

"Well, I guess I should go downstairs," he said, pulling on the doorknob.

"Get a hundred in spelling again this week," she said. "Make them all respect you for what you can do."

"School got out on Thursday," he told her very patiently. She wouldn't know because she packed no children's lunches every day. "It's Easter holidays."

"Oh," she said. She seemed disappointed. "Well, there's things you can practice up on for Camp. Like sword drills. Maybe you can win at that."

"Maybe," he said. For years, when he was learning to read, he had heard of sword drills being held in the older classes, had dreamed of clashing steel, of leaping from bench to bench in the Sunday School rooms downstairs, tipping over chairs and thrusting through the curtains. Then last year, when everyone in the class could read even the word "Habakkuk," the Sunday School teacher had organized the first sword drill in their class.

22

She divided them into two teams, opposed walls facing one another. He waited for the box of swords to be handed out. "But they'll be only wooden," he thought. "Because of the girls." Then she told them to raise their Bibles, that was all they would be using. He was deeply disappointed until he glimpsed one of the Ely boys across the way looking grimly at him. He determined then he could thump the other as stoutly with a Bible as with a blade, and he gripped the morocco binding in a thrill of excitement. "Thumbs out of the margins," the teacher said.

"Okay, it says right here in this Book that the word of God is sharper than any two-edged sword. To use your sword, you'll have to know it. Hebrews 4:12 . . . Charge!" He bounded across the small room already swinging the Book at Jeremiah Ely's head. "Joshua Cardiff!" the teacher yelled. Jeremiah was flipping in his Bible near the back, fingers rustling in the leaves. It seemed to Joshua that his arm, that his being, that all time was suspended in the one furious arrested motion of the raised book and everyone was staring at him, everyone but Jeremiah who finished presently his mad tearing through the pages and jumped to his feet already reading in the upward leap, reading the words which rushed like a cavalry charge. So he wondered what *Bible Camp* really meant, if it would be the same as the Bible Camp where Uncle Josh was drowned. In his mind he saw a picture of a tent built out of Bibles, black and blocking out the sun.

"Well, I guess I'll be going," he said.

"Goodbye," Mrs. McHarg said. "I'll see you next week." She patted down the back of her hair.

He descended into the smell of plywood and damp cement. There was a commotion being raised in the corner behind the stairway. It sounded like someone was being thrown through a door. Then he saw the boys gathered by the toilet. The bashing came from inside, interspersed with crying and some laughing. Brian McGillvary turned his head when Joshua approached. Every freckle on his face was stretched into a grin.

"We got the girls locked up," he said. "They told us to go away, they were talking, so we locked 'em up."

Just then the nail squealed on the hasp, the door rammed at it again, and the block sprang off. The girls burst through the doorway. Brian's sister ran for the stairway.

"I'm going to tell!" she cried. "I'm going to tell!"

Ruthie Anderson ran faster, seized her by the arm.

"Don't you tell," she said. "It was fun. The boys was only having fun."

It was a lot of fun the first time he went to Camp on a work-day. They turned off the white straight road a quarter-mile before the wall of trees began, and beneath it, the tall gaunt house of the Indian Agent. They drove across a field on a lane black between green drills of grain. Off to the left was a house with the wheat growing up against its grey walls. Then the field was gone, scrub poplar and high bush cranberry and low hazelnut springing up in the sandy soil. The road veered through a hollow, bushes tangling above them, and they were onto an avenue between birch and poplar, the sunlight spilling about them. The road was red and crumbly. At times big rocks were tumbled to the side. They came into a clearing where an outcropping of rock tilted up-meadow like a buried razor-back. The car passed through a gap as wide apart as gateposts.

"For a time," Grandpa said, "it looked like we might have to found our Camp upon that rock."

"Until we got dynamite," his father said, "and blew it to kingdom come."

His father was driving. Uncle Owen sat in the back seat with a tool-box that wouldn't go in the trunk. Uncle Glen was trucking summer grazing cattle today to the Community Pasture. It was the first work-day he had missed.

"It's what we should do with those Indians," Uncle Owen said. "The ones who come and smash the windows."

"They're best left alone," Grandpa said. "We can afford a few windows."

"Will they be there now?" Joshua said.

"You better hope not," his father said. "They slashed the plaster in the old schoolhouse. They'd probably slice you up with it."

The car passed through a cutbank with roots sticking out from the clay like splayed nerve ends. Then they were banking through the trees. His father shut the motor off. They rolled soundlessly now on the plunge of dirt road.

"GCX to Tower," his father said. "We're making our final landing approach."

Joshua was on the edge of his seat. The wind rushed past the windows, coming down, down, the road simply diving, and then he saw the lake again gleam blue like eternity through the trees.

They came out of a curve and the side of a building was straight ahead of them, but below. It was all windows, some jagged and dark. Their car rushed at them out of the shiny panes. For a moment Joshua thought they were going to smash through the rest of them. His father geared into low to save on the brakes. The gear-shift lever rattled and the transmission wailed. Then the dirt road peeled off and levelled out along the shore.

"Holy smokes," Joshua said. "I thought we were going to crash."

"All the time I thought so in the Air Force," Uncle Owen said. "That's the way your dad thought you were s'posed to fly."

"The way *I* thought?" his father said. "Look who's talking."

There were other cars there and other boys. So all morning long it was running and rejoicing, the hills above them gambolling like calves and the lake waving up at their feet. And the sun winked out of the waters and pelicans bellied over it; the air swam round with ferns and reeds and the grass buzzed and suddenly he was floating upon clouds of thanksgiving, no sense left at all of time passing.

The moving crew jacked a little school onto the hillside in place above the big one before lunchtime. Someone said it was hot enough for a swim, then there were clothes scattered everywhere on the grass. Naked, they ran down into the water, men and boys together. Their bodies slid through the water, leaping and falling back in a shower of clear sparkling droplets. The water looked green against the trees until the bottom mud swarmed up.

"We'll have to gravel it," Grandpa said, doing a lazy backstroke. His chest was hairy and wet.

There was a large pot of beans and wieners for lunch, kettle-warmed over a small campfire. Everyone pulled out their own sandwiches. They drank clear spring water from the dipper in a milk pail.

When Reverend Haagshed came, Joshua was with his Grandpa, father, and some other men in the little white church on the shore. His father was measuring two-by-fours to saw for bunk shelves. Up close, Reverend Haagshed's chest looked as big as a pulpit.

"Well, Brother Cardiff," he said, "this moving idea of yours was a smart one. We're going to put this church back in the business of saving souls."

He had a way of holding his head back when he spoke like he was keeping his nose above water. His eyes never left the face he was speaking to. They reminded Joshua of a pig's eyes they had once dissected in science class, bulging with jelly.

"It will do," Joshua's father said. "But it's a bunkhouse now."

The bottom half of the minister's face smiled about the room.

"I don't suppose it will be the first time folks have slept in a church."

He was looking at Joshua's father yet out of humorless eyes.

"But the Lord will use even a church for sleeping," he said. "He's not proud. We're going to make men out of the boys who lie down in this building. Put backbone and discipline into their lives, make them obedient soldiers of Christ. That's a better fate, eh, for an old country church than getting filled to the rafters with grain. We're going to put God's temple back in God's work."

"Nobody ever said growing wheat wasn't His work too," Richard Cardiff said. "Just ask my Dad here. Grain cheques pay preacher's salaries."

"Thank God for it," the preacher said. "The Lord keeps his own accounts. He knows, Cardiff, whether you're a blessing or a burden in His work. I don't have to judge." He spoke without heat, his tone barely shifting as he brought up another matter. "I've recruited a dozen men who are waiting in the dining hall," he said. "They need you to show them how to build forms down at the tabernacle."

The rest of the afternoon fell heavy as cement. The bunks were built, the centre wall taken out of the big schoolhouse, and the tabernacle floor poured by six o'clock. When they got home, Joshua's mother had milked both cows.

The next time was no fun at all. Reverend Haagshed was there when they arrived.

"The Indians have chopped down your bunks," he said to the men.

They all had to be rebuilt. A truck went to Melfort for new plywood.

There were tracks in the hardened concrete of the tabernacle. Across the middle it looked as if someone had lain in the wet cement. The impression was that of an angel in the snow, only the legs were wrong. There were two deep hollows half-way down.

"I guess that fella is stuck up," Mr. Chesterfield said. He never came to church, but volunteered to work because his kids were coming to Camp.

Some of the men guffawed.

The cement had to be filled in.

It was a damp, blustery day. The straps of the quonset rafters were hard to arch in the wind. When they began to sheet them in, a gust of wind carried off a leaf of plywood. It was shivered against the one high oak along the shore. Bits of kindling were flung out onto the water.

Even the wind is as bad as those Indians. Will they howl down like that and wipe us out too, I wonder?

Joshua watched the trees all day long to be ready to give warning.

The next time he was there was for Camp in July. No more damage had been done. It was alright again; it was even fun. There were devotions at 7:30 every morning when they had finished washing in basins of cold lake-water. The iron bell rang for breakfast at 8:00 and they marched in in teams. A team for softball and volleyball ate together, did dishes and k.p. together, learned Bible verses together, everything that was done earning points for the team.

At chapel time they sang choruses like "Do Lord, oh do Lord, oh do remember me." Most everyone liked action choruses best. They sang with their hands and feet unfettered: "I'm too young to march in the infantry (stamp, stamp, stamp), Ride in the cavalry (crouch and bounce like a kangaroo), Shoot the artillery (hands slap like musketry), I'm too young to fly o'er the enemy (hands outstretched, flown wide enough to wheel and clash with other planes), But I'm in the Lord's army (finger to breast, finger to Heaven, then open-handed salute), Praise God."

It was Saturday afternoon on the ballfield, the last day they could play at Camp, when he heard the drums. They were just there, suddenly, without preamble. He turned immediately to face the lake, ears straining like a mule's at the faintness of the sound. Somewhere a long way off he heard the crack of wood and the cry of voices. Then he even heard the plop behind him in the plowed earth. It sounded like a mallard duck gunned down onto summerfallow. The cries grew louder. He could just catch the drums at times above them. When he heard the running feet go by him, it was too late. Jimmy McGillvary picked up the dirty soft-ball, fired it as far as he could toward home. Then he wheeled on Joshua. His face was as bright for a moment as his pumpkin hair, spitting like an over-blistered pie.

"You stupid little bald-headed kid!" he yelled. He was shorter than Joshua though he was fourteen. Veins bulged out on his squat neck as he shouted, swelled like the throat of an anaconda swallowing a goat. "Three runs you give 'em, you bald-headed little" and then his voice dropped to a near-hissing whisper, "bassturd!"

He threw his glove as far as he could toward right field, then trudged after it.

"I heard something, that's all," Joshua called after him. "Just because you're too short to hear above ground . . . ."

Jimmy McGillvary did not look back.

"Hit your balls out this way," he yelled toward the infield. "If I'm gonna be the only fielder, you got to give me a chance."

For an instant Joshua was tempted to dash out through the trees. Then a girl walked meekly to the plate, an awkward bat by her hip, and the loud and scornful voices of her backers made him hold the field. The pitcher struck out on three balls, retiring the side, and he ran the long way in from left field, not looking at anyone.

At bat, Brian McGillvary grinned at him.

"What was you trying to see in them woods, Josh?" he said. "Bears?"

"I wasn't looking to see anything," he said. "I was trying to hear the drums. They've started over on the Reservation."

"They ain't real Indians any more, you know," Brian said. "Not like the ones in Zane Grey. So don't let 'em scare you. They probably wouldn't know a ambush if they was hiding at the edge of the bush."

"I ain't scared," Joshua said. "You don't see what I mean. They weren't like I thought they'd be."

They were slow and reassuring, like the sound of one's heartbeat.

"Then try not to think about them at all," Brian said. "You've got a war dance to worry about out there if you goof up any more."

They coursed through his ears like blood pumping, serene and constant and unknowing.

But he kept his face to the game. By three o'clock, the sun was a whitened blister overhead. He was glad when at last the game broke up. They walked back on the road where dust rose underfoot and hung in clouds about their ears. Then their feet ran almost out from under them on the hill with the lake and swimming hour beneath.

They beat along the waters of the lake as if the valley was their artery.

That evening, after tabernacle, he decided he could wait no longer. They had been to the dining hall already, running fast enough to outdistance the girls for the pick of salmon sandwiches or whitecake. They were lined up under the black and silent trees for a drink of water from the spring — occasionally getting drenched in a stream which leapt from the nail-hole if the drinker put his thumb over the hose the right way — in fact, they were already in devotions when he made up his mind. Through the musty odour of straw, the boys faced one another across the aisle of the bunkhouse, over the gulf which had once been formed by straight-backed pews. Now it was set off by bunks that looked like little strip farms, patch-quilts growing strangely colored crops, the pillows clustered like haystacks before a wood, except that the farms were on two levels, one above the other. The boys on each tier sat at the foot of their beds, legs dangling into the emptiness. Most sat in their shorts. Ivan read to them out of the Psalms.

"Blessed is the man that walketh not in the counsel of the ungodly," came his voice from the bench along the lower shelf. The light from the gas lantern wavered over his pages. The shadows it cast along the upper shelves were monstrous.

Ivan read on. He was not undressed. He still had on his white shirt, frayed at the collar, and his tie. Both were tucked beneath his belt, into trousers more shiny now than black, though pressed — God alone knew how — with a sharp crease every morning. Ivan was a missionary home on furlough. He too had been to Africa, with Gospel Missionary Union. He could not go home to visit his parents, although they lived only eight miles away on a farm near Nisooskan. His father had renounced him the day he left communion of the Ukrainian Catholic church to become a protestant.

"You don't come in my yard no more," he told Ivan. "I teach the dogs to piss on you."

Ivan was just twenty-two the fall he came to the youth rally in the Lacjardin Gospel Assembly and was saved. Joshua was an infant then. It was right after harvest. Grandpa got him into Bible School more than two weeks late, at Thanksgiving. Ever after, old man Gezdevitch told everyone who would stop to listen to him on the streets of Nisooskan that Bran Cardiff had robbed his cradle, but it didn't matter, what was in it was only a *paunya*. Eugene Kutsak from Nisooskan, who was at Camp, said it meant goody-goody, like in not getting piss-eyed drunk. They'd all seen old Gezdevitch buttonholing on the street over supper hour, when the beer parlour was closed.

So Ivan spent weeks at a time staying with Joshua's Grandpa and Grandma on this, his first, furlough year. Their home was home base now. It was just so wonderful, Grandma said, to have a missionary in the family again. Ivan said, although he wasn't born to them, he was reborn into their family, they were his spiritual father and mother.

Joshua liked Ivan very much. It wasn't only because he had left father, mother, and kin to do what he believed was right. Nor was it because he had been to the bright-colored (on the map, anyway) countries to which Joshua longed to go. Although it was part of it, certainly: Ivan told stories of what he had seen and done so that you could almost feel the cold slither of a snake across your feet, taste the juicy scoop of fruit plucked from a tree in your own back-yard, or see the lions play like cats in the long African grass while the sun rolled over the shoulder of the wide central plateau. But Ivan was more than either his trials or travels. The time he had come upon David McTavish and a couple of other boys chanting "Fuzzy Wuzzy was a bear, Fuzzy Wuzzy had no hair," he had taken them down to a rowboat by the shore and had read to them from the Bible. They had come back very thoughtful and quiet. They volunteered even to peel potatoes after the noon meal. And when Joshua and Brian McGillvary were caught one afternoon snitching an unsliced meat-loaf from the kitchen, Ivan had taken them as well to the rowboat, telling them as they dangled their arms in the water that Christ once died for their sins and if they truly were His children, they only crucified Him all over again with their every sinful act. He said it in such a mournful voice that Joshua felt miserable for his part in the affair.

Ivan continued reading now, his voice drifting above him into the listening darkness. "And he shall be like a tree planted by the rivers of water, that bringeth forth his fruit in his season." Each boy paid close attention. Ivan read with theatrical skill.

"For the Lord knoweth the way of the righteous: but the way of the ungodly shall perish." His cadence fell shudderingly on "ungodly." He paused, then said the last two words slowly, distinctly. The "perish" was final, as if all eternity lay right behind it. For a second Joshua lost track of the drums sounding faintly through the blank board walls. Then Ivan closed the Book.

"Does anybody know what we've just read?" he asked.

"The Bible?" said a hesitant voice in the shadows.

"That's right," Ivan said. "God's Word. Does anyone know what it means?"

"It means," Jeremiah Ely said in short bursts like gunfire, "that if we don't obey God's law, we'll go to hell."

"Yes," Ivan said, "it does mean that." He sounded sorrowful again. "God doesn't want to see that happen, though, to any of us. That's why He sent us His Son. The rest is up to you; if you don't accept Him as your personal saviour, you will surely perish. Not just your body, but your soul for all eternity, doomed among the horrible pointing flames." He paused. The shadows were monstrous on the upper wall. "But God is still trying to reach you. Tonight. Before it's too late. That's why He speaks to you in that still small voice you can hear inside you. That's why He also speaks to us from His Word." He raised his Bible; its shadow reared high on the wall.

"What does He talk about a tree for?" one boy asked, looking down into the gulf.

"A tree has roots, doesn't it," Ivan said. "So when a strong wind comes, it stays put beside the water which gives it life. Why do you suppose He goes on to mention chaff? Probably all of you who live on a farm have seen your dads combining. What happens to the chaff that comes out of the spreader?"

"It blows down your neck and makes you itchy," another boy said.

"That's right," Ivan said. "What's it good for?"

"Not much. Good for making you have to take a bath, I guess."

"It blows away," Ivan said. "You can't use it. It gets burned off the field after the harvest is in. God says the ungoldly man is like that. He blows around a lot, never very fixed in his habits and his

31

attitudes. He's not good for much. He will also be required to burn some day, when Christ comes to fill up his bins. But the godly man's another story. He's a tree, eh? He's firmly rooted beside God's waters and his leaf shall never wither. When he makes up his mind to live for God, he sticks to it. He bears fruit because he's truly alive."

Then Joshua had to know for certain. "Does God ever speak in other ways?"

"He used to," Ivan said. "He used to send angels. But not any more. We've got His Word that Gideon and Jacob and Lot weren't given. And we've got His still small voice."

"Can He use drums?" Joshua said. "Like out there?"

Every boy turned his head toward the wall where the sound lay beyond.

Ivan shook his head slightly. He was quiet for a second, his face reflecting the lamplight, and then he spoke as if some heavy thing were pressing him down.

"The Indians out there — I am anguished to say it — but I fear for them because they are lost. They are dancing to the devil's drums. In Africa, they dance the same way. The people dance all night in the heat, in the wet and enclosing darkness, and they cry out to terrible gods. I have seen them cut their arms with knives and not bleed, walk in the fire and not be burned. Satan walks among them; it's his power they're using. I've wept for them, pleaded with them, prayed for them. In the light they are wonderful people: they laugh and they love and they feel sorrow, and they are kind, oh so friendly, understanding. But in the night when they dance — like tonight — to the drums, I know they are lost."

Joshua heard no more. He did not listen when Ivan asked them to lead out in prayer as God directed. He did not hear Ivan sum it up in prayer, asking God to speak to the hearts which still yearned after him. He was thinking he would have to find out for himself, he would have to find out quickly now.

When the murmur of beseeching voices ended, there was a moment's silence. Then eyes began to open again, squinting even in the flickering lamplight. Bodies moved stiffly back over the rustling straw ticks, peeling covers open. Joshua dropped down to the bench. He had his trousers in one hand. When he pulled them on, he slipped into his shoes, then drew his jacket over his bare

32

back. He passed the missionary's bunk quietly. Already a little boy was squatting way in the back on his heels, his face screwed up in silent crying.

"Where are you going, Joshua?" Ivan asked.

"Toilet," he muttered, trying vainly to avoid his eyes.

"Don't lose your way," Ivan said quietly.

The door closed behind him and he was in darkness from the first step out from the ring of light beneath the windows. The look on Ivan's face stayed with him, the eyes so deep and caring. And then he couldn't do it. He turned off on the trail up to the toilets and sat there awhile, shivering, smelling the rottenness beneath the odor of quicklime. Still he could feel the pulse of drums without him, within him, and they seemed the same. He was surprised that he wanted so much for them to be, he didn't know why. When at last the light blew out in the bunkhouse, he headed downhill into darkness, into the throbbing sameness of sleep.

He wasn't sleeping at all in the bed with Donna and Joel, though Auntie Bee kept shrilling down stairs after him that he was, and that he was a devil's chip off the old block, the devil could have him for aught she cared, sleeping with girls at his age and dragging for bad measure her Joel after him. Get out, get out of here, she was shrilling. Go home, go out to the Indians where you belong, just get out of here. We know you, we know who you are, get out, get out of here.

They had gone into the house to get out of the cold. It was nothing bad, whatever she imagined it was. Joel had invited him in along with Donna. All morning long and half the afternoon they had skated together from town to Uncle Owen's and back, gliding over a shore like glass. Half the school were there, although it was Friday. Joshua had watched the skaters on the lake from early morning. He could see them through the living room window, looking down the hill beyond the pines. They appeared like bugs swirling at the end of a water trough. At last, Joshua's father said he could stay, although the family was going to the Remembrance Day service at Nisooskan. He knew that by the time he would get down to the beach, put on his skates, then sail over the distance to town, Joel would be skating already with Donna. She wore a red-and-white checkered scarf which trailed behind her dark hair. She smiled from a distance, striding twice on one leg to once on the other. She was the prettiest girl in the school. He smiled back as he rode up to them, not daring to look at her very long.

Joel said, "Where have you been all morning? We've been out here since nine o'clock."

Donna's face was red and smiling in the cold.

"I thought I might have to go to the service," Joshua said, panting and trying not to.

"That's for old fogies," Joel said. "They'd be out here if they really wanted to fly."

Joshua was untying his parka hood, then doing it up again close about his ears.

Then they were skating, three of them, five, fifteen of them, with their blades singing over the ice and the trees passing by as in a dream along the shore. The sun glistened on the mirrored surface of the lake, except they could look down through it to the weeds standing brown and unwaving in the water beneath them. Where ever the feathery arms touched up under the ice, it looked like jack frost on the window pane, only a different color. No one stopped all day long to eat and always Donna was with them and more than them, skating in the centre of their row with boy after boy taking turns at her hand, although sometimes she skated with her girl-friends, so that the best any boy could do was to take an outer girl in tow. When they played Choo-choo, their breath came in real puffs of steam, and when they cracked the whip, the ice would crack and hum far out into the lake.

At last when they three were alone, Joel asked them to come home with him.

Donna said smilingly, "Both your faces are red like Indians. Is mine too?"

"Beer parlour red," Joel said. "You look like an Indian who's been in the beer parlour all day."

Donna's father owned the hotel in town. Joshua knew that Joel meant only to convince her how cold she was, he wasn't even aware he'd insulted her.

He tried himself to gloss it over. "Don't they turn white? I mean, since white men turn red. Well anyway, they're out of the cold, they're one ahead of us."

They were in fact stung now for warmth, having admitted it. They walked precariously on skates up through the trees, sat down on the burning cement step, fumbled slowly and painfully out of laces and boots. There was a smell like sour milk in the landing. On the steps up into the kitchen, Joshua's footbones spread like leaden ingots. Uncle Owen's and Auntie Bee's bedroom door was closed. They took off their coats in the spare bedroom. There was a needling now in Joshua's toes.

"Why don't we go upstairs?" Joel said.

They went up the stairs quietly.

Joel had quite a few books. They were all mysteries, Hardy Boys and Nancy Drews, a few science mysteries like Tom Swift. Joshua found a paperback with an alluring title: *Alfred Hitchcock's Favorite Stories of Mystery and Suspense.* Donna had taken up a Nancy Drew story. She sat down tentatively at the desk. Joel was sitting near her on the bed. He turned back the spread.

"Why don't we get warm under here?" he said.

Donna got in between them. Joshua was nearest the door. Their faces smelled cold above the covers.

Joshua forgot about everything as he got into a story; it made him forget even the fool's heat bricking his feet. It was about a man wandering aimlessly about the Aegean, getting off one tramp steamer after another to explore any island which took his fancy. He disembarked on a deserted island where even the sailors refused to land, some of them protesting, seeming to warn him in a dialect he couldn't understand. He had noticed through the glasses on shipboard that a wall circled inland above the shore. There were figures there, statues, he had seen them in the glasses too, and as he beached and drew nearer to them he marvelled at the detailed perfection of the workmanship. They were exquisite human forms, of purest marble, Phidian masterpieces, apparently undiscovered. He entered through the gate into a little garden, contained by an inner wall. Here too were priceless statues, most of them standing in the act of arrested movement or attention, as if they had been captured on film and miraculously converted to stone. It was the same everywhere he went on the island, though as he passed through doors into interior gardens, there seemed to be a haunted look on some of the faces, growing more and more bedeviled as he progressed, until at last some of the figures were half-turned back, arrested in the moment of apparent flight. A look of horrified surprise on the faces began to take hold of him, and from somewhere deep within him he began to feel what it was, without knowing. He had to hurry now from gate to gate, passing those marbles which seemed about to run backwards over him, a few statues actually facing him now, though with their heads cast over their shoulders. He knew as he came into the final courtyard what it was, there was no door opposite and he could feel it off to one side in the shadows. He knew for certain what it was even before he heard the hiss of the snaky hair, yet somehow he couldn't stop himself, with his heart straining already to beat like clenching stone, he turned. . . .

Auntie Bee was in the doorway looking at them. Her eyes looked like steel bits that would scatter marble into dust. She said, In my own house, beneath my own roof. Sleeping with a girl we've tried to save in Sunday School. You never learned that, did you, at your mother's knee? You little reprobate.

I wasn't sleeping, he said. We weren't, were we? We were all reading a book.

That's as bald a lie as I've ever seen, she said. I can read you like a book, you bare-faced little liar. How dare you? How dare you? Eleven years old and sleeping with a girl. Then dragging down these little ones after you. There's no protection for anyone. You get out, you get out of here.

We were just reading, Mrs. Cardiff, Donna said. The books are right—

Don't lie for him, she said. Don't make it worse for yourself. His Grandpa knows who he is, we all know. It wasn't your fault, Donna dear, you couldn't know. Just don't make it worse. Stay away from him now. You get out of here, she said. You stay away from these little ones. You're damned, even Grandpa thinks so.

He fled past her then, out beneath the sloping roof, down the stairs. He carried off his parka like a stolen loaf of bread. Uncle Owen's bedroom door was ajar; he lay on the bed with his arms flung out like a man on a cross. Joshua saw nothing but the door in the kitchen. He plunged through the odor of sour milk, out onto the sidewalk which burned through his socks. He scooped up his skates like a fumbled football, his socks soaking up damp from the iron turf. He didn't stop until he sat down with his skates on the burning ice.

Why don't you go out to the Indians where you belong, she said. Why don't you try and lose your head too.

He was skating as if the ice yawned just behind him, the black, chilly water fanning out in his wake, an infinite gulf rushing around him. But he wasn't able to outskate the doomed ache

36

inside him, swallowing him up like a snake devouring its tail.

Grandpa was right. You're damned. He said as much himself.

His blades sent cold shocks from his toes to his teeth. The runners dragged and scraped now and then, but afterwards they hummed like arrows released. The woods rose ominously on either side of him, hills beetling over him. He hadn't noticed when he passed the white-painted security of home on the bluff.

His feet wouldn't stop; they flooded over the ice. The woods were dense and shadowed in the late afternoon sun. His father said the forest here was so thick in summer, even Robin Hood would get lost.

He slowed down some when he rounded the bend at the three-mile angle. His ankles ached and his chest felt lanced through.

So this is the way it must have been with arrows sticking in your chest, through your back. It sears so bad up under the breastbone. Thank goodness they finally gave it up, they don't do it any more.

Though he couldn't help thinking of Deerslayer on the houseboat, and the threat, the unending threat of arrows from the woods. It was on a long, wooded lake like this, with Deerslayer rowing, rowing and watching to save Judith and her goofy sister from the Mingoes. Just before the savages attacked, they were supposed to let out such unearthly yells.

It was quiet here now, save for the scratch of his skates and the blood thudding in his ears. There was no sound outside him. It was forbodingly still. Then he realized he was still expecting to hear the drums. The silence was what was wrong, the nothing-sound of danger.

The trees gave out on the Bible Camp along the shore. It looked like a deserted village, one street long. He skated past the dining hall over water where they swam in summer. The diving board was pitched up on the bank. Farther down, the tabernacle was flushed in the setting sun. All was perfectly still, but with a sense of rushing silence, as if he were cast and falling already into outer darkness. He didn't slow up, couldn't have if he had wanted to, though he felt the ache winding tight and bunching inside him, like an overwound flat-ribbon spring. Maybe that was it; he was a mechanical toy; he would stop when his spring ran down. If first it didn't snap and maybe rip the stuffings out of him.

He came around the last bend and the mist rising told him there was open water ahead. Then he could see it, the surface wine-dark with the sun upon it. He turned in toward the trees. Bristling willows overhung the shore; there were too many rocks to walk on skates. He climbed through the rustle of dead leaves, the snap of sleeping branches. As he faced into the west again, the sun through the trees flared in a blazing column. His heart was pumping through valves of stone. He could not stop; he despaired of it. The sun was dappled, striped, then blazing.

The fence stood him up straight and staggered him. He almost fell backwards, then gained his balance, flinging one arm out against a tree. There were spots in front of his eyes. In his mind he had envisioned the forest sweeping for miles unbroken, a tangle of grey winter wood divided only by a thread of river looping west and north toward the Saskatchewan. The Reservation was lost somewhere in that tangle, its only boundary the forest's edge. He was surprised it wasn't so.

He began very carefully to separate his parka from the barbs. Rust gritted on his leather mitts. He took one off, working carefully. The top wire was quite floppy. He pulled on it, fingers fumbling between the cotton and the hooks. He pricked his finger on one of the points and still he couldn't pull the material over it. He pulled harder. There was a dead snap of wood and then the whole wire came free. Part of the post hung on it. Only now he had a wider section of his parka caught up in the wire. He pulled in exasperation, ripping the heavy cloth front. His sleeve caught as his arm came down.

Why it's just like Tar Baby.

That settled it for him. He wormed his way out of both sleeves, managing only to tear his sweater once on the barbs.

Okay, have the parka if you want it, just so you leave me be.

But he changed his mind once he was free of it. He knew he had to have a coat for the seven or eight miles home. When it did come at last, it tore away. The stuffing poured out of one sleeve, oozed like a rake of blood over the front of the thing. He stopped shivering a little when it was on.

The fence had to lead somewhere; he couldn't just leave it be. He followed it over the face of the slope, keeping it at a safe distance on his right. The sun was down, there was only a dull glow in the west when he came out of the trees. The fence ran only a little way through the darkness. He could see the fainter gloom of the water twisting away between the willows. The fence did not

dip into it like cattle-fences do. It simply stopped on the bank
beside a clump of willows.

Skating up-lake, he did not notice the moon flying in the east,
nor did he especially hear the wavering howl of coyotes along the
shore.

*No wonder that Cree kid went beyond the roped-off swimming
part. The only way out was to swim.*

ii

There wasn't a reason, even a moderate excuse, for more than a
year by which Joshua might satisfy himself about the Cree.
Auntie Bee came over one night to apologize for the way she sent
Joshua packing out of her house. When she spoke, the cords stood
out on her neck and her eyes pouted like barely toasted marsh-
mallows. She stood in the living room, her big chin tucked in and
working, but the presence of her face drifting out through the
window, across the lake home. She said she had found the boys,
Joshua and her Joel, with Donna Klimchuk in a bed, and she had
thought . . . Well, Joel didn't have any idea what she was saying
afterwards, what the questions could mean she was putting to
him. Obviously she had been mistaken. She couldn't help but
assume . . . Would he and they forgive her? His mother looked sad
and a little tired, but when she spoke, there was real tenderness in
her voice.

"Of course we will, Bee. 'Blessed are the merciful: for they shall
obtain mercy.' I've always tried to teach my children that. You'll
forgive her, Joshua, won't you, because she asks?"

He could only nod reluctantly.

It was the same way with the parka. His father stamped the
floor like Raymond Jones's bull. The parka was brand-new,
$13.98 from Simpson's that fall. How could any eleven-year-old
kid, dead or alive, manage to make a two-week old coat look like
that? A mad-man maybe, in North Battleford. If his keepers were
crazier than he and passed out scissors, perhaps. But did he look
that crazy? He wondered sometimes. Maybe they could tell him?

Joshua was forced then to admit how it had happened. It was the way Auntie Bee kept saying Indians, he belonged with them. He didn't realize what he was doing.

"Why don't you try some Eskimoes next time?" his father said. "Or do they get their parkas now from Simpson's too?"

"I didn't mean to ruin it," he said, almost whispered. "I'm sorry."

His mother stood up then to his father. She said, if he wanted her to, she would earn the money for a new one. But sooner or later, he was going to have to learn how to forgive. He was going to have to be able to show his own son mercy first, before he could ever obtain mercy for himself.

All his father said was, "Where would you get a job?" He was a little scornful. But after supper, he did give Joshua's mother the money for another order to Simpson's. As he peeled the bills out of his wallet, he said it must be getting time for a Reformation again, what with this buying of indulgences for cash. Because he knew for sure there were folks, some of them not very old, who couldn't afford to sin at these rates any more. They'd best count their blessings while they could, because next time they'd have a whole lot more to count on.

Donna didn't come any more to Sunday School. She said her mother wouldn't allow it, she mustn't go to a place where people had minds like that. Nowadays Joshua saw her only at school. He passed the hotel evenings, hoping just to catch sight of her. Several times he met drunken Indians that way, coming out of the beer parlour. One night, it was the next June, he found an Indian lying where he'd fallen beneath the beer parlour door. He lay across one arm on the heaving sidewalk. Puke roped down his neck in a puddle under his elbow. His eyes were closed. Joshua picked up the toppled red hunting cap, lay the crown of it on the side of the man's head over the crow-black hair. The visor at least shaded the eyes from the slanting sun. It was a long time before he could make himself hunt ditches again, looking for beer bottles to earn a little spending money.

He often caught sight of Indians, however, on the road running past the farmhouse. They were scattered like saskatoons on a bush on their way into Lacjardin. They would be clumped like chokecherries though, on their way back out of town, wobbling over the road as on a branch drawn suddenly for picking. In the summertime, they sat among the roadside weeds for a rest, looking like birds on a telegraph wire, except they would pass a bottle to and fro along the edge of the ditch. Then one day, in the wintertime when it was very cold, an Indian man stood at the foot of the driveway and, facing the house, he urinated in the snow. He took his unrelieved time about it, sending up a great cloud of steam above his head, catching the last of the sunlight, so that he began to resemble the picture of an angel alighting in an old illustrated Bible. Joshua was relieved because his mother was in the kitchen at the time, peeling potatoes. He kept Janie forcibly away from the picture window. She squalled a bit, finally yelling in exasperation.

"Joshua," his mother said from the kitchen, "leave your sister alone."

"I am," he said, holding on tight to her shoulders.

"He is not," Janie yelled. "He won't let me look out the window."

"Joshua, do I have to tell your father when he comes in from the barn?" his mother said.

"No, you don't *have* to."

His mother's voice sounded tired. "I've got to tell him you've been sassing me now. Unless you would say you're sorry."

"Let *go* of me!" Janie said, trying to squirm between his legs.

He resisted for a moment, looking over his shoulder out the window again. The Indians were gone from the driveway, already disappearing down the west brow of the hill.

"I let go," he said. "I'm sorry."

Janie rushed to the window.

"There's nothing there," she said. "But there was something. You bully."

Joshua went to the kitchen.

"Would you like the woodbox filled, Mom?" he asked.

"Just go outside," his mother said. "Stay there awhile." She sounded very tired.

He put on his felt boots and his parka in the landing, then opened the back door. The storm door squealed on its icy hinges. He closed both panels on the steam rushing out into the cold. The bare electric bulb still glowed above the barn door. He went the other way, down the snow-plowed driveway toward the road.

When he reached the spot, there was a wide yellow hole in the snow. He scuffed at it only half-thinking, then began to kick fresh snow over it. After a while, he had to grade the snow in with his boot from a long way off, the hole was so big. In time, he had covered all of it. Even so, it wasn't hid; the mound of snow was too big. He started to tramp it down and the stain came mixing through. He had to mound it over again.

They hadn't seen the earthen mound before the fire. It was over the hill in the thickest wood and the fire divided around it. They only smelt the smoke when the wind swung into the northwest.

It was a Sunday afternoon, cool and clear as water. Grandpa and Grandma had come from church for dinner. Grandpa and his father were pitching and backcatching while Joshua and Janie took turns at bat.

At first, the smoke crept hazily over the yard.

"Someone's burning stubble on Sunday," Grandpa said. "You'd think at least a man would want to rest."

"It's probably Nels Pedersen," Joshua's father said. "His missus makes that man a going concern. He's still working Sundays and here it's already October."

But there was too much smoke, too near, for it to be just Nels Pedersen. The smoke closed down over the yard like a blizzard. The wind drove it so hard it stung almost like sleet on the cheeks.

"We'd better go see," Joshua's father said after a time.

They drove on the west road. Smoke billowed out of the trees like a row of explosions. They could see the flames, before they were very far down hill, eating through the bush.

"Well I'll be jiggered," his father said.

"It's going to beat the cars," Grandpa said. "We'd better get help."

They put out a general ring, as soon as they could get Mrs. Hamm off the line. She was crippled and her husband believed the moon was twenty-five miles from the earth. People rarely complained about Mrs. Hamm talking on the phone.

The flames flickered through the tallest trees like they were candles. The ground fire swirled and eddied like a pack of dogs. Joshua carried pail after pail of water from the trough. The men were wetting gunny sacks to beat out the flames. The yard was filling up with cars, trucks. Soon they were lining up down the driveway, out on the road. Men carried pails and sacks. Then for a time, Joshua simply pumped at the trough. When he did get into the woods again, he saw figures twisted in agony like devils in the lake of fire. He could see dimly the smoke-blacked skin and scorched khaki writhing on its shore. Shirts flew out through the smoke. Joshua raced to pick them up. He could hear the click of spades, sometimes see them through the smoke scooping, then scattering, as in a moving flower bed, the dirt heaping up over orange and crimson blossoms. Now the heat was solid like a wall, the smoke thick and retching.

The fire poured steadily like water, even uphill, though finally it was beginning to look like they could stem its tide. They were still two hundred yards from the barn. A man let the pigs out of their pen too soon. They ran out through the yard, then plunged downhill toward the lake. Joshua's mother and Grandma were still loading household goods onto the truck. They were helped by Auntie Carolyn and Auntie Bee, some neighbor women. Chickens flew about the yard.

Then the last file of flames was out. With the yard still under a blanket of smoke, one man said it reminded him of the mustard gas at Ypres. From the barn they could just see faintly the granaries; from the granaries the house loomed in a fog.

The women were leaving everything on the truck to make a lunch.

"Thank God we can," Joshua's mother said. "Thank God there's something left to give."

Joshua and Janie helped carry things from the deep freeze to the oven. The house was beginning to recover from its appalling silence, from the vivid pall of smoke. Little gray wisps were all that bannered past the windows any more.

Yet the smell of woodsmoke was in his pillow when Joshua went upstairs to bed. At the breakfast table, it smelled like someone had dumped the ashpan behind the stove. After school, Joshua walked with his father down through the woods to look at the waste. The leaves crackled underfoot for fifty yards, then they entered upon a shore of ash and blackened trunks.

"It sure did clean out the undergrowth, didn't it," his father said.

The ground sifted up around their faces. Joshua felt the soot almost in his sinuses.

"I'd really like to know how it started," his father said. "You

43

wouldn't have any special insights, would you?"

They came upon a wide-mouth entrance into the ground.

"I'll bet you wouldn't trust Smokey the Bear," Joshua said. But he didn't say it right out loud.

He was putting a pair of exploratory legs into the mouth of the den.

"You better not get in there Joshua. There's no telling what's holed up yet from the fire."

They walked some more. A lot of the trees were charred as high as his father's head.

"I suppose some fool on the road threw a match," his father said. "I know a car was parked there Saturday night. There were a dozen beer bottles in the ditch. Did you get them yet? Those guys probably threw a cigarette. Something like that could smolder all night, even go underground, before it blazed."

The mound rose right in their faces. It was like something Joshua knew from a dream.

"Well look what the fire uncovered," his father said. "I never knew this was here before."

Joshua wasn't sure what to call it.

"Do you know, Dad, what it is?"

"I'm not sure exactly. My guess, though, is it's a burial mound. Would you look at that. Didn't I say these woods were thick enough to get Robin Hood lost? If this was merry old England, we'd have just found the Sheriff's gold."

"But it really is an Indian mound? You mean real Indians lived here on our land?"

"And died here, it looks like. The ones that made it didn't have far to go to get to the Reserve, did they? They must have lived here for years to grow a pile like that. I bet we could find an arrowhead or two, if we only looked."

They did, scuffing one out of the dirt almost immediately.

Those Indians lived here in our bush. They're in this very ground underfoot.

"See how jagged those edges are," his father said. "They're hard as flint. I bet we could strike a fire with it."

"Who needs to?" Joshua was looking at the grey chipped stone with a kind of awe.

"That's right, who needs to. I almost forgot with all these spruce needles around. Do you see the way the fire swept by? It

44

didn't touch that spruce here at all. Isn't that odd?"

Put off the shoes from thy feet, for the place whereon thou standest is holy ground.

"Maybe it's sacred," Joshua said. "Maybe that's why it didn't burn up."

"Don't be silly," his father said. "The mound funneled the wind around it. The fire blew right past. On this spot yesterday, it would have been like the eye of a storm, with danger all about, but safety at the centre. That's due to wind funneling too, air rushing around the centre of a low."

"This is high though. How could that be the reason it's so calm?"

"It's my meteorology exam all over again. Would you like some ground school tomorrow? We could come out here with shovels and do a little digging."

But the next day it snowed and the ground turned to flint. Joshua walked out to the mound several times over the winter. More and more it seemed to him it was the eye of the storm. He walked on drifts of snow which carried him, firm ridges spun like pinwheels round the mound, so that he could walk right up the spines to where they crested, and then jump the little space to the top. The snow on the branches of the spruce lay like feathers.

It's higher than the drifts. And in the spring it will still be rising, the ground swelling and swelling. Not like Uncle Josh's grave, nor like greatgrandpa and his wife in the cemetery at Nisooskan. They're all sunk and caved like empty ribs.

The wheel of Grandpa's Oldsmobile flattened the mound on the driveway. Joshua ran behind the car.

⟍ Back to present

"Howdy doody," Grandpa said. Even his eyes were smiling. "You've got snow gophers on the driveway, I see. I'll pay a nickel a tail, five times what your Dad made in the Depression. Is that a deal?"

"Aw, Grandpa, you know there's no such thing. That's not much of a deal at all."

"It is for me. Have a humbug?"

"No. No thanks."

"I've got peppermints if you like . . ."

"Okay."

"I've got a deal for your Dad as well. Is he still in the barn or did he forget the light?"

It turned out that Grandpa had been over to St. Brieux to see the brushcutters.

"If I were to do mine at the same time," he said, "they'd do yours for fifteen dollars an acre."

"Do yours?" Joshua's father said. "I didn't know you had anything to do on that land. There can't be enough left there for a man to pick his teeth."

"There's at least a couple of acres north of the buildings. You remember what I always said: the day you break an acre is a day you won't be broke."

"But you'll be cutting down your windbreak, won't you? You'll blow away come one good blizzard."

"Not likely. The three rows of elms and maples my dad planted should hold us down, don't you think? Glen agrees with me. He just hates to lose the wild raspberry patch. You picked there, too, when you were a kid, didn't you? I sort of hate to lose them. But we can always set out a few canes. I rather like the prospect of having our fruit and eating it too."

"I don't know," Joshua's father said. "I could really use the extra acreage. The breaking would be some kind of crop, all right. But I can't afford it right now, I was going to leave that bush as pasture."

"Don't forget," Grandpa said, "what Solomon said about the ant. If you need it, I'll loan you the money. It's time you started getting ahead in the world."

The mound people. They'll be ants in the light.

The brushcutters didn't come until the week before Camp; they pulled in about noon on Joshua's birthday. They crept up the hill from the east, a caravan drawn steadily by a bladed diesel-caterpillar, with a three-gang plow and rubber-tired caboose in tow. The woods about the house echoed with their rumble-clank-prrrr on the driveway. His father met them by the well.

"Allo, m'sieur," a short, stocky man said from the back door of the caboose. He had a full black beard. "W'ere would you like dis ting?" He slapped the wall of the trailer.

"You can run it in by the tankstand over there," his father said.

The man jumped lightly down from the doorway. He didn't bother to close the door. While the cat' sputtered quietly, its exhaust cap fluttering upright above the pipe with the blue air shimmering around it, the driver, the rider, and Joshua's father

46

unhitched the caboose from the plow and rolled it back under the trees. Joshua helped to pull it.

"Dere we are," the bearded man said brightly at last. " 'Ome for us fellow pour quelques jours. What you call yourself, boy?"

"Joshua," he said. "What's your name?"

"These are the Cartier brothers," his father said. He pronounced it *Car-teer*. "Alphonse and Yves, this is my boy."

"Well den, Josh, you come see us skin down some tree if you like. We give you a ride on our cat' an' you won' be scratch."

"I might, I don't know. Thank you, Mr. Carteer."

"Sure you come. Don' be scared of dat ma-chine. Or is it us fellow, heh? Don' be scared of us: we're not goin' to eat you, you know. You'll find us fellow real gentle men, eh? Wit' anyt'ing but a tree, dat is. We bot' 'ate tree of any kind."

"I thought you might," his father said.

"Where is it dat we start?" Alphonse said.

"On the north brow of the hill. You'll have to drive down through the east pasture. But you'll take some dinner first. The wife has it on the table."

"We ate a big brek-*fass*," Yves said, not looking at anyone. He was tall, he had a big nose, and it looked like he was starting to grow a beard too.

"I'm sure the wife has it on the table already," Joshua's father said. "Come in."

There were scalloped potatoes for dinner and fried sausage, kernel corn, stringed beans, and two kinds of salad: lettuce with sugared mayonnaise and jellied fruit. When lunch was over, Joshua slipped two sausages into his hip pocket. He had to sneak them when his father wasn't looking.

Outside no breeze stirred beneath the noon sun. It was very hot. Janie rode now on the shoulders of Alphonse, squealing a little when he pretended to buck her off.

"Joshua's got a birthday," she said.

"Is dat so, boy?" said Alphonse.

"Yes, sir," Joshua said.

" 'Ow would you like to drive our cat'? My pre*sen*' to you."

"No thanks," he said. "I mean, thank you, but I guess I won't." The man looked at him like he was crazy.

"I don't feel much like it," Joshua said. "I don't know why."

"Well, it's up to you," Alphonse said, shrugging. He twisted his head up to Janie. "Are you a brave girl?" he said, smiling and carefree once more. "Would you like to come wit' us?" He was pointing to the machine where his brother sat, his hands working choke and throttle controls, rewarming the engine. Yves was partly screened by the four-poster steel frame which rose above him.

"Sure," Janie said. Her voice was all giggly.

So Janie rode with the two men on the slow-treading yellow tractor out through the pasture gate. Joshua could see her with her hands on the levers. He felt a little jealous watching them go. Then he couldn't help but follow them on the trail out through the bush. The trees, before he entered them, looked like a host of green-hooped skirts on silver legs. He followed inside a screen of trees when the cat' turned northward along the pasture.

He watched with his father from a sunny glade while the machine knocked down blackened trees before it. They fell two and three at a time and the sky opened out behind them. The bulldozer puttered steadily, butting at them, bowling them over and rolling them up into windrows in one nigh-unbroken motion. A cloud of ash lay on the air, clouding the sun. The earth sat stump- and pock-marked behind the snuffling cat'. Everywhere its tracks appeared in the dirt, crisscrossing the ground with the imprint of a tight-flexed watchband. On the piles the tree trunks lay, black soil crammed between their roots. They resembled the muddy feet of corpses. Now the damp, heavy smell of gouged earth hung above the odor of ash.

"Why did Alphonse say he hates trees?" Joshua said, drawing one of the sausages carefully from his hip pocket. It was all greasy now inside. His father squatted on his heels in the grass, watching the machine at work. Joshua placed the sausage in his mouth with a quick wiping motion of a hand across his face. He tried to munch quietly.

"Maybe one fell on him one time," his father said. "Maybe it's just a part of the job, like the preacher hating sin. I couldn't say for sure."

The second sausage slipped on its way out of Joshua's pocket. It dropped on the ground. He tried in vain to get his hand over it.

"Good night nurse," his father said. "How many times have I told you to leave something for the next meal? Do you always have to get the last bit of good stuff for yourself? Brush that thing

48

off and put it in your pocket. I want to see it on your plate come suppertime."

They watched the trees still jumbling down like pick-up-sticks. There was a lane opening up through the woods downhill. Off to the west, Joshua could see the Indian mound bulge amidst bare, dry bones. The spruce looked very green through the tangle of grey trunks and limbs.

"What about the burial mound?" Joshua said suddenly, forgetting the stigma upon him.

"What about it? Do you think you'll find pemmican there to go along with your sausage?"

"No, I mean what are we going to do? We can't plow it down, can we?"

"Why not? There hasn't been time to do any spading there yet. We might as well let the bulldozer uncover the goods for us, as do the work ourselves."

Before it came out of him, he didn't have an inkling he was going to do it, and while it happened, he wasn't even sure where the flow of words was coming from, he was simply crying out against all of it: the steady drone of the cat' on the summer air, the slow-motion swing of the earth-bound trees, the scoop of coulter and share beneath the earth-ribbed mound; and suddenly his voice carried a deeper note, as if he were crying out against time and even death itself.

Uncle Josh in the empty ground and the earth sagging through his lid but the mound here isn't buried, at least there's something springing up

His father looked at the ground a long time.

"Perhaps I could leave the mound," he said softly. "Because somebody used it once to remember their dead."

He got up, facing the cat'. His voice was brusque when he added, "I don't suppose we could ever have flattened it out. Machinery would always be getting stuck on the hump."

In the evening, the woods behind the tankstand and the caboose pitched shadows over the yard. They crept south-easterly across the trough and well; the pump, not to be outdone, threw a long-handled shadow ahead of them to the trees on the east side of the yard. Joshua sat on the wooden well-cap; he was panting still from three hundred strokes on the pump-handle. The deep-planked trough sat next him, clean and level full with water.

Beneath it, a thin stream snaked from a corner where the water had spilled over down the driveway. It left a dark stain on the gravel.

With the pump-creak and water-gush silenced once more, Joshua could hear the thin, reedy music of a harmonica which had not been playing when he started chores. The player was skilled. He could make the music quaver and hush and swell again with his hands. It sounded sad and lonesome, yet there was in it too the feeling that one gets sometimes on water, in a canoe perhaps, with the sun going down and the river drifting one along and nobody around except some birds calling and all that empty land stretching away beyond both banks. Joshua got up off the well and walked slowly, almost hesitantly, toward the caboose.

Yves was sitting in the grass, his back against an oil drum, not looking at anything, just playing. His hands were curved around the instrument and the music curved through them as his cheeks rose and fell. Joshua looked at Alphonse sitting in the doorway of the caboose. The man's face was blackened still by the day's dirt, as black almost as his beard, except around the eyes and mouth.

"He plays real good," Joshua said.

Alphonse nodded, tapping one of his dangling feet upon the air. They both listened for a time. The shadows ran past the house now, all the way into the trees.

When Yves paused for breath, Alphonse said, "Play 'appy birthday. She's almost gone."

"I'd rather hear something else," Joshua said. "You sang it at supper."

"O-hooh, yer mother, she bakes one ver-ry fine cake," Alphonse said. "I h'ate till I'm almost sick."

"I'm glad you liked it," Joshua said. "I ate lots too."

Yves looked at him questioningly.

"Play a *voyageur* song," he said. "Something from the time we learned about in school when they first came up-river."

Yves began to play a song that wailed softly in the growing darkness; it sounded more mournful than the last one. When he finished, Alphonse asked, "Did you 'ave a 'appy birthday, boy?"

"I think so," he said. "Except for the trees. Why do you hate trees?"

Alphonse looked at the ground. "Oh, I don' know exactly," he said softly. "Dey always grow up on you if you once let 'em go.

Dey won' let you farm wit'out breakin' your back. An' sometimes I jus' wan' to see somet'ing. I wan' to look as far as I can wit'out havin' somet'ing stop me."

Yves took the harmonica away from his mouth. "Notre père," he said, then stopped. After a moment he continued. "Our father is killed by a falling tree. It squash him like a bug."

"I'm awful sorry," Joshua said.

Presently Yves began to play again, and the night air was filled with a hushed and solemn music.

One morning after Camp was over, Richard Cardiff said, "We'll get some root-pickers today." He sprinkled brown sugar on his porridge, then soaked it up in cream.

"Who will we get?" Joshua asked. "Pass the brown sugar."

"Please," his mother said. She was still at the sideboard, laying out the Gideon's Bible with *Our Daily Bread.*

"You don't need the boy this morning do you, Helga?" his father asked.

"No," said his mother. "Janie will help me hoe the weeds, won't you dear?" She took a thick loaf of bread and sliced some for the toaster.

"I want to be a root-picker too," Janie said.

"There'll be lots of time for that," his father said, "when we get the worst of it out of the way. Joshua and me have to go to the Reserve for help. You don't want to work with a bunch of Indians, do you? They steal little girls away from their folks and sell them in Alberta."

"That sounds like fun," Janie said. "How much would I cost?"

"Richard," his mother said. "Don't make her believe such lies." She buttered the toast that was up.

"You'd cost more than anyone could afford to pay," his father said. "So you better stay home and hoe the garden and help your mother."

"Who are we going to get?" Joshua asked again. "Honest Indians?"

"I didn't know there were any," his father said. "I hate to drive that far just for Indians, but I guess they're all the help we can afford. We'll talk to Quinn."

Quinn lived in a white clapboard house just inside the Reservation fence. Across the road from him was the school, a squared log building which, apart from its deep-set windows, looked mostly

51

like a trading post. Quinn was the Indian Agent; he also taught the school as far as it went, to grade eight. He was a tall, robust man with a very red face, between the eyes and nose radish red. When they drove into his yard which held no barn, no granaries, only an outhouse beside the woodpile, he was there swinging an axe as easily as a semaphore. The Red Ensign was flying from a mast hasped on the gable of the house. Across the road, the school flag-pole was bare.

"Cardiff," the man said, speaking into the open window of the car. He raised the axe above his head and brought it in one glinting arc down onto the stump. The round piece of stove wood split cleanly in two. He raked the halves with his axe toward an even-toed pile.

"Know any Indians who would like some work, Pat?" Cardiff said.

"What have you got to do?" the red-faced man said, putting another round stick up on the block. "Nothing you haven't got a good week to do it in, I hope."

"A day's picking roots," Cardiff said. "Do you know anyone who wants the money bad enough? I'm paying six-bits an hour."

Quinn cleared his throat, spit on the grass. The grass was clean mown and unlumped with chicken dung. "Won't get anyone here for under a dollar," he said. "How many do you need?"

"Two, at that price," Cardiff answered. "And only if the money doesn't go for liquor."

Quinn smiled, his mouth stretching like a sealer ring. "I've two in mind," he said. He bit the axe firmly into the block, then climbed into the back seat of the car. The blanket pulled loose from the bench as he settled down; he tucked it up again.

They were driving now on a dirt road which ran straightaway, bound after bound, then veering abruptly almost at right angles like a jackrabbit turning stopping crouching into the earth then bounding again through the bush, all the while the pattern of sun-light and green shade swirling over the road and the poplar and paper birch dreaming above them, quiet beyond the clack of their passing. Joshua could see log cabins, sometimes modern box-style houses finished with siding and shingles, tucked away among the trees. None of them had lawns or fences; nor did they have flowers growing by the side of a wall. Most of them had only old cars in the yard, sometimes several of them, and then at least one would lie with its wheels in the air. Old washing machines stood off around the corners of some houses.

The car nosed into a tunnel of shadow where the trees wholly over-arched the road. Dipping down a curving slope, they burst into sunshine where a creek overran the road.

"Turn right beyond the ford," Quinn said. He rested one arm on the top of the front seat. It was covered with red bristly hair.

They drove slowly through the creek. The water murmured beneath them, running swift and bright into the trees.

"Whoa, right there," Quinn said. "You can barely see it's a lane."

The brome grass was tall between the tracks. It stood bent-headed, about as high as a wagon floor. The wheel tracks opened out in it like parts through sunbleached hair.

"Take it slow through here," Quinn said. "You hit a rock through your oil pan and those roots will be too expensive to pick."

"Don't I know it," Cardiff said.

They drove through the shade listening to the steady brush of grass beneath the car. Once a rock scraped long and slow on the frame.

"Guy who lives here, name is Joe Little-dog," Quinn said. "He works pretty good when he wants to. I have a hunch he's about ready to want to. If I'm not mistaken, we'll catch Walking Horse here today, too. Lay you four to one odds."

"I don't bet," Cardiff said. "Who's Walking Horse? What do him and Little-dog do?"

"They're Indians," Quinn said. "That's what they do best. They're keeping a treaty. Of course, sometimes to keep it, they have to go pick roots or clean some barns. It's all a part of the treaty."

"What do you mean?" Cardiff said.

"Nothing much," the man said. "They keep a treaty better than most men I know."

Where the lane ended, a broad meadow opened out among the trees. A wine-brown house stood on the right, near the edge of the woods. It was a fairly new house; the paint wasn't blistered yet. But the wooden stoop which must have stood (even leaned) by the door sill when the carpenters were finished lay on its side like a range-frozen steer. Brown grass from the previous fall curled round its stiffly-sticking legs.

"I 'spose they don't use the front door much anyway," Joshua thought. But he was surprised by the shattered glass in every window. "The rain will get in," he said to himself, "and their floor will be wrecked."

"Would you believe it?" Quinn said. "The government built these houses out of the national debt." He got out of the car and walked to the canvas tent which was pitched down the meadow from the house. He kicked aside some half-burnt wood, then some empty cans, as he tracked through an old campfire. He stood for a time, his head stooping through the flaps, his shoulders almost level with the cold stovepipe jutting through the roof. Near the tent a high-boxed wagon hunched, squatting on tall wooden wheels, tongue lying in the grass. Two horses, a grey and a drab paint, were tied to nearby trees. They were grazing in the sunlight; their tails switched briefly at the swarming flies. By the woodpile, across from the house, a junked car was rammed among the trees. It looked like pictures Joshua had seen of cars from the 'Thirties. It was black where rust hadn't spread like scabs. There were no wheels on it. The grass bunched beneath its fenders, between the bumpers. Three Indian children, two boys and a girl, sat in the front seat; one had his hands on the steering wheel; they all were looking over their shoulders at the Cardiff car. Except for the rise and fall of the cloud about the horses' tails, the yard seemed profoundly without motion.

Then an old woman trudged round a corner of the house. She wore a green kerchief on her head, knotted beneath her chin. She was fat and stiff. In her long and nondescript garment, she lumbered in short rushes towards the car. The sun glimmered on something she held together in both hands; they could see a tangle of wires curling beneath her forearm. When she drew near to Cardiff's window, they could make out at least a metal dome which had been catching the sun. She held the contraption up.

"Wannabuy dis doorbell, preacher man?" she said, in a voice as leathered as her skin. She was very old; her face was burnt brown, tracked very deeply with crowfeet about the eyes and incredibly wrinkled around the mouth. She had no teeth. "Ring real goodferyou. Ring. Ring." She tapped the bell with a fingernail. It made a dead sound.

"I'm not the preacher," Cardiff said. "I only look after the money from our church."

"Good," the old woman said. "Den you can easy buy dis door-bell."

"I don't think so," Cardiff said. "Where did you get it?"

"On d' house," the woman said. "By d' door. Ring. Ring." Her eyes looked as if they took in nothing, everything.

"Ring, ring," Cardiff mused, almost speculatively. He shook his head slightly. "Why should I buy a doorbell? None of my neighbors has one; I don't even have one."

"Buy it," she said. "Den you have one. Ring. Ring."

Cardiff looked down the meadow toward the tent where Quinn was still leaning in.

"How much?" he said. "Does it work?"

The woman held up the button-key in one hand. "Ring. Ring," she said.

"How much?" Cardiff said.

"Eight buck," the woman said.

"I'll give you two."

"Six buck. Ring. Ring."

"Two."

"Gophuckyerself."

Cardiff looked at Joshua, his eyes flicking quickly away, then back at the woman.

"What did you say to me?"

"Gophuckyerself, preacher man."

Cardiff opened the car door. The woman was already wad-dling away behind the vehicle.

"You shouldn't talk that way about the minister of God!" he called after her. "You unregenerate old squaw."

The children in the wrecked car were still steering the wheel, still looking back over their shoulders. The woman shuffled out of sight around the corner of the house. A loop of wire trailed behind her.

"That filthy woman," Cardiff said. "She has no right to lump us with the others. Not after all the stuff our women send from Mission Circle. She's got no call, either, to say those things to me. I'm not the sort of white man she can blame for that. You see what you get, don't you, when you try to help? I offered her two dollars for something I know I've paid for God knows how many times already in taxes, money which ought to have bought some handy

55

things for your mother. And she turns on me right while I'm trying to pay her again for that secondhand thing. What would we do with a doorbell anyway? Even if it did work?"

"Maybe we could put in on the house we'd buy from the Indians," Joshua said.

"Who was *asking* you?" said his father.

Quinn was coming back now toward the car. Two Indian men walked some distance behind him, side by side. Joshua could not have said how old they were, except they were grown men. They were about the same height, much shorter than Quinn, though one was quite stocky. They wore flopping khaki pants with wide belts. One had on a yellow-black plaid shirt; the stocky one wore a wrinkled white Sunday shirt, too long at the wrists, probably picked out from the clothes-barrel that the Mission Circle sent at the end of every month. Each man had pulled low over his eyes a cheap baseball cap, so they appeared to look at nothing but the ground as they walked.

Quinn got into the front seat for the first time then, cramping the boy enough so that he could not turn around. When the hired men climbed into the back seat, Quinn made the introductions without a backward look.

"Walking Horse, Joe Little-dog, this is Mr. Cardiff. He's your boss if you promise not to spend the money on booze." Quinn sounded as if he were about to laugh, only when he did it would be a very private laugh, he was going to save it until he got home.

Joshua's father turned part way round so that he could see one of the faces. "Boys," he said. There was silence then, not even the silence of polite curiosity, but a silence which seemed to grow sullen in the twelve-mile ride back to the farm. It was an adult kind of surliness, a conscious and deliberate ignoring, which Joshua dared not intrude upon, even after they had dropped the Agent. It was, in fact, only after Quinn got off at his driveway and they drove on in the silence sharper than ever before that he realized the Agent had not been a part of it, or if he had, the lines of feeling had been flickering all about the boy in their circuit to and from his father.

When they reached home, his mother was at work in the garden. She was kneeling in the row of lettuce as they passed. The sun was bright on her yellow hair. His father stopped the car by the well. He turned around.

56

"Boys," he said. "You see that thin strip of trees beyond the barn? The roots are there. Shake the dirt out before you pile them. My boy here will show you. Try to keep up with him."

Joshua could see Janie looking out the kitchen window. She held the gauze-white curtains like a veil in front of her. Then he turned away from the house. The two men walked in silence beside him. They were looking straight ahead.

Why did he have to go and say that? I want so bad to try and like them though it's going to be hard when they look like they don't care and he only cares about his money being well spent. He could smell them now more than he could in the rank silence of the car. It wasn't a beer parlour smell so much as a kitchen smell, something to do with cooking.

"Why you two?" he said at last. "Why did Quinn pick you?"

"Why shouldn' he?" the stocky one said, still not looking. "He knows."

"Knows what?" the boy said. His voice was simply curious now.

"Knows we ain't had a trip t' town fer awhile. Knows we bin lookin' fer a way."

"He knows what money's good fer," the man in the plaid shirt said abruptly. The peak of his cap still pointed at the ground.

"You mean you give him some of it?" He thought he caught it now, what his father's sullenness had been about. He began to feel angry too, at Quinn, nobody else.

"Jackfish don' catch no otter," the man in the plaid shirt said, curt as before.

"Dey jus' drink d' same water," the stocky one said, grinning.

There was silence again. They were among the trees now, treading in the dappled shade.

"Were you the ones who broke windows at the Camp a couple years ago?" he said finally. "Did you chop up the bunks my Dad was building?"

"You think we ain't got little kids too?" the sour-plaid said.

"He means," the white-shirt said grinning, "we got juv'nile frequency problems jus' like ever'body else."

They walked unspeaking for a few steps more.

Then he said, "Who's who? Who's Joe and who's Walking?"

The man in the white shirt laughed. "We're all walkin'," he said. "Only I'm a Walkin' Horse. Dis guy here, he's a walkin' dog,

I guess. Hey Joe?"

"What's d' boy?" Joe Little-dog said. "A walkin' eagle?"

"Why do you say that? My name's Joshua."

"Why you got no hair, Josh?" said Walking Horse. "Dat's all dis dog here wan's to know. He t'inks maybe yer eagle clan."

"I wish I was," Joshua said. "Then I'd have a reason to be bald. There's nobody could say different then."

"Looks ver' good," Joe Little-dog said. "Hard to scalp."

"Do you still do that?" Joshua said, growing slightly anxious.

"Nah," said Walking Horse. "Joe's jus' kiddin' you a little. He seen dis movie show in Nisooskan. Joe's only havin' fun wid you."

"Should put bear grease on it," said Joe Little-dog. "Shine like d' sun."

They had come out through the thin strip of trees now, and the field lay baking beneath the sun. It looked hopelessly big. They could hear the tractor start up in the distance, then mutter softly in the yard.

"I still don't really understand," he said, looking for the first time directly at the two men. "I'm glad he did, but why did Quinn go to you?"

Walking Horse lifted the peak of his cap. His eyes were dark, quite as dark as a field and almost as level.

"Joe an' me have done a lot of work before," he said. He paused, as if choosing his words carefully. "You see, some of Joe's family has had t' go t' work before. Dere was a time when we was changin' off regular wid a man from Nisooskan." He stopped briefly, searching, then continued again. "He come by Quinn's place lookin' fer help, you see, an' Quinn said Joe's oldes' daughter could help him most. Feschuk was dat man's name from Nisooskan. He made homebrew in his basemen', most of it no good. But he always left a jug wid Quinn w'en he come up. So Quinn had us over regilar to share it, 'til we found out Mrs. Feschuk was lookin' fer help in Nisooskan. So me an' Joe wen' down t' take d' job an' each time we was through she give us homebrew. She never give us a jug 'cause she said she couldn' have her husband findin' out. She always give it to us in pickle jars. So we would stop in at Quinn's place on our way home an' work on d' jug Feschuk had lef' on his way to see Joe's daughter, an' den we'd start on d' pickle jars we brung from our work in Nisooskan. Dat Mrs. Feschuk was sure a fine woman. Big as a cow moose an' a real hard worker. Said she liked Ind-yun help because she was Metis herself."

"So Quinn knew," the boy said. "And he did what my Dad asked him not to. What's he getting out of your work here today, anyway?"

"Nothin'," Walking Horse said. "Nothin' unless yer fad-der had some homebrew in his basemen'. But Quinn said you couldn' spec' much else when dere ain't bin no work fer such a long time. Not since Joe's daughter moved t' Sas-katoon. He said he's happy anyhow. He's bin wantin' t' do somet'ing fer d' church people ever since dey spoke t' him, you know, 'bout d' way he lets white folks git along wid us Ind-yuns."

"Then I ain't gonna let it concern me," the boy said. "That's between you and him. But what was Joe's daughter doin' for Mr. Feschuk? The same as you was doin' for Mrs. Feschuk?"

Walking Horse looked at Joe Little-dog. Joe Little-dog's cap turned out and away.

"No," Walking Horse said slowly. "No, we couldn' do d' same as her."

"Why?" Joshua said. "Was what she done so awful?"

" 'Course not," Walking Horse said. "What she done was mos' normal. Dey was in d' bush an' she was showin' him how t' trap beaver."

"Oh," Joshua said. "I thought it was something bad because of Mrs. Feschuk."

"Yer thinkin' more'n is good fer a boy yer age," Walking Horse said. "We was only doin' town work. Hoein' in d' garden. Helpin' her t' hill her potatoes."

"Then I know what it's like," the boy said. "We got an acre of Netted Gems alongside the summer spuds and I had to hill them all myself when I got home from Camp. See, I still got the blisters on my palms. They didn't break."

"You wait till you git older," Walking Horse said. "You won' git dem blisters den. You don' have t' use yer hands so much w'en you bin doin' it awhile."

Joe laughed, two barks.

It made him hesitate. Then he said, "I know what you mean. My Grandpa's been doin' it that way since before his children was born. He goes with both feet, up and down, straddling the row."

"I guest dat much w'en we met yer fad-der," Walking Horse

59

said. "I could see right away he's a big one too. Ain't dat so, Joe?"

Joe Little-dog laughed again.

Then neither man was laughing and the conversation seemed suddenly forgotten. They were all three of them gazing down an avenue which dropped from view over the edge of the hill, looking down a main street paved (though heaving already) with roots and walled up high on either side by heaped-up brush and earth. It was not the only street; beyond its walls, the burnt and burning trees from other rows jutted like block upon block of haze-bound chimneys.

"There must be a million roots," Joshua said. He sighed heavily. The dismal smell of wood ash and loam, of naked open earth, settled in his lungs; it felt like it touched bottom.

"How come yer fad-der din' plow down his garbage dump?" Walking Horse said.

"What do you mean?" the boy said.

"D' on'y place where he missed a tree." Walking Horse was pointing. "Dat dirt hill over in d' second row. Or is dat where he hides his still?"

"He doesn't have a still," Joshua said. "My mom wouldn't let him. Not even if he wanted to."

"Den I ain't gonna put my nose in no garbage dump," Joe Little-dog said. "Or in no cess pool."

"You don't understand," Joshua replied. "It's an Indian burial mound. That's your people there. I managed to save it when the brushcutters came."

"How you know dey ain't Blackfeet in dere?" Walking Horse said, grinning. "I wouldn' a bust my ass fer no Blackfeet."

A bird sang above them and behind them, hidden among the leaves. It sang six or seven notes, then ceased abruptly, as if it had choked on its own liquid gush.

"They were here first," he said at last. "Before me or my father or any white man. I thought you would understand."

"D' Crees wiped 'em out if dey was Blackfeet," Joe Little-dog said. "Maybe it was my grandfad-der dat killed 'em off." He looked at the burial mound for a moment as if he owned it.

Then they could hear the tractor coming up the east side of the bush.

"Dat yer fad-der comin'?" Walking Horse said.

"He's bringing a chain," Joshua said. "To pull the stumps.

That's fun to watch." But all the fun seemed spoiled for him now.

"Sittin' in d' shade, maybe," Joe Little-dog said. "Dis is hotter out here dan a hoo-ers pants."

"Than a what?" he asked, remotely interested.

"It's somet'ing hot," Walking Horse said. "When it ain't got hoo-er frost on it."

They walked on in silence for a time. Then, with the tractor nearing the corner of the bush, Walking Horse spoke again.

"You still ain't said, Josh, why you got no hair."

Joshua felt a little uncomfortable. "It just fell out," he said. "Night after night it was layin' there on the pillow."

Both men stood very quietly for a moment. Somewhere overhead a kildeer cried, perched in the air itself.

"I bet you," Walking Horse said finally, "dat dem white kids laughed you around a lot."

He nodded, more self-conscious than ever now. Then the two men stooped toward the roots.

When Richard Cardiff rounded the turn of the woods, all three of them were beginning to smell their sweat mix with earth and drifting smoke. The John Deere bore on steadily toward them, its cylinders detonating like two rapid hammers on a lead roof. Jets of dust wheeled up behind the rubber lugs of the big rear tires and plumed like the tail of some dirty comet. When it was almost upon them, Cardiff clutched and braked the machine, pulling back in the same motion on the throttle.

"Joshua!" he called from the tractor seat. The idling engine pounded around his voice. "Come up here." He motioned with his hand.

Joshua heaved a bumpy piece of wood on his pile and ran over. He climbed up on the drawbar hitch so he could hear.

"What have they been doing out here?" his father said. "You've only got three little piles."

"We didn't know where to start," he shouted above the steady din. "I wasn't sure *where*." He had to lean toward his father's ear with the last word.

"At your feet. Anywhere, all around. I want you to keep them working as fast as you can. I'm going to pull some stumps." He pointed northward over the brow of the hill. "Down there. Remember now. As fast as you can. I'm putting you in charge."

Joshua got down. The tractor engine throbbed like a headache.

"We're s'posed to go faster," he told the two Indian men who worked without looking at the tractor.

Cardiff sat on the blunt-faced engine, watching them. Walking Horse was working now at a full gallop, flinging the earth-clinging roots into round tipi-mounds for burning. Joe Little-dog moved at one speed, SLOW, but he was thorough: bending from the waist, reaching, closing, disposing, then reaching again, as though he were clearing a floor of broken glass. At last when Cardiff rode off on the tractor (every second the thunder of hammers on sheet metal growing quieter —'til, with the curve of earth between them, the sound coming up like drums, only much quicker, sharper), Walking Horse slowed to the enduring pace of his partner.

Finally the sound of the John Deere beat too thinly on the summer air — it was simply gone — as if its very bulk, the solidity which made it powerful, had dissolved in the wide-open spaces.

"Le's take a rest," Joe Little-dog said flatly. He was already walking toward the trees, wiping his palms up and down, up and down on his pants as he went.

Walking Horse started a new pile with a club-root.

"Come on wid us," he said. "You'll go funny in dis sun."

"I can't," the boy said. "You better not either. He put me in charge."

"*Moostosomay,*" Walking Horse said sharply. "Tell 'im we dragged you away. No man c'n stand in dis heat all day. Tell 'im you had to go find shade fer yer head."

"If you got to take a rest," he said, "don't be too long," bending to hide his shame. He persisted for a time in dragging roots as big as himself to his pile, hauling on the dark, dank wood which seemed an embarrassment above ground, like women's panties hung on a clothesline. Each backward step he took was earned in sweat out of the crumbling soil; the dust, at times wind-whipped, burned in his eye-sockets. It was not long, however, before the roots and sun and wind made him change his mind. The threat of his father's wrath grew distant, remote, and he too turned to the trees.

The men sat in a patch of shaded grass inside the shrunken pasture. Joe Little-dog rested with his back against a white poplar. Joshua stood outside the fence for a moment, trying to hold the eyes that took in nothing, everything.

"My father might come back soon."

"Den we work," Joe Little-dog said.

The boy stepped through the barb wire fence, spreading it like a bow. He sat down in the speckled shade, facing the men though not looking at them now. He looked through the few standing trees into the yard, saw the red-painted granaries and the unpainted barn. The barn was partly screened by a hazelnut bush.

"I picked a milk pail full of hazelnuts here before the fire," he said. "And my mom and me picked six milk pails full of saskatoons. There won't be nothing like that left in this bit of bush."

The men said nothing.

He thought for a long time about what he might say next. At last he said, "Can white people ever go to a Sun Dance?"

Walking Horse didn't seem to hear him for a moment. Then he said brusquely, "You mean it was jus' layin' dere on d' pillow?" He was looking intently now at Joshua's head which felt suddenly as if it were afire. The boy nodded ever so slightly.

Them too then, even they won't let me be; there ain't nobody in the world who'll leave it alone. He felt for a moment like Joel sitting on the barber's stool.

Walking Horse looked at Joe Little-dog.

"*Mistikwan*. A head like dat," he said gravely. "Scalp by Manito. An' he ain't even Ind-yun."

Joe Little-dog nodded, not looking.

"*Muskikeweyinew*," Walking Horse said softly. He let his breath out as if he had been holding it. "Medicine-man."

He took a brown, squarish bottle out of his pocket from behind the drawn-up knees. There was no label on it; bits of white glue-paper stuck on the glass. He uncapped it, raised it to his lips. His Adam's apple jerked as he swallowed. Then, wiping his mouth and chin with the underside of his arm, he passed the bottle to Joe Little-dog. Joe Little-dog did not wipe the mouth of the glass; he took two great pulls at it, bellowing his cheeks. Then he licked his lips and held out the bottle to the boy. Joshua hesitated. *The very woods, the air, the sun flee away, they vanish. Old Bran's body lies off from his head, the eyes closed and the neck-stump still draining into the grass, only it isn't blood exactly, it looks thinner like maybe it's colored alcohol. Grandpa says it's what you should expect, it's what's coming to you if you drink with Indians, and these are the ones. The judge hung their chief almost fifty years ago, hung him by the neck 'til he was dead.*

For an instant, Joshua could see a kind of photograph of himself, lying on the grass, his own severed head paler than his ancestor's had been. His world hung for him like a ball in the balance. Then he reached for the bottle, touching the stub brown fingers, still not looking at Joe Little-dog's face. Without wiping the top, he drew violently from it.

The liquid spurted to the back of his throat. It burned sweetly at first, then with a tinge of bittersweet, and he had to swallow quickly to keep from choking on it. It reminded him vaguely of whitecake. He gulped once more from it to be equal with the men. Then quickly, a little awkwardly perhaps, he passed the bottle to Walking Horse who nodded, lifted it to his lips once more. Joe Little-dog took it in turn, one more swallow, and then he was peering down inside the bottleneck. He grunted. Then he stood up. Joshua began to get to his feet too, except that Walking Horse was already beside him, one hand on his shoulder, and he was shoved gently down again.

"Scalp-by-Manito," Walking Horse said. "Dat's your name now." Then the liquid was cascading on his head, warm and sticky, and it trickled behind his ears, down his neck like flies walking on his skin. He did not pull away. Though even now, with his head itching like he'd stuck it in a honey pail, he did not fully understand.

"The drums," he said in a small voice. "What do they mean?"

"Dey don' mean nothin'," Walking Horse said softly.

"*Mistikwuskik,*" Joe Little-dog said. "Jus' drums."

They were all standing now, with Joshua searching the two fat-cheeked faces for a sign, and there was nothing. Walking Horse capped the empty bottle, put it in his pocket.

"Le's pick d' roots," he said. "We don' wan' you t' git a lickin' from yer fad-der."

"He wouldn't lick me for the roots," Joshua said. "He'd just be mad. What he'd really lick me for is the drinking. Though I ain't drunk."

" 'Course you ain't," Joe Little-dog said. "None of us ain't. Dat's d' trouble. But d' quicker we get dis fuckin' mess cleaned up, d' less he will be able to suspec'. He won' know nothin'."

"There's this stuff on my head. I must smell like a layer cake."

"You jus' say it's to keep d' bugs off. Say we give it to you — it's

64

an old Ind-yun treatmint."

But by the time the tractor returned, the sun had already dried his head. It didn't matter that when he moved his lips, his whole scalp moved like a crust of ice.

At dinner time, his father brought lunch pails on the tractor. They knelt then in the shade of the silent machine, smelling the gasoline and the cooling metal, and Cardiff said, "You're picking up a bit. But we've got a long way to go." They were at the crest of the hill now; all the way behind them, their boulevard appeared to be dotted with stooks ready for harvest. Farther down the slope, the land looked more like a hailed-out crop.

Cardiff had brought three quart jars of Kool-Aid — raspberry, grape and lemon — and they all drank a great deal before they felt ready to eat. There were thick slices of Prem, buttered home-made bread, deltas of apple pie, and chocolate cake. They washed it all down with Kool-Aid; as the meal dwindled, there were more and more crumbs left floating in the jar.

The boy's father left the tractor sitting there after lunch. He worked beside them through the suffocating hours of the after-noon. They stooped and rose and stooped until it seemed they could not rise again, as if their backbones had been drawn like bows. But they straightened up and went on and on and on like that. The sun poured down like lava, though it did not burn the boy's polished skull.

At supper time, in the golden light of late afternoon, the Indian men asked for their pay. They were in the second last avenue, near the bottom of the hill. Cardiff stopped working, looked up the long slope at the rows of wooden mounds. There was urgency yet in his sweat-blinking eyes, a kind of madness to be finished with it now instead of later. The look lingered for a moment, then his face relaxed.

"We've done enough," he said. "My boy and me can finish this bit tomorrow." He reached for his wallet. His hands were black with mud. He took two crisp notes out very gingerly. They were purple. "I'm giving you a bit of a bonus," he said. "I didn't figure you'd work so hard. You boys are the best hired men I ever had. In fact, I never dreamed of getting this far today."

Walking Horse reached for his money, then Joe Little-dog. Each mumbled something, not looking him in the face.

"I'll give you a ride back to the Reserve right away," Cardiff said.

"Nah," said Walking Horse. "Gotta check d' mail."

"You want a ride to town first?"

"Nah," Joe Little-dog said. "We're used t' walkin'."

"Well so long den," Walking Horse said. They were both looking at the boy. Then they were gone, walking across the bottom of the field to the railway track. Their shadows stretched before them as they went.

Cardiff looked for a moment as if he would change his mind. Then he looked up the hill.

"Well, they earned it," he said briskly. He did not look at the boy.

They were already scrubbing their hands and faces in the washroom next to the kitchen when Joshua's mother came in.

"Where are the hired men?" she said.

"They left," Cardiff said.

"You mean you didn't ask them to stay to supper?"

"I couldn't," he said at last. "They wanted to go to town."

"You didn't even ask them," she said. "That's the reason they're walking into town. Those poor men. They're going to miss their supper after the kind of day they put in. And then they'll have to walk home at the end of it. Lord knows they'll be drunk. Those poor men."

"I'm not going after them now," Cardiff said, wiping hands that were still muddy on the towel. "Probably they wouldn't have got into the car anyhow." A hint of a smile jerked at the corners of his mouth.

"You could have at least paid them after you took them home," she said, her face flushed as if she were going to cry. She turned away into the kitchen and the boy could hear the pots being clinked at the stove.

There was far too much of everything on the table. Joshua felt almost too weary to eat. He stayed at it a long time; finally he was too full. Then he felt ashamed because the men had had no supper. " 'Course they got money," he thought. "They must serve something in the beer parlour besides beer."

But in the end, no matter how many times he thought about their money, it was not enough. He looked into the living room where his father lay on the rug beneath the radio. The CBC announcer droned like a fly in a coffin.

I got to walk the second mile then though I'm not even sure I'll find them there, and I ache too much to walk at all. They ain't asking me either to walk that second mile they ain't even asking me to walk the first. But I got to I got to now

The remains of supper lay cold on the table. His mother was milking the cows, letting his father rest after the day in the field. He could hear Janie talking to the cats in the yard. He peeped in at his father once more; Cardiff lay sunk into the floor, sagging in almost-sleep. Swiftly then, he crammed pork chops into his pockets. He thought about mashed potatoes as well but he couldn't carry a serving dish in plain sight.

Would they be safe in a pocket I wonder or would they soak through the cloth and run down my leg? I don't want no potatoes in my socks when I'm walking, that's the last thing I need and besides they're white; they'd show the lint too bad. He settled finally for the six pork chops. His buttocks felt like sausages inside his jeans.

Janie looked up as he came out the back door. She was sitting on the grass with a lap-cat, stroking its fur.

"Where you going, Josh?" she called at once.

"Crazy," he said. "Wanna come?"

"No," she said. "You look crazy. How come yer pants are so funny?"

But he was beyond the house already, on the gravelled drive.

It was a long walk, ten black hydro-poles to the railway tracks, turning, then nineteen more poles to his Uncle Owen's gate. From there it would be a half-mile into town. Every foot of the way had ceased long ago to be conscious to him; he paced himself by the poles, one hundred-fifty steps when he was in a hurry, one hundred-seventy if he was dawdling, and the numbers clicked unseen in his mind, never aware that he was even counting. This evening, although he did not see it, he registered below one-fifty.

The air was tender now, caressing, like salve upon sunburn. A soft breeze drifted from the south. The earth was alive again; the crisped and drooping wheat woke up in the wind, it clashed like tiny troops of spear. Insects swarmed above the road, head-high; at times they needed brushing aside, like cob-webs hung in a door-way. He heard a meadowlark drool its song; he caught sight of it at last atop a thick, square post along the railway fence. On each side, field mice scoured in quick rushes through the ditch-grass. He thought they must be feeding before the night and owls winged over the earth. His shadow lengthened in the adjacent field; he chased its giant strides, hoping he would be in time.

Joel saw him first, across the track embankment.

"Hey Josh!" he yelled. "Come on an' play high-skyers."

He looked into Uncle Owen's yard. Joel was waving a bat. Auntie Bee looked out through curtains.

"Can't now," he called. "Got to go to town."

Joel was running after him.

"You can be Yankees if you want. I'll be Dodgers."

"Thanks," he said. "But I got to get to town real quick."

"Hey, Josh, did you poop yer pants? They're all mussy. Wait up. Hey come on, Greasy Legs! Hey, I really think you crapped yourself! Is that why you got to get to town so fast?"

He was running himself now to get out of reach. His pants bulged behind him, strained on his thighs. He touched his seat with one hand; it was oily and wet.

The hotel, when he reached it, was dark. There wasn't a sign of Donna. Not a window in three stories was lit. But the low adjoining shed was aglow with lamplight and with voices. He stepped across the threshold of the porch. As he pushed on the inner door, a weight drew up on a pulley. The voices came suddenly loud and mingled. It was dark at first inside; he could see the faceless clumps of people about the room. Gradually, his eyes took in the squat round tables, then the bright glasses of beer, then the faces of farmers and townsmen whom he knew. He had never been inside the beer parlour before. It was sunk beneath the level of the sidewalk. On the right, a short stairway led up to a thick oak door. He had seen the other side of it in the hotel lobby. Opposite the street entrance stood the bar. It opened through a frame into a cubby-hole enclosure, like the hot-dog booth in the curling rink. Mr. Klimchuk was back there now. But he wasn't making hot dogs. He was drawing beer from a tap into glasses. He set the bubble-streaming glasses onto a tray. His bare arms moved very quickly.

Then he was carrying the tray with the clustered glasses into the room. He was a tall, thin, handsome man. He wore a white shirt rolled to the elbows, a black string-tie. He walked with a trace of a limp; he had taken a hit in the knee on D-Day.

"Well Josh," he said, "have you Cardiffs taken to drink at last? Glad to have you. I've been waiting a long time for your people's business. You'll have to do me one favor, though, before I take your order. Show me your birth certificate. I can't take a chance on losing my license, you know. Even though you folks come in here so seldom."

A number of men had stopped talking. They were watching, grinning.

"Please sir," he said. "I'm not here for that. I'm looking for Walking Horse and Joe Little-dog."

"I thought it was too good to last," the bartender said. "Ought to know you church-folk would come chasing after Indians before you'd drink with white people. Them boys is back there in that corner. Wake 'em up sort of gentle. I can't afford no more busted furniture. You come to hire them on again tomorrow, did you?"

"No sir. I brought them somethin' they forgot."

Mr. Klimchuk was setting the bright glasses on a table.

"What's that?" he said. "Their bottle of vanilla extract? That's all I need."

But Joshua didn't have to answer. He was already weaving through the scatter of voices and chairs. Eyes followed him as he passed. He heard running titters, short claps of amusement. Then a hand touched his shoulder from behind.

"Sonny," the voice said, "the shithouse is in that ere di-rection. Do ya need a spoon ta scoop it out?"

He looked back; the man was old, grizzled-cheeked. All the men were grinning broadly. They didn't look toward his eyes; they were staring at his behind. He put his hands into his back pockets. They were sopping.

Joe Little-dog was sitting with his forehead on the table. His crow-black hair drooped over his money. A blue note and some silver lay among the empty glasses across the table. The empty chair was pushed back, as though its occupant were about to return.

He hesitated beside Joe Little-dog for an instant. He didn't want to rouse him suddenly. Then Walking Horse appeared next to him, buttoning his fly. His eyes were streaked with red.

"*Tshay,*" he said. "Yer shouldn' drink so much d' first day. Yer better go home."

"You needed something to eat," he said. "I brought you some supper."

Walking Horse squeezed his shoulder.

69

"Somet'ing to eat," he said very slowly. "Yer a real Ind-yun."

The pork chops caught in his pockets as he tugged at them. They hung for an instant on the lining, then slipped like six-guns from their well-oiled holsters. He held them, dripping, in both hands; they cast blunt shadows on the walls. A burst of laughter slapped at his behind. Walking Horse smiled level with his eyes, not much taller than him, and his eyes were red.

"*Hi!*" he said. "Somet'ing to eat." He sat down abruptly. For a moment he sat very still, blinking as though trying to hold something back, then he fell with a wooden sound onto the table. His head spilled the glasses aside.

Joshua set the pork chops down beside the heavy-breathing faces, away from the long straight locks of crow-black hair. The laughter leaped all around him. He turned and ran then, eyes on the floor, out through the single voice of the room. The laughter licked at his heels like bright flames.

As he neared home again, the sun stood like a pillar of fire on the joist of dark horizon, and its blaze ran lightly overhead on cirrus rafters. Stones in the road stood out sharply in its glare; weeds by the roadside took on new definition, dimension. The bush around the house looked black against the burning sky. By the time he reached the yard, the earth itself was afire.

"Joshua!" Janie yelled from somewhere in the shadows. "Joshua, Mom's real mad at you. She had to separate the milk herself. I helped."

I didn't do none of us any good then; Mom had to do my work plus dishes too and I failed even to get there in time to help the men. I didn't accomplish nothing but trouble; and wait until she sees my pants

He went directly to the well and, hooking the piece of eaves-troughing over the spout, he began to pump the trough full for the week. It took a long time. He was very tired. When the water splashed at last over onto the gravel, he sat down on the platform. He watched the color fading from the earth, from blues and violets to black. The sky drained like a sinking pool of light; it was the last thing to hold color, turning clinker-grey before the stars came out.

The back door opened briefly.

"Joshua," his mother said, "come in here right away." Her voice sounded thin more than it did angry. "I'm tired, I hoed all day and now I've worked half the night besides. I won't wait much longer to have a talk with you. Come in before I decide to speak to your father."

"Okay," he said, wearily.

The screen door closed. At that moment he saw two men pass in the highroad beyond the garden. Their gait was uneven and they lurched at times as if fighting the stiff-backed road. He waved, standing on the elevated cap of the well, and one of them, it looked like a white-shirted arm, waved in return. He watched after them until they had vanished in the gathering darkness. He hoped they would make it back all right to the Reserve.

So maybe it wasn't for nothing, they did come to; and when she knows at least there is a reason.

iii

"I hear in town," Grandpa said, "that you've been in the pub with Indians."

"I had to," Joshua said, looking into the grass-green eyes which, if they weren't much taller than him any more, still seemed to look down at him from a height. "They'd worked all day and didn't get no supper. So I took in pork chops."

Joshua's arm and shoulder ached. For thirty minutes, he had churned cream for Grandma in the kitchen. He wandered out to the sun porch only after the cream slapped hard to butter. Grandma said Grandpa was taking his rest from summerfallow.

"I heard that too," Grandpa said, still looking like it was from on high. "But don't you fear for your very soul? Haven't you considered your great-Grandpa, my own father, what happened to him because he drank with Indians?"

Joshua was tempted to say he had only been a delivery boy, he hadn't stopped to drink in the beer parlour. But he could not say it with the picture still in his mind of the brown hands passing him the bottle and the surprising taste of whitecake, hot and burning, out there in the field of roots.

But how could he know that? He doesn't even know about the

71

name. I can't let him find out about that, ever.

Grandpa was speaking again before Joshua could say anything. It was like he wanted to be certain that the choices were clear, that there could be no middle ground.

"Do you really want, like him, to spend eternity in hell?" His tone implied, grave as it was, that he could not be held responsible, should Joshua wake up one day and find himself in torment; it would have to be his own wilful doing, nothing more or less.

"No," Joshua said softly, looking out the window of the sun porch. His fingers skidded down the jumps on the siding of the old homestead-house. The horseshoe pits where he tried to play (though he could not win) against Grandpa stood out darkly in the grass beneath the lilac hedge.

The set of Grandpa's jaw relaxed slowly. He didn't smile, but the lines began to show again, like warm furrows turned from the hummock of nose down past the draw of his lips. His face brightened like a June pasture.

"I always figured you were a good boy at heart," he said. "Even if you did inherit my obstinacy."

"But why's it got to be Indians?" Joshua said. "Why're you just against *them?*"

"I'm not," Grandpa said finally. "I'm against all drunkards, whoever they are. Remember the Proverb, 'Wine is a mocker, strong drink is raging.' Those Indians brought out the worst in my dad with their drinking and fornicating, they made him mock and rage like he hadn't done since he came over. He would have been all right if it hadn't been for them. But they were here and he acted no better than a wildman until the time they killed him. He had it coming to him. Though I can't forget about it. You couldn't know what that has meant to me."

Joshua was stung by the sudden pain in his Grandpa's voice, and it irritated him a little, as if it were unfair that anyone should feel they'd suffered as much as he. Then his face must have registered his disbelief.

"I knew you couldn't realize it," Grandpa said. "You didn't know him like I do. I don't know if I can even make you see him like he was, with Indians or without them, though they made him much, much worse. Most of it I even hate to say. Do you think it would help you understand at all how I feel? I wouldn't tell it otherwise."

72

"Sure it would," Joshua said, hoping to hear finally what it was about old Bran with the Indians. Maybe, that way, he could avoid it himself. "How will I know what's good and what's evil unless you tell me exactly?"

"Well," Grandpa said slowly, his calm costing him some effort, "for one thing, he couldn't sit still, he was always running somewhere. Wherever he was wasn't good enough. You might put it that he was going to and fro in the earth, he was always walking up and down in it. He was only seventeen years old, just four years older than you, when he left Wales in 1884, we don't know why for certain, although I'm sure he didn't have time to snatch up a second pair of trousers, he was in that much of a hurry. I've heard since from the Gwynnes — you know them, the ones in Melfort, they come from a neighboring shire in Wales — that he somehow gave outrage to his elder brother, to some right or other, and knowing what comes later I can guess what it might be, so that even his father wanted him gone at once, never to show his face in the house again. That's where we come from; that's the kind of blood we have to live down."

Grandpa looked down at him a good while before he went on. Joshua could hear the wind through the screen door rushing in the trees. Then, when Grandpa started up again, it was like his face was floating free of his body, looming at first above him, then carrying Joshua with him, and he forgot the walls around them, the wind outside, he was riding only on the fall and rise of Grandpa's words.

"He came running with the terror behind him, not even daring to look back, and when he stopped the first time, he was in Toronto. He couldn't have stayed long, because he was next on a troop train bound for the West (himself a West Country man), apparently not even caring which side of the fight he'd be on.

running old Bran hurtling on flatcars through the black of night through rock and bog and ice and snow to where the rails ended then not even pausing for breath but flying over the burning ice until there was track again and racing once more to get into the quiet immensity of the land

"He didn't even know," Grandpa said, "who Louis Riel was. And for once in his life he was on the right side, most likely because he didn't know. But I suppose you know your history, it didn't take long at all to defeat a ragged crew of half-breeds and cowardly Indians. And of course the Canadians had the man with the gun, the Gatling machine gun; my Dad said he handled it each time Howard took a rest. He said he even got pretty good with it."

running old Bran rushing with the gun around Batoche and pumping pumping it spurting lead from the hot barrel until it shone like a halo around him

"Afterwards the Crown expressed its gratitude in land, a quarter of sod near Saskatoon, but he wouldn't stay on the prairie, he tried two whole summers to stick it out, then he had to come north and east this time to be in the woods once more, settling down for a change right here on this spot, but almost at once running again, this time to the Reservation, going there over and over though now he homesteaded the land, cut down the bush, that the Indians he consorted with had once hunted in."

running with the terror dragged like a blade behind him, knocking down trees in his wake, laying clear the earth, and he farming now furiously by day the broken land that he might drink by night as furiously of the wild, almost Celtic, spirit in the woods, then running back in almost dawn to race over a field with a disc and horses

"My mother would always be waiting for him then. She would have the cows milked already and the horses waiting in harness when he returned at sunrise, his eyes inflamed with sleeplessness and drink, to ride whatever implement she would hitch for him in hurried clatter to the fields. Lord knows how she put up with it. I often wonder why she married him, what she saw in him in the first place. She was so slow, so quiet, such a homebody herself. From the outset she must have forborne him. I suppose, too, that she must have known something of the old, terrible rituals in the woods, having come herself from the forests of Bavaria. Anyway, she never went with him, never once asked him even to keep account. As she might so well have done."

running from one squaw to the other barely stopped before he was off again running to another

"I was just fifteen when he died. I've never told anyone this before, Joshua, not anyone. I try — never — to think of it. But I saw him . . . I saw him there in the grass and I tried to stop him. He wouldn't hear of it. Almost right away he was off again, don't you see, there was nothing I could do. He met the Chief's wife, a fat ugly squaw under the trees, and he was gone . . ."

barely stopped before he was off again driving into . . . the blunt axe bite falling running hot and sticky for an instant through the roots of the grass before . . . blackness

"I was still running when I got home. There was no one ever to let her know, don't you see? She could die not having to find out the truth. It was only a year later she passed away, never having to picture for herself the hell he went to. She died believing in Jesus. We both got saved, you see, after the funeral, in the tent of an evangelist who had come to the town sports-grounds. So do you see a little now of what this means to me? Do you see why I don't want you going to those Indians?"

Grandpa's face was dearer to him suddenly than it had ever been. Yet he heard himself say, knowing even as the words tripped off his tongue how cruel it was, "If it meant so much to you, why did you let my uncle go back with the Indians. Why didn't you try to stop him too?"

Grandpa's face was scrubbed with sorrow.

"Because," he said, "I knew he wasn't going there to act like them. God led him to that camp at Ft. a La Corne to save them from sin, not to add to it."

Something stiff and stubborn, mere logic, perhaps, was driving Joshua on. He couldn't escape it.

"But didn't you lose the one as much as the other? I never knew my uncle any more than I did great-Grandpa."

"No," Grandpa said steadily. "I know my son is in heaven; I know my father went to hell. Him, I hope, you will never meet. If you remain true to the Lord like you said you would that day when, at the age of six by my knee, you took Him into your heart, then I know you'll meet your Uncle Joshua in heaven. He's there right now, where God has wiped the tears forever from his eyes and he's waiting only for the rest of us who're coming from the other shore. He'll be playing along with Gabriel until the trumpet of the Lord shall sound."

Grandpa's hands gripped the wooden scrolls on the front of the armchair. His knuckles were tanned as dark as the maple. They unclenched slowly as the hope, like sudden hunger, on his face turned in his eyes to thoughtfulness. After a time he got up spryly and went over to the roll-top writing desk. He took a key from a packet of envelopes and squatted on his heels before the lowest drawer. When he stood up again, he had a silver trumpet in his hands.

"This was your Uncle Joshua's," he said softly, holding it like it was crafted out of egg-shell. "A Getzen. The finest trumpet money could buy. I bought it at a music store in Saskatoon for his thirteenth birthday. He'd been taking lessons on a used one for five years. He learned to play this one so it would melt the heart of a stoic. I used to think it sounded like the morning stars sang together. Every note seemed to go inside you. It hasn't been played since the day he died. Look here on the bell where it's dented, where the brass is crimped. He had it with him at Ft. a La Corne. The Indians put it in the pine-box with him. I guess they thought we were going to bury him with the horn in his hands. It was their old pagan notions yet, though they said afterwards, when some of them were saved, that he seemed to bring all heaven down to them when he played it in the big tent. Somebody closed the lid on it when they were nailing it down."

He held out with both hands the instrument to Joshua, waiting carefully until the boy had placed in turn both hands on it.

"I want you to have it," he said. "To keep it for him. To learn to play it as well as you can. There's a lady in Nisooskan who gave him his lessons. She's still living and, as far as I know, still playing. She was a wonderful teacher. Josh said everything he knew he learned from her."

Joshua straightened the trumpet out before him, getting the feel of it in his hands. Still there was something inside him as cool and unyielding as the metal.

"Now I think I know what you mean," he said, "about great-Grandpa. But what about the Indians? You said yourself that some of them were saved because of Uncle Josh."

Grandpa looked long and closely at the trumpet.

"They were a different band. They weren't contaminated by my father's evil."

"But these ones weren't even living then. They're younger than you. I know some of them; they know me even by name."

"Then you'd best walk on the other side of the street from them. There are Indians out there as old as me. They were living when it happened. I know them better than you; you're in danger, make no mistake. You ought to be recalling that Proverb: 'Make

no friendship with an angry man; and with a furious man thou
shalt not go: lest thou learn his ways, and get a snare to thy soul.'
Remember that; I don't want to argue with you about it. You're in
danger, real danger, of your immortal soul."

Grandpa's face was quiet, but its gravity outweighed him. The
spine of his logic broke into pieces. He was quiet, hearing only the
heaviness of Grandpa's breathing.

*Blessed are the peacemakers: for they shall be called the children
of God.*

Then he remembered. And he said so. He added, too, for good
measure, what his mother said about doing unto others as we
would *have* them do, not like they do in fact.

"What would you think," he said, "if it was the other way
around and they just left us to hell?"

Grandpa looked away.

"Your mother's right," he said after a time. "I guess all this
time I've been thinking just about us. I've been wrong for the right
reason."

He looked at the trumpet, the shining silver of it lying in the
boy's hands.

"You still haven't said you'll try to learn it. Do you feel at all
you might want to?"

There was something warm and welling inside Joshua. He was
nodding like his head was the tail of a dog, it wouldn't stop.

"All right then, I'll tell you what. You try this instrument over
the winter, all I ask is that you be faithful in your lessons, and I'll
see what I can do about bringing an Indian boy to Camp. You've
helped me open my eyes; there's no reason why we shouldn't
suffer the little children, as Jesus commanded us. Do we have a
deal?"

"Boy, do we ever. I'll try my best, Grandpa. I hope I can learn
how to play like Uncle Josh did. I hope you'll still like the sound
of it." The dent felt like only the slightest crease beneath his
searching fingers.

"Just don't let anything happen to it, that's all I ask of you.
That trumpet is worth more to me than all my land and buildings."

"I'll try, Grandpa. I'll do my level best."

That night, as soon as his father came in off the summerfallow,
Joshua ran to the tankstand where the tractor was being refueled.

"Look," he said. The sun sparkled through the trees onto it.

His father looked down from the tractor out of his blackened face. His eyes were red inside the lower lids.

"What on earth," he began, then stopped. "Did Grandpa give you that?"

"He sure did. He wants me to learn to play."

His father closed the valve on the tank, then arched the hose to let it drain.

"I wonder what came over him?" he said, but not to Joshua.

At the suppertable his mother said, "We should take it back as soon as the dishes are done."

"Why?" his father said, sawing with a butter knife at the brown-inside of his steak. "He actually wants him to have it. I never thought he would, after he didn't make a present of it the day Joshua was named."

"But he wants him to learn to play it," his mother said, dishing creamed corn onto Janie's plate.

"What's wrong with that? He can get lessons in Nisooskan."

"He can't; he's no way to get there."

"Yes he has. I'm going to drive him."

"Then I don't understand you. Not at all. You won't even drive that far so I can visit my sister. Only when the car has to be fixed or you need fertilizer."

"I want music lessons too," Janie said. "Can I have a guitar?"

"You're too little to hold one," her father said. "You couldn't reach." He looked back at Joshua's mother. "We'll buy our groceries at the Co-op instead of here in town. They may not be any cheaper than at Goodman's but there's the dividend. You see?"

"I don't, not really. I don't understand why you're suddenly willing to drive that far once a week."

"Because it's only eight miles after all. He'll be able to learn from Mrs. Carlson, the lady who taught my brother years ago."

The tone of his father's voice sounded like it did when he talked of his first solo flight.

One morning when the air was filled with the smell of pumpkins and potatoes—the second Saturday in September—they dressed up to go to Nisooskan. When they had turned off the highway onto the bald knoll of the town, his father drove down wide, sunlit streets lined with stunted maples. The leaves had turned a dirty yellow, in places a coppery color, and a few were pasted in the dew against the sidewalk, lying like postage stamps on forgotten letters. The car turned several times and stopped at last in front of a small white house with flowers trellised on the fence.

"This is it," his father said, looking out the window at the gate. He had parked the car with the driver's door against the curb. He didn't say any more.

"Have you got your money?" his mother said as he got out of the car, holding the frayed black case carefully before him.

"I put it in my wallet. I've got it."

"Okay. Listen when she tells you. Do what she says."

"Let's go," his father said.

"Don't be scared, Josh," Janie said, just before they drove away.

There was nothing to be afraid of. Mrs. Carlson was old, but kind. She was a stout woman and wore a print dress which bagged around her feet. At first he thought she would look silly with a trumpet at her lips, but her fingers moved so lightly and her cheeks bulged out like apples, and then the music came so clear that he knew she would be a sterling teacher. She played with her eyes closed and the music seemed to rise out of an endless dream.

"I guess I must look funny," she said when she was finished. "An old lady like me good for nothing and still trying to play like it's a big concert."

"No," he said quickly. "I'll bet even the angels envy you."

"Ha!" she laughed, shaking up and down in front. "I don't think the angels would like to be as fat as me. Even though I was as slender as a reed, when I played as a girl all around the country for dances."

Joshua learned that morning the notes of the scale at the piano, and how to read those notes on the page.

"The notes on the lines," Mrs. Carlson told him, "are E G B D F, reading up from the bottom. But that's hard to remember. Let's call them 'Every Good Boy Does Fine.' You're the boy on the middle line and when you play the note on the top line, you'll do fine. You see? And the notes inbetween are like a face sketched in. F A C E. E goes at the top for eyes. Say it now so I can hear."

Near the end of the lesson she said, "Next week we'll talk about notes and time. But now I should give you something you can practice."

She told him about the mouthpiece and how it worked, then showed him how to hold his lips as tight as a paper against a comb. When he blew into the trumpet, it felt like trying to spit through a dishrag. The gleaming bell made a windy, dirty sound. He looked at her in embarrassment, even with the trumpet still at his lips. She was laughing, shaking up and down again.

"You'll learn," she said. "At first, you know, it's worse than having diarrhoea."

She played again just before he left and he walked along the street as if he were floating on her music. When he turned the corner at the Telephone Office, he touched the concrete again. Three girls walking with a boy toward him seemed to be watching him and whispering together. They laughed and giggled. He cut diagonally across the street, not looking back, with his case bumping on his thigh and his scalp beginning to feel red as the bulb above the Fire Hall door.

In the weeks to come, he practiced every day after school. His father was busy combining with Grandpa and his uncles, and when Joshua had finished his half-hour of practice, he would ride in the truck with Grandpa and tell him everything. Grandpa would smile and nod and it would be so comfortable in the truck with the sun slanting now through the windshield and Grandpa's jacket warm on the seat between them. And when they drove into the yard, Joshua would run from the auger to the house to hear the World Series score, what inning it was, because the World Series was something that Grandpa only missed for harvesting, nothing else. And together they would go into the house for the box with supper in it, Grandpa smiling and saying he was tickled to get some of Helga's cooking for a change, and if the game would be on, they would wait just another pitch to hear if the tension in the announcer's voice would crack like a bat, or if it would close out bright and formal into the Gillette barbershop song. Together, they two would bring the supper to the men, and the combines would stop, and Uncle Glen would bring the truck from the far combine with Richard or Uncle Owen riding passenger for a turn, sitting dethroned, at the same height now as everybody else. And Uncle Glen and Grandpa would take their time to eat, Richard and Uncle Owen scooping the food off their plates, Richard in a hurry to get his field off before it got tough, Uncle Owen hoping they might make it yet onto his tonight if the dew would only hang back. Then in the evening, with the moon rising like blood over the hill, Grandpa would sing to him, "When the m-m-m-m-oon shines over the c-c-c-c-cowshed, I'll be waiting at the k-k-k-kitchen door for you." It always made him laugh, and then Grandpa couldn't help himself, he'd laugh too, and then Joshua would ask for more. Later he would fall asleep, looking at the red and white lights of the combines muttering around the field, smelling the air, and hearing Grandpa sing beneath the soaring moon.

But when combining was finished at last and his father was in the house after school, the practising of the trumpet drove Richard out to the barn.

"It's not nearly so pleasant as a moose in season," he would say in the kitchen.

"Give him time," his mother said. "Rome wasn't built—only burnt—in a day."

"At least Nero could play the violin," his father said.

Nevertheless, his father still drove him faithfully to Nisooskan every Saturday morning. On the days when the family came along, he would drive directly to the Co-op and Joshua would walk. But on the days when they went alone, his father would drive him to Mrs. Carlson's door and sit looking after him until he was in the house. Once, before Joshua had gotten out of the car, he said, "It's funny, you know. I can still see him going up the steps when my Dad dropped him off."

The following spring, by Mother's Day, Joshua was at least competent enough to try to play in church. He practised for weeks. Then on that Sunday morning, standing suddenly before the rows of faces at the front of the church, things went badly for him. The first three notes sounded strangled, he got behind the piano, and he couldn't quite catch up to Auntie Bee whose arms rose up and down like Clydesdale hooves galloping, galloping. He sang in the inter-stanza, his voice a little clearer than the trumpet had been.

> *Tell mother I'll be there,*
> *In answer to her prayer,*
> *O tell my darling mother I'll be there.*

The last verse went a little better, the notes beginning to carry softly at the end. He saw Grandma weeping silently before he sat down. She kept blowing her nose so that Reverend Haagshed had to wait with the sermon.

After church, Grandpa put both hands on his shoulders. He just looked and looked at him. There was something approaching recognition, a flighting of memory, in his eyes, and tenderness was upturned in every furrow of his skin.

"You sounded almost like him when he was your age," was all he said.

But the next Sunday, after church, Grandpa said, "I've been out to talk to Chief Coming-day. They've got a boy coming for sure. I just now put his registration fee on the offering plate."

That July Thomas Singletree came to camp, riding on the wagonboard beside his immense and immovable father, the boy holding in one brown fist the rope reins on the trudging beasts while the man looked straight ahead at the buttocks of the horses. When the wagon appeared, it came through a wall of rain as if a curtain had divided to let it pass. Joshua just saw it there, it was outside the dining hall where, ever since the ball game was rained out, the campers played between benches stacked on tables, rattling as they ran the dishes in the open cupboards. The wagon pulled up by the door and stopped.

Joshua stood in the doorway, barely out of the wet. The Indian boy's father was the biggest man he had ever seen. Joshua guessed he must weigh four hundred pounds. The Indian man looked down at him and water tunnelled off the brim of his black felt hat, spilling in one quick river onto his enormous belly. His grey hair hung limply over each of his shirt-bursting shoulders. He didn't say anything; he just looked. He looked for a second, long enough to be satisfied, and then he wasn't looking at anything at all.

The Indian boy reached back into the wagon, withdrew a paper shopping bag from beneath a piece of canvas. He got down on the hill side of the vehicle. Above him the leaves on the trees pointed like tiny shovels; they dripped bright, steady drops. The old man moved suddenly then, shifting his weight to near the centre of the board for ballast and, making his flannel belly comfortable again on his knees, he set the wagon in motion with a flick of the rope. He didn't look back. The wagon rolled away into the drizzle; it left two thin tracks in the mud, two lengthening lines scored with hoofprints. After a moment, the rain-wall shut down, washing the wagon from sight.

Thomas stood at the edge of the road, his back to the rain-dark-

82

ened trees as if he had just come out of the woods. The rain spotted up his shopping bag with splotches of bright brown.

"Come out of the rain," Joshua called. "You'll wreck yer stuff."

Thomas came across the road and over the threshold. Joshua stepped back. Thomas shook himself like a dog, spraying water in a little cloud. His khaki shirt clung to his skin, dripping in a tail behind him. His jeans were too long for him, dragging in the mud below his heels. They stretched almost like overshoes over his toes.

"I come t' go swimmin'," he said. "Notice how I was gettin' ready fer it all d' way? Call me Thomas."

"Hello Thomas," he said right back. "I'm Joshua Cardiff." He didn't know yet whether Indians shook hands or not. He watched for a moment, then let his arm relax.

Thomas grinned widely, his teeth gleaming as brightly as the silver trumpet.

"I know yer real name," he said.

Other campers were beginning to gather around them. He didn't say any more.

"This here's Thomas," Joshua said to them. He was afraid Thomas would say more and suddenly he felt a little nervous with him there. But Thomas stood quietly beside him as campers and grownups now pressed close. In the warmth of the dining hall his body gave off a dark, heavy smell, not like soiled clothing, but like the soil itself. Thomas was by no means heavy, though, far from it; he was as thin as a willow picket. He had not stopped smiling since he entered the room, his teeth flashing in a double crescent. His eyes moved over the faces surrounding him, the light as bright on them as upon his open mouth, but his eyes less perfect, the left one straying inward so that Joshua had the uncanny feeling Thomas was watching him in the same instant that he was looking everybody over.

"Hello Thomas," the Teen-boys' counsellor said. He was well-muscled, tall, and wore a white tee shirt with the green crest of a Bible School on it. He was from Oregon and a powerful swimmer. Joshua had watched him before devotions one morning swim the lake six times, back and forth. "We're glad to have you. Did I hear you say you came here to go swimming?"

Thomas wasn't given a chance to speak. One of the cooks

caught sight of him as she came from the kitchen.

"The poor dear!" she said. She put down her stack of plates. "You're all wet, child. Has no one taken care of you yet? Just look at that wet hair an' those wet clothes. Never mind a cold, you'll catch whooping cough if you don't get dried off."

"He's not that bad, Mrs. Robinson," the counsellor said. "It's only a little rain water. We'll have him wrung out before you can say your husband's name."

"It's Alfred Robinson," the cook said, not able to keep from smiling. "Don't you make jokes about folks' names."

"You see?" the counsellor said. "He's nearly dry already."

"Alright," she said. "But you get that boy into clean togs, anyway, as soon as possible. Do you have a change of clothes, child? Of course you have. I suppose they're wet too in that shopping bag."

"It's okay," Thomas said. "What I got on's my swimmin' clodes. W'en do we start?"

The cook was opening her mouth to protest; the counsellor headed her off.

"Right now, if you want," he said. "This is regular swimming time, for the next hour. We were going to cancel it on account of the rain."

"It's all water, ain't it," Thomas said.

"You bet," the counsellor replied.

So they went swimming, Thomas, Joshua, and the counsellor. Thomas took off only his shirt to go in. Some girls were standing in the rain to watch.

"I don' wear nothin' as a rule," he said, grinning.

The girls tittered like swallows on a wire. Thomas ran straight into the lake, water churning out from his legs, and then he stumbled and went under. Joshua went in after him, splashing to catch up. By the time he had ducked under, then up again, Thomas was out to the diving raft. His blue jeans clung tightly to his legs when he stood up. The grey rain slanted against the water, needling it with endless pin-points. Thomas swam like a dog, arms treading the water beneath his chin, a continual grin across his jaw. The counsellor swam in wide circles about them, sliding like a porpoise through the water.

Later, Joshua rummaged a straw tick to lay out beside his own on the bunkhouse shelf. Thomas was drying off with a Cardiff family towel. His thin jaw chattered, clicking his teeth. Joshua was up on the top shelf, arranging blankets on the mattress.

"Scalp," Thomas said. He said it like he was maybe making fun. "Dat's yer real name."

Joshua looked down.

"My fad-der tol' us how dey talked about you in d' Council." Thomas was grinning up at him, arching the towel across his back. " 'Scalp-by-Manito': it's what Walkin' Horse said." He pulled a bright plaid shirt out of his shopping bag. " 'Yer a real Ind-yun': dat's what Walkin' Horse said too."

Joshua unstiffened a little from the suspicion of ridicule.

"I don't look like it," was all he said. "I don't even look like a regular white person." He was embarrassed that they should have to talk about it so soon.

"Dat's what I was sayin'," Thomas grinned. " 'Course you don'. You wouldn wan' t' look like a reg'ler white person, would you? So what's left? Jus' Ind-yuns aroun' here."

Joshua was grateful that they had wanted to include him, but there was something about the way Thomas spoke of it, his casual breeziness as if it wasn't all that significant, that irritated him.

"If I don't look Indian," he said, "then I can't *be* Indian. Not any more than I can be a normal white person. I'm not sure you understand."

"Shit, yer Scalp, ain't you? If you gotta 'n Ind-yun stamp like dat on you, yer mixed up somehow wid Ind-yuns. Dere ain't no goddam way aroun' dat."

He had the shirt buttoned up now; he was stepping into the wet, long-legged jeans.

Joshua felt horribly uncomfortable about the language. Now he couldn't feel close at all to Thomas. He wasn't even sure he wanted to spend the week having to be around him. "You're not supposed to take God's name in vain," he said quietly. He wasn't looking at Thomas at all any more.

"I din' know you called him shit," Thomas said.

Joshua was thunderstruck. He caught himself looking to see if Thomas was hit by lightning. Then he noticed the boy hitching up the sopping wet trousers across his loins.

"You're not going to put on those wet jeans, are you?"

Probably he's got lice too, if that's the way they wash clothes. I should really move my tick, and have that towel sterilized.

"Why not? Dey ain't lettin' folks run aroun' here nakid yet, are dey?"

In his voice, Joshua could hear the shame, for himself and Thomas both.

"You mean that's all you got? Why doesn't your mother take better care of you?"

Thomas looked away. At last he said, "She wen' crazy. She's locked up in Nord Battleferd. All we got's my little sister."

Then the distance fled away. "I'm sorry. I didn't know. My Grandpa never said nothin' about it. I am really sorry."

There was silence between them for a moment. Then Thomas said, "W'en do we eat?"

"Hang on; take them wet jeans off. I got a pair in my suitcase that oughta fit."

By nightfall, Thomas shaped for him already the brother he had never had but always wanted. Though in the days to come, there were things, little occurrences really, in word or deed, in the expression of an attitude, which gave him pause. They were at the dock the next afternoon, waiting for the canoes to come in. A dozen other campers were there too, just sitting around waiting. A short red canoe came off the lake before the others. When the paddlers had beached it, two campers first in line took hold of the prow. Thomas splashed through the water and jumped into the stern. "Hey, whaddya think you're doing?" one of the boys at the prow said. "It's our turn."

"No it ain't," Thomas said, still smiling. "I got it first."

The two boys were taller than he, though Thomas stood on the ribs of the canoe. Now their voices dropped very low so that Joshua could not hear from the dock what they were saying. But their faces were equally threatening. At last the two outside the boat let go their hold. One of them just shrugged, but the other said something quietly to Thomas.

"Fuck yerself," Thomas said aloud, then looked over his shoulder to see if the counsellor had heard. "Come on," he said to Joshua.

They paddled about the sun-glinting lake, trying to slip up behind a mother duck with four ducklings. The mother would call in her strange, hoarse quack and the ducklings would dive beneath the water. She would lead the canoe on farther before she went down herself, and it would be a minute or so before the ducks bobbed up like corks on all sides out from the boat. But Joshua didn't enjoy it very much. He was thinking of the look in Thomas' eyes when he swore at the boy on shore.

Later that afternoon, they were at the paddock on the north side of the tabernacle, where the Shetland ponies were. They each had ridden already and Thomas stood watching now from the top of the gatepost beside the building. The riding counsellor leaned with her back against the wall.

"How come you got nothin' but mares here?" Thomas said.

"We don't have only mares," the young lady said. "The brown one's not."

Thomas was silent for a time.

"Boy he sure is some stud, eh?" he said at last.

Some of the boys laughed. The instructor looked embarrassed, but she smiled.

Thomas turned around on the gatepost and began to pull at a loose strap of board sprung from the quonset. He was hauling himself like a mountain climber up a rope when the instructor said, "Thomas, come down. You might get hurt."

"I c'n tear dis t'ing down wid my bare hands," he said, grinning.

"Do you figure you're climbing Jacob's ladder or something? Come on down."

"I'll climb up an' jump down on yer head." His jaw was still set in a grin.

The instructor only smiled and turned away.

Or, when they were supposed to be at morning tabernacle, Thomas said, "Le's go fishin'. Sittin' in dat hotbox wid sawdust on yer feet ain't camp. It ain't even a Blackfoot i-deer of a camp." Joshua felt uneasy at first, but he couldn't stay behind.

They found a grassy bank and they cast with rods and reels they hadn't asked to borrow from boys in the dormitory. They caught two good-sized pickerel and eight perch. Thomas made Joshua throw an eight-inch jack back. It was the first fish he had ever caught. About an hour later, Joshua caught one of the big ones. He played it in with trembling hands. It flopped and wriggled while he tried to get the hook out of its mouth. They agreed, then, they had caught enough. Thomas showed him how to clean the fish, cutting with his jack-knife into the gill against the head, the ugly face falling away and blood running over his fingers.

87

They built a fire on a rocky bed (Thomas had matches; he sneaked off a dozen times a day for a smoke) and when the fire burned down they roasted the fish on the coals.

"Ever tasted smoke' fish?" Thomas said.

Joshua shook his head.

"It's really, really good," Thomas said. "Better even 'n pork chops. Smoke it wid green willow, wid poplar bark. Better 'n cigarettes."

The roast fish was delicious. It was a little bit smoked. The smell stayed on Joshua's hands all that day. When they got thirsty, they drank from the lake. Thomas showed him how to hold his hands so he could drink from the wrists. The water was clear and bright.

But they had to go back. It was supper-time when they returned.

"Where have you been?" the counsellor with the Bible School tee shirt (he had three of them) said. "You even missed swimming. I'm disappointed in you boys. Reverend Haagshed is more than disappointed. He wants to see you in his cabin. Come on."

The cabin was very dim inside. It was an old fishing shack, built of lime-chinked log, the only structure that had come with the property. One narrow window opened on the east side. Reverend Haagshed sat on his cot with the blankets folded Army style, his feet planted firmly on the floor in front of him. His black boots shone even in the dim light. His huge Bible lay open on his knees. The counsellor pushed them toward him, then drew back himself out through the door.

The minister's eyes were cold and blunt. His jowls trembled a little before he spoke. "Where have you boys been?" he said at last.

"Fishin'," Thomas said brightly. "You should of bin dere. We caught two pick—"

"Joshua Cardiff," the minister said sternly, "I expected you to be a blessing instead of a burden. I expected you to be a good example, not a bad one. Instead, you take this Indian boy who can't possibly know any better and you go running off for the day." For a moment his eyes searched Joshua's face. Then his expression softened. "Are you trying to run away from the Lord, boy? Is that it? Is He calling you like He did Jonah?"

"No, He isn't," Joshua said. He felt extremely uncomfortable.

"Then it's outright wickedness," Reverend Haagshed said. *"By their fruits ye shall know them.* What have you got to say for yourself, boy?" The preacher had his head tilted back; his eyes hooked for a moment into the eyes beneath him.

Joshua looked away, his now-swimming vision sliding up and out with a desperate wriggle. "Nothin'," he said.

" 'Course you do," Thomas said. "Tell 'im you had a good time. Tell 'im you roasted fish an' ate 'em while dey was roastin' deirselves in dat plywood box."

"Don't you interfere," the minister said. "Or I'll give you his punishment too."

"You better," Thomas said, smiling. "I don' know nobody else here to do it wid."

"Then I won't," Reverend Haagshed said. "It's time you met a few more edifying children. As for you, young Joshua Cardiff, you've got some history you're going to have to live up to. You're not going to disgrace your grandfather who founded our church in Lacjardin. Tonight, after supper, I want to see you at the washtubs behind the dining hall. And tomorrow after breakfast and dinner as well."

Joshua grimaced, trying even to hold that back, unsuccessfully.

"After supper then, too. You can wash dishes until you learn what it means to serve the Lord."

"What about me?" Thomas said. "I don' mind dishes."

"We'll see," the preacher said. "There's plenty of chances yet for you."

When the boys reached the dining hall, there were long rows lined up, waiting for the cook to open the double doors. They had fried bologna and baked beans for supper. There were huge enamel pots of steaming beans. Thomas ate five plates; Joshua picked at one helping.

"Eat some a dis goddam stuff," Thomas said, grinning over a slice of bread. A counsellor looked down the table at them. He seemed to be trying to hear what was just beyond his hearing.

"I ain't hungry," Joshua said.

"Don' get feelin' sorry fer yerself," Thomas said. He dribbled beans off his fork and down his chin.

"I ain't any more," Joshua replied. "I'm just as plugged as a toilet with fish."

"Good beans," Thomas said, his mouth full.

They weren't as good in the evening service. Standing for the singing of "Showers of Blessing" which came before the sermon, Joshua smelled something vile. He looked sideways at Thomas. The Indian boy had a smile on his face. He looked self-satisfied about the eyes and nose. Joshua stopped singing, held his breath. Then the people behind them tapered off real quick. Soon no one was singing for three rows around them. Joshua looked at Thomas. The corner of his mouth twitched, like he was trying to hold something back. When the outer congregation came to "Mercy drops round us are falling," Joshua snorted. Then there was just no holding it, neither for him nor for Thomas. He was laughing and laughing as noses up and down the aisles turned toward them, then away. Thomas sounded a loud one as the songleader stopped waving his arms, his mouth half-open and confused with singing. Three short ones followed, sort of whistling against the pine-plank bench. Joshua was laughing and laughing, long after the preacher looked around from the front row and stood watching him.

That night the dormitory jiggled with laughter in the darkness. The counsellor in his crested tee shirt could not quiet them.

"Hey Thomas," a voice called, "croon us yer tune."

"Play 'Christian Soldiers' so we can march ya to th' toilet."

"No, no. Play 'I'm Forever Blowing Bubbles'," another voice cried, breathless with giggling.

Thomas laughed somewhere up in the blackness. Then he stepped on Joshua's leg crossing over. "Gonna sit on yer face," he said to the speaker farther down the bedrolls.

The whole bunkhouse was yelling when Reverend Haagshed came in. The night smell of the lake came in with him. It was cool and fresh. He snapped on a flashlight. Thomas sat astride a boy's chest like he rode a horse.

"I've had enough," the minister said in a voice like a bagpipe. "QUIET! There now, I said I've had enough of this."

"So've I," said the boy on whom Thomas was sitting. Several boys splattered their pillows with laughter.

"That's fine with me," the preacher said. "You've all just lost your swimming privileges tomorrow."

"Aww," said a voice, "we were only foolin' around."

"You mean fartin' around," another voice gasped, helpless with laughter.

"All right, ENOUGH! There'll be no one here swimming for the next two days." They could see the minister's jowls trembling in the beam of light as he spoke. "You've done nothing but ruin the effect of God's Word that you heard tonight. We'll learn Bible verses in the next two days, enough of them to make up for this abomination."

"You mean we got to memorize?" one boy said.

"Against thee, thee only, have I sinned," the preacher said. "That's the first one you'll learn. You're not in trouble with me; you've gotten into desperate trouble with God."

"This is worse 'n school," the boy said. He never came to Sunday School; his folks weren't saved.

"It's better," the preacher said. "School can't save you from hell."

He was standing now below Joshua's bunk. He lifted the flashlight above the foot of the blankets.

"Shall I send you home from camp?" he said. His voice slanted up as cold as a chisel.

"No," Joshua said at once. He blinked against the beam of light.

"Tell me why not."

"I—. I haven't—." Then he couldn't say any more.

After a long pause the preacher said, "I won't this time. I'll give you one more chance. But I'm going to tell your father. You must be disciplined."

The next day after lunch Thomas waited on the side of the hill, where the spring came out of moss and leaves, for Joshua to be finished at the dish-tubs.

"Dat's *really* good," he said when Joshua came through the bush. "We c'n fergit about swimmin' today." He was grinning around his whole jaw.

"You don't mean that, do you? I thought you liked swimmin'. You said things like smoked fish an' swimmin' was really good."

"No I ain't," Thomas answered. "I said dey was really, really good. If it ain't dat, all dat's lef' is really good."

"Oh," Joshua didn't understand.

Thomas said, "Is d' preacher goin' where I t'ink he's goin' w'en he dies?"

"Yeah," Joshua said slowly. "That's where preachers go for sure. Every one I ever heard says that."

91

"Dat's *really* good," said Thomas. "We wan' t' go where it's really, really good, don' we? So dere ain't much use in gittin' ready to go wid 'im. Why'nt we go fishin'?"

"I can't. He'd send me home. Besides, they're meetin' in the bunkhouse where the rods are."

"Oh," said Thomas. "Well, le's sneak off in d' bush fer awhile."

"I can't. I'm scared he really will send me home. You heard what he said last night. He's already gonna tell my dad."

"Aw, dat's chicken shit. Yer home ain't so bad dat it's worse 'n dis, is it? You ain't got nothin' t' worry about, Scalp."

"I got my soul. I really don't want no desp'rate trouble with God."

"You don' t'ink," Thomas said grinning, "dat a guy who took yer swimmin' away could give you back anyt'ing dat was really, really good? You don' t'ink dat, do ya? So if yer in trouble wid God, yer in trouble fer good."

They were already sitting in a sunny glade when they heard tramping in the underbrush of the hill.

"Git behind dat tree," Thomas whispered.

In a few moments Reverend Haagshed came out at the foot of the clearing. He stopped, looking about him. The sun shone full on his sweating face. He seemed now to take his bearings by the sun and the trees. He swished through the long grass to the centre of the clearing. Thomas threw a pebble to one side and behind the man. Reverend Haagshed stopped, looking. He peered into an empty thicket.

"I know you boys are in there," he said softly. He spoke in measured rhythms. "I'm warning you for the last time. They start learning their verses in five more minutes." '

Thomas wickt a stone off a tree close beside the man. His dark face wasn't tense any more; he was grinning slightly. The preacher turned around, startled.

"Come out where I can see you," he said. "God sees anyway where you are, so you can't escape."

Thomas skipped a rock near his feet. It skittered through the grass.

"Joshua Cardiff," the man said, "I command you in the name of everything holy to come out of that bush."

Thomas put a hand on his arm as he was rising. His jaw seemed cemented in a strange smile. The next stone barked the minister's

92

shins. The man danced in the sun.

"Joshua Cardiff," he said in a voice filled with pain, "I'm sending you home from camp." His words jerked out in the convulsion of his legs. "You'll face God for this even if you won't face me."

Then he disappeared into the shade. He was bent over hopping, still rubbing his shins, the last they saw of him.

After an agonizing while Joshua said, "Now I'm in desp'rate trouble. You shouldn't of thrown stones."

"Don' be so worried," Thomas said, grinning fully again. "He talks a lot. He'll give you another chance."

"But stones," Joshua said. "He's God's minister. You really did it this time."

There was nothing for it now but go down to the bunkhouse. Thomas didn't even try to stop him, walking beside him in the sun-streaked green of the woods. Reverend Haagshed was reading aloud from his Bible when they opened the door. Boys lined the aisle like birds on a fence.

"Thank God you came back," the minister said gravely. "Take over," he said to the tee-shirted counsellor. "Come with me," he said to Joshua and Thomas. His Bible came with him. They had to walk on either side of him along the shore, his presence like electricity between them. When they reached the log cabin, he climbed the stoop in advance of them, opened the X-planked door, and motioned them in. "Now," he said. "You boys have gone too far. God will put up with disobedience for a time. He'll put up with even a moment of irreverence. For He knows your heart; He knows what deep down chance there is of your repenting. But when you take to abusing His gospel minister, you're reaching the point of no return. You, Joshua Cardiff, of all people ought to know that. You've had advantage of the Bible stories: you know what happened to the boys who mocked God's prophet Elisha. You know how He destroyed them. I'm afraid you've almost been treading upon that point of no return. I'm afraid it's happening to you right here in a Christian camp. I wouldn't have believed it, a child of Christian parents throwing stones at a servant of God. I'm afraid you might be in Satan's power without knowing it. So it probably won't do any good to reason with you or with Thomas. Probably the one thing left to do is to pray the devil out of you. That's what I've got to try to do. So I ask you to kneel down. Just get down on your knees by these chairs. That's it. Just get down on your knees. You, Thomas Singletree. KNEEL DOWN! Now both of you bow your heads and may God take hold of you." In the warm air of the cabin the minister prayed a long time. His voice rushed and turned and returned like a cavalry charge. His sentences were full of the power of the blood of Christ. He spoke strange names, Belial, Beelzebub and Rimmon, Moloch, Mammon and Dagon, and his voice took on an incantatory tone, chanting in rhythms beyond language. In the warm air Joshua felt chilled. After a long while, the prayer was ended. They all got stiffly to their feet.

"You may go now, Thomas," the preacher said.

Thomas hesitated for a second, then went out the door. Joshua heard his feet on the porch, then down the steps and lost in the grass.

"Somethin's happened to you, Joshua," the minister said. "You were always a sort of distant child, off by yourself even when you were among folks. I always accounted it to your hair, to the loss of it. But you've turned wild since this Indian lad came." His jowls quivered while he spoke; there was an earnest and solemn look in his eye. "Beware of what's happening to you, boy. I thought until just a moment ago, when I asked you both to kneel, that it was your fault. I suspected you were leading him astray, that you were using him for an excuse, because he didn't know better, to let loose. I thought it was you who threw those stones. But the look in his eye when I asked him to kneel . . . Well, at any rate, fear for your immortal soul. I felt the presence of Satan in this room like I have never felt it before. Look to your salvation while there still is time."

Joshua could not tear his eyes away from the man's. At last the minister moved.

"I'm going to separate you two for the remainder of Camp," he said. "I don't know if there's hope for Thomas on his own. But I do know there's hope for you. You must look to your immortal soul. I'll help you, if you want, to move your things away to the other bunkhouse."

That night before service, the drums came to life again down the lake. Joshua met Thomas just for a moment by the drinking fountain.

"I'm goin' back to d' Reserve now," Thomas said. "But I'll

come nex' year fer d' start of Camp. After dat, yer t' come wid me by night to d' Sun Dance."

"Do you have to go?" Joshua said. "Do you have to leave because he moved us?"

Thomas nodded. He wasn't smiling any more.

"It's okay. D' Sun Dance is startin'. I got lots t' go back to. I'm jus' sorry you gotta stay. But dey said one more year. Dey said not yet."

Grandpa's right about this band of Indians, there's no changing them without getting contaminated first yourself.

"Well, goodbye, then. I'll be seeing you around, I guess."

"S' long 'til nex' year, Scalp. S' long, my frien'."

They clasped hands for an instant in the shadows.

But my soul my eternal soul

iv

"Don't be so nervous," Peter said. "There's nothing to be nervous about."

Peter was smiling, assurance flooding like light from his heart-shaped face. He had thick, wavy hair, lots of it, combed just so in a glistening ducktail. The style was like something on a face looming before oil wells, before designs of cars and motorcycles, from the billboard outside the Roxy Theatre in Nisooskan. But the rest of his face was different, not smouldering with defiance nor turned impersonal as a mask, but easy-going, pleasant, relaxed.

"You should try to take it easy before they get here," he said, "or you'll go bananas up a tree."

"What makes you think I'm not?" Joshua said. "Taking it easy, I mean."

"Because you look a nervous wreck. If I hadn't been bunking next to you, I'd think you'd had something going with Old Lady Five Fingers."

"With—" and then he stopped, fearful of betraying himself.

"Does be—ing your me— ma— you —f?" Peter said seriously.

"What?"

"I said does beating your meat make you deaf?" Peter was grinning without malice. "Gotcha. You better be careful. The long-handed mistress will kill you, the old solitary vice."

"I haven't," he said. "I haven't been doing it." It was true, though he felt his ears burning like he told a lie. "I knew it was supposed to be bad for you, it could stop your bones from growing, maybe drive you insane, and here I see it's already gone and given you a speech impediment."

"Aha," Peter said easily. "You know it's all baloney. It can't even make you a nervous wreck, I was only kidding. Just relax, there's nothing to worry about. Leah's a nice girl, she won't bite. Not unless you're — well, you know." He grinned good-naturedly.

"She doesn't look that kind at all."

"No, you're right, she doesn't. But they're all the same, you know, under their clothes. If she sees you're willing, she'll say 'Hug me quick,' don't worry. Any of them would. So just don't worry."

Your will is supreme, young man, you can do as you please.

"I'm not worried," he said. Although he was, and more than just about Leah. It came in waves which seemed almost to clutch him under, down down beneath the throb of the drums. The Sun Dance, if his promise to Thomas meant anything, was starting tonight after service.

You can wreck your virtue, if you want to; you can go after her whose feet go down to death, and whose steps take hold on hell, if you want to; there is no power on earth to stop you

"That's just fine," Peter said. "Only don't you think you should let your face in on it? You're still a terrible sight."

but know thou, that for all these things God will bring thee into judgment.

"I know it. I think I better just go back and wait awhile . . . ."

"Wait for what? This is it, right now," Peter said kindly. "Tell me honest, Josh, have you ever been out with a girl?"

Peter was seventeen, these two years immeasurable between them. He had never, like Leah, been at Camp before, but he had obviously been in situations Joshua could only imagine. Peter and Leah both came from Louis Lake, a town forty-five miles away. Grandpa had been over there to invite their assembly to come in with them.

"Ye — sure, I have. Skating on the lake, stuff like that, lots."

"Good, that's good. Have you — well, ever necked, or anything like that? Well, it doesn't matter. I guess you've broken the ice, so to speak."

Peter's laugh went up softly among the leaves. The sun lay flat now upon the horizon, burning in scarlet promise through the bush.

"Like I said," Peter said after a time, "she's like any other woman. She wants you to talk at first, about school and friends, both hers and yours. About family, her father, but she'll talk a lot about her brothers too, she's got seven of them, so listen real close and ask questions, act like they all matter to you, every last one of them, but especially her favorite, the one she'll describe as good-looking, a hit with the girls. Then come on that way with her yourself, make her look in her own eyes as much like him as you can, only, you know, from the other side, pretend you're a little jealous of how many guys she must have on the line, and then put your arm around her, she'll get a thrill out of that. Then as soon as you feel she's ready for it, stop dead in your tracks and wait for her eyes to come up into yours. Lean right into the kiss and hold her close. What you get after that," Peter's voice assumed suddenly a pulpit tone, "is the gift of God, God willing."

His head cocked to one side and his smile was as if meant for a confrere.

in these several stages of seduction . . . at the young man's command . . . permitting the first kiss . . . she surrenders the outpost of her chastity.

"You twisted that around," Joshua said. "It's from *The Way of a Man With a Maid,* every bit of it. Or *A Virtuous Woman,* I forget which." It made him feel almost confident.

"Sorry," Peter said, grinning widely now, his lips stretching the valentine outline until it threatened to rupture. "I never heard of those stuffed animals."

Grandpa and Grandma had given him the books after Donna left school that winter. She was supposed to be finishing, have finished, her year at an aunt's house in Flin Flon. His father and mother, when he brought the books home, maintained a discreet silence. There was none like them on his father's shelf, only Reader's Digest Condensed Books and a few collections, several with just photographs, on the war. Grandpa and Grandma had offered these in almost an offhand way, saying, if he liked, he could pass them on when he was through with them to Joel — he should soon be ready for them. Joshua could only remember fragments of them, since he got rid of them as quickly as he could, but several fragments cut like glass: *this sexual instinct . . . the stirring of a divine impulse . . . exalts us above the angels in heaven to create . . . but the unlawful use . . . sinful in the sight of God, leads finally to the destruction of both soul and body in hell. For could such a one have forgotten his mother's purity? Jesus said that whosoever looketh on a woman to lust after her hath committed adultery with her already in his heart. If thy right hand offend thee, cut it off and cast it from thee: for it is better for thee that one of thy members should perish, and not that thy whole body should be cast into hell.* He would have believed little of it, even though the stories were frightening: of young people gone insane or idiotic, of young women living miserably in houses of shame, filled with diseases, dying horribly under assumed names, buried in a Potter's field, and finally of young men cursed in hell by women so seduced. But always there were the reproving scriptures. At bottom he could still doubt everything, everything but the verses and the example of his great-grandfather.

"So," Peter said. "Since you already know everything there is to know, you don't have to worry. She'll eat it up like cake."

Joshua's ears went hot again, but he tried as best he could for nonchalance.

"How're you so sure, Peter? Maybe you took her out yourself, eh?"

if any hell to be shunned more than another . . . hell of him . . . trampled a mother's hopes, a sister's sweet kiss . . . a loving maiden's pure confidence

"No," Peter was saying, "no, I haven't done that. For one thing, though, she as good as told me. Even if I'm not supposed to say anything to you, she told me how you'd been watching her every day, only you weren't making any move at all. That ought to be enough then to let you know she's normal, even under those ankle skirts. But I also know her family pretty well. Her dad works with mine on the railway, you see. They live along the tracks in the company house right outside town and her father never lets boys come round, not anywhere near the house. You know those

European fathers, they're Czechs or something. I suppose he's worried, too, about living on the wrong side of the tracks. So you've got a double blessing: she's dying to go out and she hardly knows the score, just her woman's instincts."

Peter gave him the chocolate box smile.

Then they could both hear footsteps on the hill, so much nearer and heavier than the drums. The trees were screening their vision. Joshua stiffened a little, feeling his breath come shorter, then shorter yet.

Through the birches, Auntie Bee came into view. She stepped behind the outhouse, wiping her feet on the grass beside the door. She was looking back down the hill, her head swivelling like a radar dish.

"That poor Joel," Peter whispered. "I'm surprised she even comes to the toilet without him."

Joshua waited until she closed the door.

"It's not just him she keeps track of," he said, trying to stay below a whisper. "You haven't been fooled into that, have you?"

They could smell, after the door was closed, the quicklime come a little stronger. At least the quicklime was highest, the sharpest part of the smell. A slap, like an inner tube jerked from a tire, reported through the wood at the same instant they heard voices, girls' voices, coming up the path through the trees. Joshua felt as if he had to go to the bathroom too. The girls were chattering quickly. Suddenly Auntie Bee was humming, he thought it sounded like "I Come to the Garden Alone." Then it was; her voice, straining a little, sang out, "And he walks with me, And he talks with me, And he tells me I am his own ..."

The toilets in the basement of the school, their grey painted walls and concrete floors with white chilly porcelain beneath mahogany lids, and hardly any room in the stalls.

At recess, when the thermometer was thirty below, the five boys in his grade no longer went with the little kids outside to play soccer. They went down the creaking stairs where the dust in the air was already burning dry in their nostrils. At first they would play basketball, as much as they could anyway beneath the classroom floor which squatted over them. The pebbled leather stung on his fingers in the cold, and his lungs burned high and hard from the running, the dust. It was best when the girls came down to watch. They stood in the doorway by the toilets and they looked and didn't look. Donna was in the front rank of them. He felt his scalp burning, with her standing there.

One day, Donna ran into the room and knocked the ball away from Dennis McInnis and then started for the door again, but not as fast as she had come out of it. She was laughing and running, the tail of her blouse out and streaming behind her, the silk front taut against the breast he could see. The other girls squealed when Dennis went after her and they both fell down with him on top. They wrestled, laughing and giggling and breathing hard on the floor as everyone circled around. Dennis had her pinned on her back, his hands holding her wrists together over her head, his knees between her knees, her skirt pushing higher on her thighs and somebody, a boy's deepening voice that cracked in mid-sentence, yelled "Jack her up!" And the girls giggled and squealed so much that the sound of the hard breathing on the floor was lost and after a time Donna was not so much writhing away from McInnis as into him. When the hand-bell clapped-to upstairs, nobody moved very much except the couple on the court. After what seemed a long while the biggest boy said, "We better git up there before the old bag decides to keep us outa the basement."

Dennis got up very slowly from his knees, looking all the time out of his arrogant eyes at the girl lying on her back. She had her eyes closed and she remained very still. He had to put his hands in his pockets when he stood up straight. Nobody helped the girl get to her feet. Her blouse was streaked with dirt where she had lain on it. Joshua watched both of them from behind as they all climbed up the squeaking stairs. He could feel his scalp blushing out to the cartilage in his throbbing ear-tips.

Donna put on her coat in the cloakroom among the red-faced children taking off scarves and parkas from outdoors, stamping snow from their boots. The boy saw her through the window run in and out of the icy mist. She came in again half-way through the algebra lesson, her cheeks flushed by the cold.

"Where on earth have you been, Donna?" Miss Johnstone said when the girl stepped into the aisle between the knife-chewed desks. Every boy in the room was turning his head to follow her with his eyes wistful and burning.

"Home," Donna said, looking her full in the face. "I ripped my blouse in the basement."

"You shouldn't play with the boys," Miss Johnstone said in the voice like barley dust. She hadn't had a boy friend since the first World War when the farmboy who had been her single hope had died in a mine-explosion in a French field of grain. So for forty years, in front of the same blackboard or, like now, standing at the room's edge with the same windows at her back, she went on talking. "Their sports grow rougher every year, my dear," she said. "You could be knocked down and done an injury."

"Thank you, ma'am," Donna said. "I'll keep it in mind."

She sat down in her desk in front of Joshua and assurance sat with her, in every swell of her smooth flesh. The coil of her sable hair had fallen. It touched the table of his desk when she sat upright in her chair, looking at the ridiculous scrawled blackboard he could not see for her head beyond him. There was perfume now, the first he had ever smelled in school, save for the closet odor of talcum dust that Miss Johnstone left in the aisles. The scent grieved him, for Donna at first because she had left her familiar childhood, and then it goaded him into wild and hopeless despair because she had crossed in a quarter of an hour into regions of mystery where he was not ordained to follow. She sat enveloped in a glow of fragrance, and his desk, sometimes brushed by her hair, might as well have sat in China.

In the toilets in the dirty cold and cramped toilets with even the words gouged on the walls and the lingering smell of urine around and the concrete floors like ice.

At noon, when he had chewed the last thawing sandwich spread with chokecherry jam and had put the lard pail with the hoop-wire handle back in the cloakroom, he went down the sway-backed stairs to the basement. Only three boys were playing basketball, but they weren't playing rules. They laughed a lot. Big Carl Sorgenson had just taken control of the ball when Dennis McInnis and another boy walked out of the boy's toilet. Carl stopped in mid-stride, the ball in both hands. There was a gap in his teeth where his lips stretched open.

Dennis was swaggering. He looked at no one in particular when he said, "You might as well all go in now. Me and Ronnie left some for yous."

Carl guffawed, his eyes glinting momentarily like the sun on clean cultivator shovels. Then he threw the basketball from his chest to Joshua.

"Hold our ball for us, Baldy, while we're gone," he said.

On the icy floor with the words on the walls and the toilet reeking.

He did not hear the ball tapping on the floor behind him where he dropped it, he wasn't conscious even of his feet taking leave of the floor; there was only the smooth contemptuous face of McInnis backward-falling before him, hawk-nose jetting blood in the downward instant, and his hand not yet registering the bone shock as he scrabbled toward big Carl's fists. The dim light bulbs in their wire cages spun. He could feel his scalp scrape the stucco on the way down, then he couldn't get up again, it felt like the floor was coming through his cheekbone. Big Carl leaned over him. He wasn't even breathing hard.

"You okay, Baldy?" he asked. It was not his voice so much as the attitude of stooping that betrayed his concern.

"Get away I'm okay," Joshua said. His voice was muffled by the wall. Boots clumped the floor, coming around him. Their sound spilled something hot into his stomach, rising above the roaring in his head.

It took only one of them to knock me down; it will take the whole damn school and more to let them all stand over me.

He rolled onto his hands, pushing at the floor. Then a hand was under his armpit, raising him up.

"Lemme alone," he cried.

"Can you walk?" big Carl asked.

"I guess I'll walk," he said. "I'll walk to school after this."

He walked all winter. It was only two and a half miles. The first day afterward, the Sorgenson caboose stopped after they had passed Janie and him. The horses were stamping in the drifts to stay warm. They looked small against the white expanse of open land, horses in miniature, the last team in use outside the Reservation. The back door on the caboose swung open, warm air streaming out, and one of the girls stooped out of the dim interior, calling them both in. "I guess I'll walk," was all Joshua said. Even as the words smoked out, he knew the awfulness of their implacability. It was not the beating that mattered. But he never could forgive the other thing.

Janie was already disappearing into the dim aisle.

"Are you sure?" the girl said, reaching for the door-latch.

"Sure," he said and the door snapped shut.

The caboose jerked into motion again, its runners squealing for an instant on the iron snow. Then it drew steadily onward, woodsmoke wisping behind its passing, already bent rearward in the moment it reached the stovepipe's rim. Then only the cold remained, dancing in redness behind his frozen eyelids, save around him the silence, not even his boots on the snow now sounding as something heard, but only the crunch of bone in his teeth and skull.

The girls stepped around the corner of the outhouse. Somehow it didn't surprise him that Miss Ruthie was in the lead. Her white sweater showed up clear through the trees. The door of the sentry box squeaked open just then and they stopped short. Auntie Bee stepped out, adjusting her dress.

"Hello girls," she said. "How'jew enjoy your supper?" Her face was screwed into a steady smile.

"Real good," Miss Ruthie said. "I liked the sliced baloney real good."

"I liked the potato salad myself," Auntie Bee said. "Does your momma make potato salad, Leah?"

The other girl nodded. Her white face bobbed against the darkening leaves, floating beyond questions and answers.

"We'll have to get her up here next year to help," Auntie Bee said, laughing that odd laugh. "The devil looks for idle hands. Which reminds me, I should get back to the kitchen pretty quick. The preacher's got that Injun boy washing dishes tonight and I should be there to save a few. You were going in here, weren't you? Maybe I'd wait a minute if I was you."

She turned to brace her feet on the slope of the path, then looked back at them. "Leah, if there's a chance during the service tonight, we'd sure like to hear you testify. We don't know much about you people over at Louis Lake and it would be nice to hear how God is working there. If you have any problems at all, we could pray about them. Because we're all God's children, aren't we." Her tone was confidential, reassuring, except for the slight laugh at the end.

Leah didn't speak, but her white face nodded again out of the darkness.

Auntie Bee didn't look at Miss Ruthie. Then she was descending the hill, her head turning slightly from side to side, surveying the road. The girls waited until she had reached the bottom, walking on the road and singing once more, before they left the patch of grass and began to climb through the trees. Boys'

103

voices drifted up from the road, organizational. There was a sudden clunk of wood on tin, and a voice counting fast and loud.

"See," Peter said softly, "she's not hanging back. Just stay easy and you'll make out fine." He gave out a last winning grin.

"Hssst!" he said. "Up here, you girls. Do you think we're turkeys or something, roosting on the backhouse roof?"

Both girls heard his whisper, looked higher up the hill, eyes lost in the gloom.

"I figured we'd find a wolf way back in the bushes," Miss Ruthie said aloud. "They don't dare come closer to where people go."

"Did you ever know a wolf that sat on a toilet, Josh?" Peter said.

"They only go in the bushes," Miss Ruthie said, nearer now.

Miss Ruthie and Leah were separating themselves from the gloom, emerging between tines of birch. The white sweater was still in the lead. Miss Ruthie stepped on a dead branch in the undergrowth. She seemed indifferent to its snap; she tramped on another one right away. Leah followed soundlessly in the same trail. Joshua thought how it would look to run. Then Peter stepped out to meet them and he was following, getting closer, his heart thudding like drums against his ribs.

"You boys sure make it hard for a girl to have a date," Miss Ruthie said. Her eyes were on Peter. "I'm so tired I could sit down somewhere for a rest."

"Next time we'll meet you by the lake," Peter said. "If you hate climbing a little hill so much. Leah, it was nice of you to come. Leah Krajci, Joshua Cardiff. Though you sort of know one another already."

"Hi," they each said shyly.

Joshua watched her eyes attempting to stray to the top of his head. She looked directly into his vision for an instant until he glanced away. When he looked back again, she had already lost the struggle and her eyes were steadying where they must go, like water reaching its own level. Miss Ruthie came past him, Peter following, and she didn't even look at him. He had known her all his life.

"See you in church," Peter said. "Don't get saved before then."

He already had Miss Ruthie by the hand. The next moment

was like jumping from an elevator. Joshua looked at Leah. She was no longer looking anywhere, least of all at him. He thought frantically whether he would dare just sneak up on her hand and grab it. Then Peter and Miss Ruthie were getting away from them at an alarming rate. Leah still would not look at him. He looked at her hand. He felt suddenly loose-bowelled. He had a horrifying vision of having to struggle with the hand, like reaching for a weasel in a burrow.

Peter and Miss Ruthie were just a tableau of joined hands mounting the hill. Suddenly they turned out of sight. Joshua reached out blindly, caught too far down at first on her fingers. Then it was like a bird huddled in his hand. They climbed through the trees without talking yet. He wondered if he would even hear her, with the drums beating like trip-hammers in his ears.

"Do you have a lot of brothers and sisters?" he said, but he wasn't clear on every word. He had to repeat it, mortified. Though he managed to add, "I've seen you a lot with your little brother here. At least I guess he's your brother."

"Yes," Leah said softly. "He's my youngest brother, the littlest of seven. I should have him meet you, his name is Benjamin. You might keep an eye on him for me in places I can't go."

"I noticed you looked after him a lot, he always sits with you in church."

"And sleeps. Sometimes he's a real embarrassment to my father. But he's our dearest one: the child, my father says, of his sorrow. My mother died giving birth to him."

Leah's voice was simple, quiet, without any posturing.

"I didn't know," Joshua said quietly. "I'm sorry. That must have been tough on you."

Leah's fingers pressed lightly on his.

They had turned into the road, walking deep in the dust and shadows. He could feel her beside him, her hand hardly touching his yet, though she had not once drawn away, the sound of their voices meeting more than the touch of their skin.

"You have some older brothers, then?" he asked.

"Yes, five. But two are married. I get a lot of help from my sisters-in-law. They've been like older sisters to the family."

"I'd sort of like an older brother who was good at sports, maybe, and good at telling you what to do."

"It's not as much fun as it sounds," Leah said. There was a pleasant laugh in her voice, not right out loud, but a sound which promised laughter. "Sometimes they think they own you. My brother Bal—Theobald is like that. He's always telling me how I should dress if I want to go out with boys, and what I should say. I much prefer a boy to be a little reserved, even shy."

"Well, at least I know now why you'd go out with me when I just stared at you."

Leah was smiling at him, an odd smile which seemed to involve her long, slender nose. Suddenly he no longer minded what was coming.

"You called—" he said, then rephrased it. "You started to call Theobald Baldy, didn't you? It's all right, you know, you can say things like that in front of me, it won't crack my skull like an egg."

Leah looked full at him for the first time. Her face was as white and fragile as bone china; only her eyes were dark and warm like coffee.

"I'm glad," she said. "Because I didn't mean to be hinting or prying. I wasn't really thinking. We just call him Baldy, that's all. His name and his hair are both too long."

"If his hair is anything like yours, he's lucky. I couldn't help notice it since you came."

"I wasn't quite sure where you were looking much of the time. Sometimes I thought you were staring past me at someone else."

"I'm glad we cleared that up," he said.

They were quiet for a time. Up ahead, Peter had his arm around Miss Ruthie's waist. Her head was on his shoulder.

"I can't tell you why," he said. "I guess it doesn't matter. Maybe it was a fever, maybe I inherited it, nobody knows. My mother used to say it was meant as a test of faith because God wasn't cruel. I was special in His sight, she said. He wanted to prove me, like in the Bible."

Leah nodded.

"My father says things like that still happen. He says the Age of Revelation isn't over yet. It could be you've been set apart to accomplish something for God. Have you prayed to know His will?"

"Mostly," Joshua said, "I used to pray to get my hair back."

But it was like a gate had been opened in him, he wanted now to tell her how it had been.

"One night, when I was nine," he said, thinking himself into it so completely that it came to pass as he told it — came to pass because he was telling it, though he didn't know any more if that was the way it had happened — "I had all the faith in the world it was going to grow back. My Grandpa had invited an evangelist to hold revival services in Lacjardin and in his first service, the evangelist told the story of how the children mocked Elisha. He kept saying how they yelled after him, 'Go up, thou bald head, go up, thou bald head.' That man looked at me all the time he was talking. 'Bears came and ate those wicked boys,' he said. 'They rushed out and tore up forty-two of them. There those boys were, maybe walking home after school, and there Elisha was, he didn't know why it should be so, but God had reserved him unto His grace. And there also were those bears, picking berries in the bush, not even capable of knowing who it was passing them by nor what the shrill voices were saying that would send them galloping out to the road. "For be not deceived; God is not mocked: whatsoever a man soweth, that shall he also reap." I tell you God sent those bears as a punishment, as a judgment upon all those who scorn Him or deny Him, as well as a proof of His watch over them who fear Him and honour Him.'

"Well, I didn't much want bears coming out of the trees to eat the kids at school. It seemed a terrible kind of punishment just for being a kid. I'm not sure, I guess now I was even hoping to get out from under His eye where He could always spot me so quick. Anyway, it left me sort of hopeful. If Elisha was bald and was mocked and could get what he wanted just by asking God, maybe I could too."

"I know," Leah said, "I know just how you feel. But it doesn't always work that way."

"Don't you know it," Joshua said. "Because when we got home after that meeting, I knelt beside my bed the whole night long. It was April and there was a hole sawed in the roof where my father was putting a dormer in. It was freezing. But I prayed the same words over and over with my teeth clicking until I couldn't speak them loud enough any more, I just thought them again and again. When I woke up, the sun was shining through the roof but it was still real cold. I was stiff. My knees were dented by the floor. I thought my arms would go up to my head if I made them. But I wanted to see all that mess of hair in the mirror first, before I felt

107

it. So I limped down the stairs. The bones in my feet felt like hot rods of iron. When I got into the hallway, the bathroom door was closed. My mom was scraping toast in the kitchen. I smelt it before I heard it. So I went into my sister's bedroom. She was real little yet and didn't have to get up to go to school. But she was awake, looking at the door when I opened it.

"Is it Crissmus?' she said.

" 'It sure is,' I said back. 'God give me hair. It's Crissmus at Easter.'

" 'Can I see it then?'

" 'See what?'

" 'The hair God give you for Crissmus?'

" 'You mean you can't see it yet?' I was already running to the dresser. I could see her in the mirror, the bed clothes rumpled around her waist. Her mouth sagged open.

" 'It's not Crissmus,' she said. Then her face got bright just as quick. 'Don't cry, Josh. It's just not Crissmus yet. Say, did that Rabbit leave eggs today like He was s'posed to?'

" 'He already left me mine,' I said. It was smooth and shiny in the mirror. The sun beamed on it from the bush by the window and lit it up.

" 'Don't cry,' she said. 'It takes a long time for Crissmus to come.' "

Joshua looked at Leah's white face in the darkness. It seemed to have come very near to him, though it had not moved forward.

"I guess it's fair to say," he went on, "that Christmas hasn't come yet. I'd have to say that it doesn't do much good to pray for things like that. Like my Grandpa told me afterwards, 'Thank God He's not the Simpson's Christmas Catalogue. The stuff you ordered would just be broken anyway come next Christmastime. And by then, you might not want it.' "

Leah laughed, her breath warm against him.

"Your Grandpa sounds a lot like my father. But I didn't say, Josh, to pray to get your hair back. There's nothing wrong with the way you are. I said, Have you prayed to know God's will for you? Have you prayed to find out what He has in store?"

"No. No, I haven't done that."

"You should," she said. "Every Christian should live that way. We can pray right here, if—"

He was as surprised as she when he kissed her. He met her

108

mouth full on his own while she was still talking. For a moment her lips parted and she was kissing him back. Then she pulled away. He could see her fighting for breath. Her voice, when she spoke, sounded small and hurt.

"Why did you —"

"I'm sorry," he said quickly. "I didn't want you to say any more. I just wanted to let things be."

"But my father —"

"I know," he said. "Peter told me how your father's afraid of how boys will treat you because you're from — well, out there on the railway and all."

"He said that?" she said, her voice stinging like a slap. "Is that what you thought?"

"No," he said. "No, at first I liked you because of how you looked at me. Now it's because — well —"

"Because of what?"

"Mostly because I can talk to you. But also because of the way you kissed —"

"I was going to say," Leah said distantly, "that my father believes we should seek God's will in everything we do. It's his job, I guess, or didn't Peter tell you that too? No, Peter wouldn't, because he's been back-slidden now for a year. My father works on the railway just to help with our support; his real work is as minister of our church."

"I'm sorry," Joshua said. "I really am. I didn't think —"

"I know," Leah said. "I've liked so much talking to you." He could barely see her face; from the sound of her voice he was afraid she would cry.

There was silence, save for the distant beat of drums, all about them. He waited and so did she, apparently. When the cry of a loon from down across the lake broke their private hush, she stepped back.

"I have to go," she said. "I must wash my hair before chapel."

Then she was simply gone. He could hear her footsteps in the dirt, getting farther and farther away, and the drums now swelling.

"I'm sorry," he called through the darkness. "I really am."

He stood for a time surrounded by a darkness almost visible. He could think of nothing but the way her mouth brought fire to his lips.

Go thou up bald head. You'll be damned if you go, but damned
worse if you stay. For should you bring to shame this girl who
believes in you, the lowest hell would not, could not be deep enough

V

"There are towns," the preacher said, "which remind me of Jericho. There are places of iniquity like that not too far from here."

He paused, and the sound of the drums soaked through the
unpainted plywood once more without interference. The roof
arched down over the seated people into concrete footings buried
in the earth; it left the edges of the congregation in shadow.
Joshua sat tight against the wall curving in by his head. He was
almost beyond reach of the gas lanterns which hissed along the
length of the nave. Thomas fidgeted beside him, looking around.
His movement shook the plank bench.

"Young people," Reverend Haagshed said, "times haven't
changed very much. Don't let the world sell you on progress; we
haven't gone anywhere in all the years since Jericho. There are
still fortifications right about us accursed in the sight of the Lord."
He gripped the pulpit with both hands, leaning toward them.
"You see, we haven't yet regained the Promised Land. We haven't
conquered Canaan. Do you realize that the very name of our
country retains the memory of Canaan? There's only a *d* difference. *D* for an *n*. And I don't need to spell for you the letters which
come between. The Catholics who called it Canada damned this
country in the beginning."

Joshua heard the preacher's voice in only a dim and random
way. He could see Leah four rows ahead, sitting demurely in a
group of girls. The light glistened in her long brown hair.

The scent of pine came suddenly stronger than it always was.
He looked down where Thomas was plowing up with both feet a
pile of shavings from the level scattering on the floor.

The preacher's voice waited. When it came again, it was softer.
"But this, my beloved young people, is not the Age of Law. It is
the Age of Grace; it is the era of Christ's tender mercy. God n

longer asks us to march around Jericho for the destruction of the heathen. He does not ask us to raze with fire and with the sword. If we are at war (and we ought to be if we are Christian soldiers), we are at war only in the Spirit. We have been called of God to claim the empire within us, within man everywhere; it is not for us to gain the Promised Land on earth. Now don't get to thinking, from this, that God's wrath is a thing of the past. God is not mocked; there is a day of Judgment coming. It may be very soon. It could be tonight. We don't know; it has not been given unto us to know. But until it comes, our assault on Jericho must be with the sword of the Word, and with the flame of the Holy Spirit.

"I want, therefore, to talk to you tonight about two things. They really are at last the same thing. I want to speak of Jericho — the city walled against God — and I want to speak of what one of the children of Israel did when Jericho was taken. You remember, I hope, the story of Achan. He stole the accursed thing, the thing which God forbade any private man to touch."

He looked across his audience; his jowls were trembling. He spoke again, very solemnly. "There are some of you young people here tonight who were caught stealing in this camp."

Thomas stopped jerking on the bench. His whole body became rigid; he watched the minister's face.

"I know that most of you have already received your punishment. Some of you washed dishes. Some of you had to pick up litter around the camp. None of you was burned, like Achan was, to death. Because God has not marked off anything here as the accursed thing. He doesn't tell us things like that any more. It's simply wrong to steal. But there is a day coming when the sins you have committed will be accursed if you don't repent."

Thomas nudged Joshua. "Dat bohunk baloney," he whispered, "was d' cursed t'ing. It give me real bad gas. An' I had to do all d' goddamn dishes anyway. I thought dey was never gonna end."

Joshua nodded without turning his head, shrinking a little out of the line of frontward vision.

The preacher was looking their way, staring into the shadows. They sat very still. At last he glanced down at the pulpit.

"Our text for this evening," he said, "comes from Joshua chapter six, the eighteenth verse. There we read, 'And ye, in any wise keep yourselves from the accursed thing, lest ye make your-

111

selves accursed, when ye take of the accursed thing, and make the camp of Israel a curse, and trouble it.' "

For a long moment he looked out over the congregation, seeming to stand now on nothing but the Word he had just read. Then he stepped aside from the scarred yet thickly varnished pulpit.

"This, young people, is a critical moment in the history of the children of Israel. If you remember the story, the Chosen People have just set out on their first combat encounter with the Enemy of Souls. They are trying to regain the Promised Land. They stand at the walls of Jericho, the fortress of Canaan, not with battering rams nor catapults nor ladders, but with trumpets and the Ark of the Covenant. Maybe the warriors of Israel are impatient because their might is subservient to the slow trudging of the priests. Their bone-chilling shouts are silenced by the outstretched arm of Joshua. They walk in meek submission with the women and children in that dusty daily trek around the thick rock walls. It is a strange way to run an army, they mutter. They fear that the Canaanites up there in their high walled city will look down on them like they're a bunch of stubble-jumpers. Still there is something ominous in their deliberate measured march each morning and their appalling silence grows unbearable to the townsmen huddled within the city walls."

Out of the corner of his eye, Joshua saw Miss Ruthie slip into the last row of benches across the aisle. Her white sweater was inside out; a patch of dirty dampness showed through the wool. Little bits of twigs and leaves clung in her hair. A mother with two young daughters looked her full in the face as she sat down. Miss Ruthie seemed to cringe at the glance. Her fingers ran up and down up and down on her tan skirt as if she were trying to smooth it.

"How about each of you, young people?" Reverend Haagshed was saying. "Have you built walls about yourself to shut God out? Are you a spiritual Jericho?"

His hands moved, shaping the air in front of him as though he were building from some unseen blueprint. The shadows which moved on the walls and among the listeners gave to his shapes instant dimension.

"There are lots of ways you can put up walls, you know. Disobedience is the surest foundation of all. When you pay no heed to God's claim on your life, you have measured out the footings. In no time at all, you are pouring the concrete of a stubborn will into the forms you've set. And every time you sin after that, with your mouth, with your eyes, your hands, your heart, you lay another row of stones in the mortar of your will. It ends with you living alone (or maybe with some of your sinful fellows) inside the rock walls you have built. You might think you are safe. But a day is coming when your citadel must face the iron voice of God Himself.

"Beware of that day, young people. For our God is not mocked. He can topple your wall with a single word. That's what he did to the people in Jericho. Maybe they laughed at those tedious people tramping around the walls. Maybe they joked in the streets and in the markets. But I'll bet they shivered in their beds at dawn when the Israelites started up their slow tramp tramp again. They knew down deep at last that nothing could make them safe. They had closed their doors too long upon God. And God destroyed them. He wiped them out with a shout. He didn't use weapons, just a shout. You see, He didn't want any man to take the glory. He wanted man to know what a weak and puny thing he is. One shout, and Jericho was ruined. And most terrible of all, young people, the fortress which the Jerichoites built to save them fell down and crushed them in the end. God turned their hope and pride into their disaster. All along, while they were thinking to preserve themselves, God was shutting them up — that none might escape. Beware, then, of closing your doors too long against God. Jesus said, 'Behold I stand at the door and knock. And if any man hear my voice and shall open the door, I will come in to him, and will sup with him, and he with me.' But you must open your own door. He hasn't promised to knock forever. You've got to answer soon, while He's still there. You have to catch Him while He's calling."

All of a sudden Joshua realized that Peter was sitting, had been sitting for some time it seemed, on the end of their bench. He was half looking toward them, and there was a terrible smile on his face like he was trying to laugh about something only he couldn't look any one in the eye.

"Let's get out of Jericho now while we are able," the preacher said, "and join up with God's Chosen People. We advance to the morning of the seventh day. We are with Joshua. We have just

113

completed an exhausting seven circuits of the city. In that fore-boding stillness before the blast from the seven trumpets of rams' horns crashes against the vault of heaven, Joshua counsels his people as a good minister must do: 'And ye, in any wise keep yourselves from the accursed thing, lest ye make yourselves accursed.' It's the last thing he says to the children of God before the terrible shout rips out from their throats. Why do you think he says it? What is this 'accursed thing' which we hear so much about? What makes it accursed?

"Beloved young people, the accursed thing is that thing which Achan took out of the city of Jericho. It is nothing more than a Babylonish garment, two hundred shekels of silver, and a wedge of gold worth fifty shekels. It is only a little thing. But it causes Achan to be burnt in the fire. O dear young people, the wrath of God is a fearful, flaming, dreadful thing and ye who are not in Christ must tremble for your eternal souls! And even if, like Achan, you are one of God's children, you will still meet his fate by touching the things of Jericho. For remember, young people, one of the things which Achan took was a Babylonish garment. A *Babylonish* garment, young people. Slipped from the scented flesh of the whore herself. Get this straight too, that you don't need to commit with her the deeds of darkness to be lost. If you even enjoy the company of those who are without, you teeter on the brink of eternal damnation. If you put on her garments or the sinful lipstick and perfume, then you walk like Achan with the fire all around you. But if you go inside the city of Jericho, you are already buried beneath its walls, you are devoured and all your seed with you. Then, young people, you already know what it means to die eternal death. I implore you, do not go into Jericho."

He paused, and the room floated on the backwash of his language. In the front row Auntie Bee clasped herself in her big arms and she swayed from side to side. She was weeping softly. Joshua sat squirming in the shadows and every word, every glance, seemed meant for him alone. He did not see Peter's face twisted like a gargoyle; he did not hear Miss Ruthie coughing and crying in the same breath; he did not even feel Thomas any more jerking against the bench.

"I have only a little more to tell you," Reverend Haagshed said. "But it is the worst thing of all. Do you remember the end of Joshua's warning? He says don't take up the accursed thing, 'Lest ye make yourselves accursed'? But what is worse, much worse, he says, 'Lest ye make the camp of Israel a curse, and trouble it.' Think about that. Think about what happens after the mighty catastrophe at Jericho. The scouts go to Ai, the next city. And they come back smiling. 'It's only half as big,' they say. 'It's as good as in God's hand right now. Let's send only two, maybe three thousand men up there. The rest can take the day off.' But at Ai, thirty-six Israelites are killed. The rest of the army panics; they scatter like flies before the warriors of Ai. Whereupon Joshua hurls himself to the ground and in a loud wailing voice, he beseeches God. 'Why, O Lord,' he cries, 'have You deserted us?' Then his anguish gets the best of him; he begins to doubt God. 'Wherefore,' he complains, 'didst Thou lead us over Jordan into the midst of our enemies, O Lord, that our name might be cut off from the earth?' And the Lord says, 'Get up off the cold ground, Joshua. Israel hath sinned.'

"*Israel hath sinned.* O, the enormity of those words! Not Achan has sinned. Not, There is sin among you. But *Israel* hath sinned. What one man does affects his whole nation. *'Lest ye make the camp of Israel a curse, and trouble it.'* How about it, young people? Is there an Achan among you who can make the whole camp a curse? Maybe you hardly care about yourself. Maybe it doesn't matter to you if you have to die, or even (though I doubt it) if you have to spend eternity in torment. But are you willing to take the blame for the destruction of those around you? Could you live with yourself, knowing your family or someone you loved died because of you? Worst of all, could you face someone in hell who was there because here tonight your hardness kept him from saying Yes to the voice of Jesus? Woe unto you, dear young people, if you should be responsible for the damnation of another!

"I think we all know the rest of the story, how each of the tribes came one by one before Joshua until God told him 'This is the one' and they laid hands on Achan. Be certain, young people, that God knows who you are. If He knew the heart of Achan out of all the tribes of Israel for its iniquity, be sure He knows your heart this very moment.

"Achan — I tremble to say it — was led outside the camp and they stoned him first until his body was badly bruised. Then they committed him to the pangs of the fire. And the swift and terrible vengeance of the Lord was visited upon him at the last, upon him and all his family. And they piled up a heap of stones over his flesh until the last Judgment Day.

"Walk softly then, ye unrepentant, in fear and trembling, for the fiery floods of the fierceness and wrath of God are about to rush upon you with inconceivable fury and in omnipotent power. The hour of harvest is almost at hand when God shall lay you mightily upon the threshing floor and He shall thresh you with prodigious strength. He shall thresh you without mercy against the boards with His flaming flail. If ye are but husks and full of emptiness, He will pound in His fury until the rotten planking gives way and you are plummeted into the bottomless pit, not to fall in a swift shrieking rush to your death and merciful oblivion, but to be precipitated headlong in hideous ruin down to dwell in awful knowledge of your endless doom. And the flames shall wash about your being. And they will flood throughout your substance until your soul remains alive only in the writhing agony of fire. And you will lie for all eternity chained to the blazing rock. But woe, worse than woe, unto you should a loved one be chained beside you. For what you have known here as love will be converted into deadly hate, except of hate shall be no end, and none of you will die.

"Is this, then, your eternal choice? Well might this night determine your endless destiny. This night you are forced to choose. God has said 'My spirit shall not always strive with men.' Yet at this hour, He is holding out his uplifting hands, perhaps for the last time. In the words of the chorus,

> Turn your eyes upon Jesus,
> Look full in His wonderful face,
> And the things of earth will grow strangely dim
> In the light of His glory and grace.

Come, you who are hid in sin, come down here beneath the altar, as we stand together and sing. Come down in front and take a stand before your friends. For Jesus said, 'Whosoever shall confess me before men, him will I confess also before my Father which is in heaven. Take the first step and the rest will be easy. Come down here and find peace in Jesus. *Ju-ust as I aa-am without one plea*"

Then they were all singing, soft quiet voices mingling with the deeper voice of the preacher. The contraltos and tenors caressed the melody, drifting beside it in one moving voice, and the song

116

seemed more than they were, somehow outside of them, looking down. *Aa-nd that thou bi-idst me come to thee-ee —O lamb of Gaw-od I come . . . I come.* Then a few were coming, with the second verse mounting slowly through the melody once more. They were walking as if in a dream and some were stumbling, tears streaming down their faces. Miss Ruthie was among the first to step into the aisle. Her fingers clutched at her skirt all the way to the front. She stood with her head bowed and the pulpit rose above her. Others closed around her and the damp, dirty circle on her sweater was blotted from all sight. Above the cluster of heads, the preacher looked out across the rows. His mouth was wide with singing.

Ju-ust as I aa-am and waa-aiting not . . . to ri-id my soulll of one dark blot

Then Peter was gone, slipped into the flow of people still moving toward the front. Joel was down there already, standing beside Auntie Bee. Thomas was looking around.

Those harvest-hot Sunday afternoons, the dead days, when not even a tractor moves on the land, and riding my bike through the breathless air, with the heat waves shining on the gravel like a road of ice. Uncle Owen's place. Joel waiting in the shade of the tank-stand. Slipping into the cool shadows of the garage; it's dark at first with the sliding door closed behind us. The smell of oil on the dirt floor. Joel says his folks are sleeping, at least the bedroom door is closed. We squeeze around the car, along the wall. Above the work bench, between the shelves of paint cans bins of nails and bolts, the flies drone against the speckled windowpane. Out there the trees and bright grass. On this side the flies crawling on the dirty glass, butting against it, buzzing. They strain at the light. They are so easy to catch by the wings, their blue bodies blurring like tuning forks between the pinching thumbs and fingers. Then lowering them one at a time. Turning the cold steel handle of the vise. It clamps the lower wing; the buzzing stops. A final wrench of the handle, so tight, then the fingers' release; the buzz begun again by the upper wing, the fly pitched on its side amidst the smell of steel and oil and dirt. The match flares, reek of sulphur. The fly leaps in the fire, its buzz increasing like a rising siren. The air stinks. Then only the silence. It is finished. No, that's a lie, it's not finished, not for me anyway, even if for Joel, because it's gone inside, I can't get rid of it. That fly won't die until I do. And what if I don't then

Thomas was touching his arm.

"Hey, it's over," he said. "Le's get outa dis Jerky-yo."

The singing had stopped. About twenty people were down in front of the pulpit. But it wasn't finished yet.

"Let us pray together," Reverend Haagshed said. The standing people bowed their heads. The preacher didn't close his eyes. He looked at certain faces in the congregation.

"There are some of you," he said, "in this audience who have not answered God's calling. There is still room for you down here in front." He was looking right at Joshua for a moment. "Tonight might be the last time God ever knocks at your heart's door. Don't be caught dead in Jericho." He closed his eyes and his chin jutted upward. "Father, we have heard your voice speaking to us tonight. We have heard you knock and some of us have answered. We praise you for your mercy, Lord, and we pray you to be merciful to them who have not answered you. Wait yet a little while. In Jesus name. Amen."

"Come on," Thomas whispered. "Dey're gonna wait dat Sun Dance fer us only a little while."

Joshua looked down toward the front. All at once he wished Thomas had never come to camp. This grubby Indian kid left him feeling worse than uneasy, in a way that threatened now to be obscure to him. It wasn't the spastic disrespect any more, the wild uncaring for the opinion of elders, which more than once had pulled Joshua into the path of sober stares. It was — it was — he didn't want to think it. Because Huck Finn had had it a whole lot easier than he did, that was for sure; all he had to do was remember the way Nigger Jim was always so concerned about him. But Thomas show concern? It was as if he didn't even have a soul, because if he did, he couldn't care so little about it at a time like this. This was it. He was embarrassed in the sight of God, finally, to be seen with Thomas, because his personal soul's urgings might be mistaken for the same no-soul at all, or if individual, a squalid and smelly one.

"Hey," Thomas said, almost out loud. "You ain't gonna turn chicken shit, are you? Not after all dis time?" His pupils narrowed to flinty points. Joshua felt both his shoulder blades touch the wall. *Why, he doesn't care at all about a person; I suppose none of them do. It was never like I thought. So now I've got to get away.*

"Hold your shirt," he said as gruffly as he could. "I got to go back to the bunkhouse for one minute."

"Sure," Thomas said, turning, giving him room. He looked back over his shoulder, grinning once more. "So long as we get outa dis Jerky-yo."

In the grassy mud of the lakeshore, Joshua tried to outpace the sound of the drums. Thomas stuck beside him, closer than a brother. *If he would just go to the toilet,* Joshua thought.

When the cry of the loon came to them across the dark water, long, drawn-out, fluttering between laughter and great sorrow, Joshua was taken by a sudden pang of shame. *He doesn't understand,* he thought. *It ain't his fault. He ain't been civilized, no more than that bird has. And all these years with a mother gone loony in North Battleford.*

"Can I tell you something honest?" he said to the outline of the face beside him. The sound of the mud sucking at their shoes stopped as they reached the flat-bottom skiff drawn up across the beach. Joshua stepped into it and sat down. There was water on the floor, trapped between the last two ribs. Thomas stood outside.

"What?" he said. His voice was even.

"I don't think I can go," Joshua said.

Just then the crying of the loon rose again over the water, sudden, brief, but echoing against the sloping walls of the valley. Something inside him, he didn't know what because it surprised him, rose to meet it, something way deep hooting at the known part of him, though with the loon's sadness and its sympathy.

"Is it 'cause of all d' loon shit dat preacher was shov'lin'?"

The irreverence of it shocked Joshua, yet he felt an insane urge to laugh. Then the very lightness of the impulse made him feel as if he were fallen already into eternal regions of fire. The faces of his Grandpa and Grandma, his father and mother, his sister, and his long-dead uncle seemed to look down at him from an enormous height, looking after him at first with concern, but receding ever more into final bliss. Then he was alone in darkness, belonging there. Only there. Except that Thomas, he realized, was still beside him.

"Maybe you're right," he said swiftly. "Maybe nothin' ever will go good for me. But what about you? Maybe you can be the one to dine in Paradise."

Even as he said it, he knew he didn't mean it. Joshua Cardiff was the one he cared about, and if he had to go to hell, he didn't want Thomas Singletree there cursing him, saying horrible things through all eternity.

"I'm tryin' to quit," Thomas said. "I ain't so fond of bohunk baloney. You see, it gives me gas, really good."

Then Joshua could no longer help himself; laughter was betraying him, bubbling up through his throat and nose. Thomas pulled the last stop there might have been by joining in. After that there was no stopping. Joshua had his knees drawn tight against his stomach. He laughed until his guts felt light and twisted.

"Who's there?" a voice called down from the road. "Did you boys skip out on the sermon?"

"No, but I guess it ain't too late now," Joshua said softly. "If you still think—"

Thomas' feet hit the floor of the skiff and they were both out of it and running, sprinting along the shore to the bend where the trees stuck out against the glassy lake. The voice behind them stopped at the boat, baying like a hound which had lost the scent. Then they were swallowed up in the thick darkness of the trees. Soon they couldn't hear the calling any more.

"I'm really, really sorry," Joshua said.

"Why? It was d' way you was brought up," Thomas said. "I knew it all along."

"How could you? I didn't know myself. I wasn't even ready for that girl when she come along."

"Who'd need to be? Wid a girl dat looked like dat?"

Though Joshua could not bring himself now to say the rest of it. He knew he had made Thomas over in his own secret image, graven along the same ugly lines of hatred and self-concern, and he was deeply ashamed. He wanted to tell Thomas how it had been, but he didn't know the way.

"Hey," Thomas said, "Walkin' Horse was right. Yer comin' fer sure to d' Sun Dance. You din' get up no wrong tree. Yer a real Ind-yun after all."

They could hear the drums almost distinctly now. But they seemed to come from over the water.

"Which way?" Joshua said. In the same instant he regretted this final avoidance. Then it was too late; the moment was lost. "Do we go toward the end of the lake?"

"Yep," Thomas said. "You can bet yer long Sun Dance pole."

But when they had crossed the point and reached the shore again, they could not walk there for the low bushes tangling out from the bank.

"I guess we gotta take to d' trees," Thomas said.

Joshua looked back down the lake, expecting to see only lighter shades of darkness behind him. Colors swirled and danced upon the water.

"Hey!" he said, startled. Then he saw the Northern Lights whirl strangely to the east of them, blue ice-greens swept round in the silence to extraordinary glints of red. For an awful moment they reminded him of a great and flaming sword.

Thomas said something in the queer language of his ancestors. To Joshua it sounded as if he'd brought up clay from his throat.

"What," he said, feeling thousands of years out of place between the alien tongue and the timeless aurora.

"*Chepuyuk nemihitoowuk.* D' spirits are dancin'. Dat means yer in fer one hell of a Sun Dance. An' you was sayin' nothin' could go good fer you. You see?"

"It's just a sun spot," Joshua said, as resistant now to his own superstition as to that of Thomas. "Radiation above the earth's poles. We took about it in science class."

"Dey're spirits," Thomas said slowly, unshakably. "You'll find out fer yerself."

"They're sun spots."

Thomas' voice burst around him.

"Shit, you don' wanna take hold of nothin' alive an' hang on, do ya? Jesus, you can be a stuck up shirt sometimes."

The words cut Joshua to the centre. He would have struck out immediately at anyone else, but he repented now with almost an equal quickness. Though he could not bring himself yet to say anything out loud.

"Well," Thomas said after a sufficient pause, "I guess d' ones who're goin' should get goin'."

The going was quite difficult in the bush. At first it was the coarse grass pleached about their legs; as they swished through it, mosquitoes rose in a thin hum about their heads. Canada thistles bit their shins at almost every step. Soon they came up against the fence on which Joshua had once lost his parka. They jackknifed over it with ease. Shortly after, they had to stoop beneath the cover of spreading bushes which felt as durable as grillework and

121

almost as pliable. Green chokecherries rolled like ball-bearing clusters against their ears; jointed willows and saskatoon bushes with twigs like coarsely bristled hair scraped their cheekbones. The farther they went the lower and tighter the lattice grew. At last Thomas stopped.

"We can't get through," he said.

"Well, I ain't goin' back. I feel like I been clawed at."

"We could try goin' up d' hill."

"Do you know the way?"

"Sure," Thomas said.

Against the slope they had to crawl out of the overhang.

"Like as not we're covered with poison ivy," Joshua said.

"Like as not we ain't. At least we got rid of dem goddamn mosquitoes."

But they had not. Climbing through tall grass again, the hum grew thick around them. They were slapping necks now, and arms, faces, shoulders with both arms. When they tried once more to follow the contour of the hill, they could not penetrate the twisted brake. There was nothing for it but to go on climbing, weaving among the trees, plowing in and out of grassy patches, swinging at mosquitoes, ducking branches, and feeling all the while the hill coming through their legs up into their straining faces.

They were lost not long after they had cleared the upper ridge. The trees overhead stood so closely ranked that they could not find either Dipper, try as they might. They listened for the drums to take direction by them, but the sound seemed to radiate all around them.

"What do we do now?" Joshua said.

"Keep walkin', I guess. Try t' find an open place in dis hoo-er of a bush."

Joshua felt like sitting where he stood. The needling of mosquitoes drove him on, though now more slowly. He no longer even cared when they blundered into a thicket of wild roses, the pointy bushes nettling on his thighs calves ankles yet the flowers smelling like a woman's perfume after the dank gloom of the woods. When they had pierced the thicket, they were suddenly among ferns growing almost in their faces, breathing them cool and green. Then the trees spread away.

They both turned round, scanning the heavens.

"I see the North Star."

"Den our camp is dat way."

"Are you sure?"

The sound of repeated slapping was the only noise for a while except for the pulsing insect-whine.

"Sure I'm sure."

"That's what you said last time. I thought Indians knew their way around in the bush."

"No Ind-yun I ever saw 'ud listen to a preacher yap 'til . . . Aw, nevermine. Le's get our way straight in our heads an' den go by it."

They left the clearing, taking one last look at the stars through a moving cloud of mosquitoes. After that they tramped on, standing at times to rest, though barely able to draw their breath without swatting, then boring on again into the tangled darkness. When they pressed waist-high into a thicket of roses once more, Joshua stopped.

"I ain't surprised," he said. "They always say you go in a circle when you're lost in the woods. I'm waitin' here for dawn."

"Okay," Thomas said, surprisingly compliant. "Le's bed down under dese here pricklers, an' maybe d' mosquitoes won' get us."

They pried the bushes aside with their shoes, opening cramped holes. After they were sunk into the cave dark beneath the blossoms, they found it impossible to turn or move without feeling some part of their flesh goaded by the unyielding thorns. They sat that way, chilling with the motion of night, pinching the occasional mosquito, until the stars grew pale and the birds began to chirp.

In the advancing light they could see a meadow widen beyond the last stand of trees.

"Dat's it," Thomas said. He was struggling carefully to his feet. "Goddamn. Dat's it. We di'n't go in no circle after all."

Joshua stumbled up from his lair, the night earth seeming yet to drag at his hips and shoulders and the painful blood pricking more now than the thorns through his legs and feet.

They walked out through the aspens, shivering unawares with them, and it was as if they were entered upon the beginning of the world. The sun was not quite risen, but the view of the valley in the morning light tingled in Joshua's belly as though he were eyeing it through his navel. The slopes swelled green with grass;

123

boulders dotted the far hill like sleeping sheep. Beyond that the fields rolled through clumps of trees to the last dim stars in the west. Down on the valley floor the lake opened gently onto a river. The river passed full and plump through the reedy marshland and then turned straight toward the foot of the near hill. It touched the slope directly beneath them and then spun out in sluggish coils across the plain. Grey puffs of wolf willow hedged it at every turn. He lost sight of it only where the valley swept round in a northward bend.

"Boy," he said, "this is beautiful."

Thomas nodded slightly, his eyes (even the crossed one) losing their fixed challenge now. He didn't bother to hold Joshua's glance and something in his high-boned face, perhaps the absence of any expression, made it useless to speak. Against the sky Joshua watched a herring gull sail aimlessly, or so he thought until it stooped beneath the land, skimming lake air now with the green slope rushing by it. It flew over a pair of great white birds swimming at the head of the river. He could make out their throaty bulge of bills even at this distance. Listening to the chatter of blackbirds and the drumsound, both of which seemed to rise out of the earth, he felt for the first time something he could almost have described as heart's ease.

A bird which he could not have named sang four slow notes, one lower, then three the same, with the cleanness of a silver pitch pipe. Thomas was moving then, like he had just stepped out of a painting.

"C'mon," he said. "Dey'll start widout us if we ain't dere by sunup."

As they crossed the shoulder of the hill where the valley swung north, Joshua saw the dark tips of spruce rise out of the grass with every step. They reared shoulder to shoulder, pointy-headed and faceless like old giants, each growing many- then hundred-armed, and all of them clad in furs. The drums were somewhere near to them. Then he could see all of it. A tent city was pitched on the grassy floor away from the spruce trees. It reminded him of the fair grounds at the Melfort Exhibition: the white tipis breathing smoke out from their wooden beaks and cabin tents squatting like little bird houses not meant for great snowy owls: except that the ferris and roulette wheels and all the painted steel and canvas of the Art B. Thomas shows made here no avenue lined with

124

flashing lights and barking voices or the hum of revolving machinery. There were still the cars, though, of a thrill-seeking crowd, cars nosed against the slope or angled any way as if the last drivers had been in too big a hurry to worry how someone else might get out. There were wagons too, nearer the tipis, their unpainted boxes pointed every which way in the grass. Horses were tethered and grazing from most of the wagon tongues and wheels and tailgates. People moved about among the tents. Even as Joshua and Thomas watched, a new bonfire opened up into a tiger lily blossom. A number of figures were also moving in and around what looked like high-domed merry-go-rounds — three of them spined with poles like grownup tinker-toys. They stood beyond the spruce trees in a straight line to the north of the camp. The beat of the drums pumped out between their spaces.

"We made it," Thomas said softly now. "Scalp, we finally made it to yer first Sun Dance. I'm glad you come." There was neither distance nor defiance left in his face as he smiled. He seemed intent only on pleasing, as if he were concerned that his friend might not like it here. Their roles, Joshua could see, had at some point reversed, except that Thomas was much more gracious and cordial as a host.

"Me too," he said, wishing he could unbend, let it show a little more.

"You got some frien's down dere bin waitin' to see you. I t'ink you got a few you ain't even met yet. Walkin' Horse done a lot of talkin'. Whaddya say we try an' find him before I shows you aroun' to d' rest?"

By the time they reached the foot of the hill a fog of mosquitoes had swirled up round their heads. The swarm came off the long grass, right down to the sowthistle clumps, as they waded through. Their jeans grew cold and heavy with the morning dew.

"Hey," a dark-faced man in a peaked cap called from the front of the nearest tent, "don't you bring them goddamn bug clouds into camp!"

Then a squat man was running through the camp toward them, disappearing between or behind some tents but never slowing, and a pack of dirty yellow dogs seemed to turn it into a race. All at once the man ducked beneath the flap of a tipi. The dogs poured in like mud after him. They backed out abruptly, the near ones still not catching on and starting to wash up against the leaders, as a plump woman dressed in slacks and a blouse emerged swinging a heavy kettle. One dog yelped when the black ironware caught him on the nose and then the whole pack eddied away between the tents. The squat man sidestepped the slowing pot on his way out again. A lean man following him ran right into it. He let out a yell, clutching at one knee, and then hopped backwards on one leg, speaking loudly to the woman in Cree. She shrugged, holding the pot behind her, and stood to watch as the staggered men ran toward the edge of camp. Both carried in one hand something that looked like a sheaf of grass. Before he could see their faces closely, Joshua knew it was Walking Horse and Joe Little-dog.

"Le's wait out here," Thomas said. He slapped with either hand at his forehead, his ears. There were bright smears of blood on his face.

"Hi dere," Walking Horse said in jerks, still running. "You boys look like you jus' come through hell."

"We pretty near did," Thomas said, grinning. "A preacher give us d'rections."

Walking Horse was there.

"Holy hoo-ers," he said, dropping the grass. He was slapping now too. "Jus' look at you two. Dere's as much blood as if you fought yer way outa dat Bible Camp. Scalp, you got bumps on yer head."

He dropped to his knees. He was thumbing the stone of a cigarette lighter.

"Git down here wid me. Dis sweetgrass will smoke 'em out."

Joe Little-dog came up just as the smudge caught fire.

"Look who cut hisself shavin'," he said. Then he was being bit. "Goddamn little bugger m'squitoes!"

The heady smoke began to mingle quickly with the insect-whine, absorbing and muffling it. Soon not many mosquitoes were left, though with his eyes smarting and his lungs choking, Joshua wondered which cloud was worse.

"We've had t' make smudges all over camp," Walking Horse said through a haze. "If you din' smoke before, you do now."

"We ain't smoked out all dem freeloadin' Piegans," Joe Little-dog said.

"I never expected near so many people," Joshua said. "Where did everybody come from?"

"A lot of 'em from Alberta," Walking Horse said. "B.C. A few

126

from Manitoba."

Joe Little-dog snorted like a horse. "Most of dem buggers would spen' a hunderd bucks just t' get someplace where dere might be free drinks an' a meal."

"We gotta put 'em up," Walking Horse said. "W'en you got d' goods, you can't turn people away, can you?"

Joe Little-dog coughed. They all stood up then.

"Now we c'n breathe easier," Walking Horse said. "Whyn't we take you to meet Comin'-day? He's makin' dis here Sun Dance dis year."

On the way through the camp, a man's voice spoke through the mosquito netting of aluminum-frame tent.

"Hey son! The white boy, what're you doing here?"

Joshua looked past Joe Little-dog through the netting. Hands were unzipping the screen and a copper-faced man stooped through the doorway. He had to duck very low to get his white cowboy hat out safely on his head. When he stood up before them, Joshua saw that his riding boots made him even taller.

"Say now, I didn't expect to see regular people here. Where do you live?"

"Lacjardin," Joshua said, faintly embarrassed.

"Is that in Saskatchewan?" the man said. His hair hung like raven feathers beneath the hat.

"It's right near here," Joshua said, his voice a little stronger. "At the other end of the lake."

"Oh. Nice land you got here. Is your dad in cattle?"

Joshua shook his head. "Mostly grain."

"I guess that's the trouble here, eh? No cattle, no oil. People so poor. Still, could you tell me why the govermint of this province don't do something for you people? You don't even have decent roads. Man, I hit a hole near Kindersley yesterday damn near took my wheels off. And the gravel! Hell, I got three cracks in the windshield startin' to run like a spider web. See the white one over there? That's my car. It's a new Cadillac. I guess I'll have to sell it for junk if I drive it back to Alberta."

"Well, I should go," Joshua said. He bumped into Thomas behind him.

"Sure," the man said. "Nice talkin' to you. See you around. Maybe you'd like a ride in the Caddy some night. If you can find us some good roads."

127

"I don't think there are any," Joshua said. "Well, so long."

Before they were out of earshot Joe Little-dog said, "Goddamn Blackfeet. We should of finished 'em off before d' white man came."

"You don' know he was a Blackfoot," Walking Horse said. "You can't tell what a man is by d' color he polishes his boots."

"If he was a Blackfoot," Joshua said, "why would you let him stay at a Cree Sun Dance?"

" 'Cause he ain't white," Joe Little-dog said.

"Joe don' mean dat d' way it sounds," said Thomas.

"I couldn' tell wid all d' blood on your head," Joe Little-dog said.

They all laughed. Joshua looked about him, beginning to feel somewhat at home in spite of the coarse black hair and strange walnut faces everywhere he looked. He saw a thin suck-cheeked woman wearing glasses whom he would have mistaken, were her hair to turn white and her skin the color of parchment, for his Grandma. Some young men were fitted out in headbands and fresh denim suits. They stood variously together looking at girls in print dresses or tight-fitting jeans as each worked about a fire. Most of the young men carried boldness about them as if to announce that they came from distant and exciting places. They took no notice of the dirty children digging in the dirt by some of the fires.

"I bet we have trouble," Walking Horse said, "wid some of dese young bucks. You ain't buckin' yet, are you Scalp?"

"He give it up," Thomas said. "At leas' on white women. It's jus' as good, you should of seen what he went out wid at camp. Ain't dat so, Scalp?"

"I guess so," Joshua said. "I don't know. There was this one I took a walk with there. She was real nice, but maybe I didn't fit in."

"Ain't no use stayin'," said Joe Little-dog, "if you don'. Dat's what it's all—"

"Okay, Joe," said Walking Horse. "Le's not make it worse fer 'im. We're gonna make 'im wanna go home."

"No I won't," Joshua said. "Though it ain't what I expected."

"It ain't really begun yet," Thomas said. "Don' say nothin' yet."

"I won't," he said. Though with the sun flooding over the ridge, he couldn't help but be disappointed when the polebuildings were suddenly illumined like X-rays of old bones. He could see now in the first structure men on chairs, four men pounding out the beat from a bass drum in their midst. They wore windbreakers against the morning air and they seemed totally uninspired, their faces set like carpenters hammering nails. The drumbeat was loud and monotonous. As he stood with the others in the doorway for a time, the noise gave him a headache.

"Comin' Day ain't here yet," Walking Horse said.

There was one other man in the lodge. He stared at them out of eyes which seemed to have popped from an enormous potato. Thick lips did not hide the dark gap in the upper middle of his teeth. Nor was a foul tee shirt enough to cover the chokecherry stain of his hanging belly, even though a band of white cloth, Joshua could see, had been stitched to the bottom of the shirt.

"Did you see d' drum up close yet?" Thomas said. "Dat man standin' dere wid 'em brought it. It's his own. He's takin' care of it."

Joshua craned to see between the drummers. He looked round at Thomas in disbelief.

"It says 'Saskatoon Police Boys Band.' Don't tell me that guy was ever a Police Boy?"

"We won'," Walking Horse broke in. "But he's bin t' Saskatoon."

"I figured that," Joshua said. "How'd he get it? They don't advertise those things in the Simpson's catalogue, you know. Tell me, did he steal it?"

"His name is Night Traveller," Thomas said. "He wen' t' d' Traveller's Day parade in Sas-katoon."

"That's all?" Joshua said. "How come I missed them handing out the drums the time I went?"

"You don't have a name, d'ough, like Night Traveller. You see? It makes a big diff'rence."

"He thought it was fer him," Walking Horse said. "He heard on d' radio how all Travellers were invited t' march in d' parade. He decided t' go."

Joe Little-dog cleared his throat and spit. But he also spoke at the ground.

"He's a stupid sonuvabitch. You ain't bin to a horse show, not dat I heard of. An' I don' go to no dog shows. So he deserved what he got."

"He got a drum," Walking Horse said. "So at leas' lemme tell about it."

"He's a real dumb bugger," Joe Little-dog said, still talking into the ground.

Night Traveller watched them still out of the bumpy potato face.

"He got t' Sas-katoon," Walking Horse said, "w'en his parade was already started. He got off d' bus an' dey was jus' marchin' up d' street. So he watched how dey was doin' it an' den he pushed through d' crowd an' stepped out in front. At first, he said, people were laughin' an' clappin'. But w'en he kept doin' it, d' cops come and shoved 'im back behind d' line of d' crowd. He couldn' figger it out but he watched dem cops fer awhile an' dey watched him an' w'en it looked like he was gonna stay put, dey wen' away. So he started pushin' through to get back into d' run of it, w'en two big white guys grabbed 'im an' roughed 'im up a bit. People called 'im names. Dirty drunk Ind-yun. Ever body laughed w'en dey t'rew 'im in an alley."

"Why didn't he fight back?" Joshua said. "He's so big."

"He never wanted to hurt nobody," Walking Horse said.

" 'Til den" said Joe Little-dog.

"Joe's jus' sour," Walking Horse said, " 'cause Night Traveller shook 'im up a bit w'en Joe threw his drumstick away one year at d' Sun Dance."

"D' handle slipped," Joe Little-dog said. " 'Cause he's greasy as a pig. Dat stupid bugger."

"Anyways," Walking Horse said, "he wen' through d' alley an' met d' parade comin' up d' other street. He figgered dis time if he was gonna stay in it (an' he should 'cause dey was usin' his name) he'd have t' get somet'ing t' play. D' Police Boys Band was goin' by jus' den. So he picked on d' drummerboy, seein' as how he'd played drums before, an' knocked 'im down an' started up wid d' beat. Dey chased 'im all over town. He run like a moose, luggin' dat big drum in front of 'im, through one of dese big gardens, you know, near a hotel wid fancy towers on d' river bank, an' w'en dere weren't no place else to go, he jumped in d' river on top of his drum. People run alongside 'im on d' bank yellin' an' jumpin' up an' down an' a few waded after 'im up to dere knees but Night Traveller jus' paddled out into d' centre of d' river an' hung on.

W'en he couldn' hear 'em no more, he thought he'd make it no trouble atall. Den he started hearin' d' noise from d' dam. Dere wasn't much he could do but get down into d' water an' hold dat drum like a — what do you call it?" looking at Thomas, *"nuka-hekun?"*

"Shield," Thomas said.

"Yeah, dat's it. Like a shield in front of 'im. W'en he wen' over, he bust his front teeth on d' rim of d' drum. D' people chasin' 'im lost sight of 'im after d' falls, I guess, an' dey wen' back to dere parade thinkin' dey could pick up dat Police Boy's drum some-times before it got to Nipawin. Night Traveller pulled off into d' bushes as soon as he could an' waited all day. He started home w'en it got dark. It took 'im three nights, one on d' river an' two more walkin' through plowed fields, t' make it. But he lugged dat big white drum home wid 'im. He ain't bin t' no parade since."

When Joshua looked again at Night Traveller, the bumpy face was alight with a grin. It gave him the strange impression of a potato jack-o'-lantern; the whole story began to take on the com-plexion of a masked trick or treat.

"It's good he got away with it," he said.

"Dat's fer sure," Walking Horse said. "Dat's our best drum."

"Brung by our stupidest bonehead," Joe Little-dog said. "I don' mean you, Scalp, you ain't stupid."

"I couldn't have carried it that far."

"You bin doin' okay," Walking Horse said, "carryin' what you got on yer shoulders. Hey, I t'ink I see Comin'-day."

Through the open poles Joshua noticed a man walking alone up from the grove of spruce. The sun glinted upon his eyes, glass lenses. When he had come near to them, Joshua saw a man of medium height and build, though with heavy shoulders and arms which must once have been powerful. His face was seamed with weather as much as with age. Two sharp creases marked the span of his brow; they were tied by short crossing marks, as if railroad track had been laid in the clay-dark flesh. Joshua looked into the man's eyes and found himself suddenly held up short, the eyes quiet and serious but probing. They seemed to look right inside him, not missing a thing outside but needing to know the level of his accountability, his turn-tail-and-run point. Then he felt him-self just as quietly released.

"Dis is d' boy," Walking Horse said. "Scalp-by-Manito. He

brought us pork chops t' eat w'en we was drunk widdout no supper. He started right away t' live up t' d' name dat we give 'im."

Coming-day looked at him again.

"Come an' have a smoke," he said.

"I don't smoke," Joshua said in a small voice. "I didn't use to drink."

It's no more than that then? An old Indian wanting just like anyone else to pass on his bad habits before they kill him off. Because I could have smoked any time at school when they all went behind the bar. Or drank in cars when they parked at the hall for a dance.

Thomas said quietly beside him, "He don't mean t' smoke from a pack. Go wid 'im an' do what he says."

Coming-day appeared not to have heard (or to have noticed, perhaps that was it) his hesitant objection. So Joshua went beside him when the old man turned. He had to walk quickly to keep up with the old man. Not a word was spoken. Coming-day walked directly for the open flap of a sail-white tipi.

"C'mon wid me," he said, ducking beneath the furl of the flaps.

Joshua ducked behind him, entering the yellow-white light. It smelled in the tent like leather and grass and soap, and something behind that, a stale odor like bygone decay. An old woman lay on blankets between two poles, as on a stretcher. Her face was creviced like spruce bark.

Coming-day spoke to her in Cree. There was intense life in her eyes, and her lips moved thinly, though making no sound. Her arms looked like rotten sticks. Joshua heard his new name mentioned.

"Dis is my wife," Coming-day said to him. "*Uskatik.*"

Her eyes seemed to touch his face very gently, all over. He smiled in a rush of sympathy, though his bowels twitched at the sight of her rotting limbs. He was filled with the sudden sense of what it meant to care for this woman. *Uskatik* just looked and looked at him.

Coming-day took up a leather trucker's wallet from his own roll of blankets. He unzipped it and pulled out a cheap cob pipe. He motioned the boy to sit at the foot of the blankets as he sat down at their head.

"Why'd a white boy want t' come to a Sun Dance?" he said slowly, his yellow-stained fingers now packing the broad pipe-

132

bowl with sweetgrass.

Joshua had not been prepared for the question. His tongue felt as weak as the musky grass.

"I—" he said, and that was all.

They sat in the silence, the stained fingers still pushing grass down into the bowl.

"Was it 'cause yer bald?" Coming-day said, looking directly but not pryingly into his eyes. " 'Cause a lot of white folks looked at you like you was queer?" He paused, tamping down the grass with a wooden match. "You got to agree dat folks don' see a bald-headed boy ever' day."

"No," Joshua said. "Only I do. But it wasn't that." His voice fell away uncertainly.

After a pause Coming-day said, "You can tell me d' rest."

"It ... it wasn't ...."

"Only dat? I knew it w'en I first saw you. So say d' other t'ing even if I might know dat too."

"Well," Joshua said, not wanting to sound foolish, "it was the drums. Like they were in me too, and I had to come. I don't know why."

"What d' you t'ink, now dat yer here?"

Joshua looked down at the washed wine of the blanket.

"I don't know," he said quietly. "They're not what I thought." He pulled at the grass by the side of the blanket.

"Say it out loud so you c'n hear it fer yerself."

Joshua shook his head slightly.

" 'Cause dey weren't no mistry no more," Coming-day said. " 'Cause somebody stole one of 'em an' dey all sounded too loud."

"How did you know?" Joshua said, looking swiftly into those old eyes.

"I saw yer face," Coming-day said. "Yer too young yet t' know how t' hide it." He set the pipe down on the blanket. There was silence for a time. Joshua felt something gathering to be spoken and he sensed what it would be.

"D' you wan' t' stay, even wid us bein' like we are?"

"Yes," he said when he knew he had waited long enough.

"Did you tell yer fad-der or yer grand-fad-der you was comin'?"

"No," he said, looking at the beaver-pelt-brown eyes.

"A man should have d' right to know what he's bin raisin'."

"They wouldn't of let me come," Joshua said. "I know that for sure."

"Den you'll have t' become yer own man," Coming-day answered, said it unalterably. "It's an awful tough job."

"I'll have t' try," Joshua said. "I can't do much else."

"Le's have dat smoke," Coming-day said. He struck the match with the scrape of a thumbnail. When he dipped it in the bowl he held it a long time, his cheeks sucking and sucking. At last the smoke curled up. He pinched out the top of the match with his fingers. Then, looking at the hole in the top of the tent, he held the stem of the pipe to the air. "Come an' have a smoke," he said.

Joshua was getting up on his knees to go over when Coming-day motioned him away. The boy watched him, confused, yet something in him beginning to understand. Coming-day held the pipe-bowl out from his eyes and talked, it seemed to no one, in Cree. The smoke climbed on a wispy thread into the light. Then Coming-day shifted on the blankets so that now the boy could see his profile, and the man spoke again in the strange tongue of his fathers. When Coming-day turned his back on him, head up-tilted, spine curving in like a snow-bent birch, Joshua knew the man would go the whole way round before he returned. Then it was done and Coming-day drew from the pipe himself in short cumulus puffs. He looked at the boy before he passed it over.

"I heard d' sun singin'," he said. "in d' spring w'en I was followin' rabbit tracks in d' snow. D' sun climbed above d' trees an' started singin' to me, 'Now is d' comin' day w'en d' Sun Dance is talked about.' So I knew dat I was chose to be d' Maker."

The pipe-stem burned on Joshua's tongue, the smoke in his throat, as he sucked at it. Coming-day swam in his water-blurred eyes. He could not, in the face of this grave old man, say that the sun had no voice. The very look of the man made him feel that it had.

Then they were getting up, the pipe gone out now, and Joshua looked at the woman lying on the litter. Her eyes shone like the sun setting behind trees.

When they came out of the tent again, horsemen were riding about the merry-go-round poles. The drumming of their hooves came up through the grass. When the lead horseman saw Coming-day, he clamped his heels into his horse's belly. The pie

134

bald spurted toward them.

"Hi! Hi!," the man said as he jerked his horse's neck back and slipped down, all in the same motion. The speed of the horse made him run when he hit the ground.

"Okay, okay, I see you," Coming-day said. "Tell me yer story but take it easy."

Thomas appeared at Joshua's elbow.

"D' scout is a man who likes t' tell stories," he said, grinning. "C'mon, I want you t' meet my fam'ly."

"Scout?" Joshua said as they walked among the tents. "What for? Are you gonna fight the Blackfeet?"

"Maybe," Thomas said, white teeth gleaming in a sudden grimace. "But we don' need no scout fer dat, jus' a few two-by-fours. D' reason fer a scout is, he's s'posed t' find d' Sun Dance pole."

"You mean they ain't got it yet, when they're already started?"

" 'Course not," Thomas said. "Even if dey do grow on trees."

In front of a dust-splotched tipi Joshua saw three people arranged as if for a family portrait. The man sat on a plank set over two rusty pails. His chest hung in his shirt like sagging breasts.

"Dis here's my fad-der," Thomas said. "My frien' Scalp-by-Manito. You seen each other but you ain't met."

"Hello, Mr. Singletree," Joshua said. The man looked out at him beneath the brim of his black felt hat. His eyes squinted into the sun. Then he dipped his hat brim in a slight nod.

"An' dis is my little brud-der Joey," Thomas said, his hand nesting in the black head of hair which had moved close beside his waist. Joey looked gravely at Joshua from beneath Thomas' spreadeagled hand.

"Our only woman in d' family," Thomas said. "My sister Lulu."

The girl's brown feet were bare; her toes turned down into the grass as if they were rooted there. Her shins were lean and smooth as saplings, covered half-way upward in lime-green slacks. She was slender in the body, still small-breasted, and as his eyes continued to climb, he realized she was tall, taller than any girl or woman he had ever stood before. He had to look up a little at her nose (it was flat, not very pretty) and he felt defeated already, too young to grow up to her. The hair which lay upon her shoulders hung dark as night between them. Her face, taken at a glance,

135

looked like all the rest of them, somewhat fat-cheeked, the skin wine-dark like dried saskatoons, except that in her eyes there waited the same light he had seen in the eyes of Coming-day's emaciated wife.

"Hi Scalp," she said, smiling at once. And then she did something which left him feeling almost naked. She reached out and stroked his skin-tight skull. "It's smooth," she said, her eyes grown radiant. "It makes me wan' t' rub it wid my knees."

"Lulu's boy crazy," Thomas said. "You better watch out fer her."

"Shut up, Thomas," Lulu said, as if it were the nicest thing he could have said.

Joshua was grieved by her familiarity with him, yet unexpectedly, he found it difficult to feel ill at ease with her.

"You got a crazy brother," he said, sensing she would be pleased. "I think he's good for me."

"I'm glad," she said. "I t'ink he's bin good fer all of us."

"No I ain't," Thomas said. "If I was, you wouldn't say all d'time dat I'm good fer nothin'. I done more dishes in three days of camp dan I done at home in a year. An' nobody said I did 'em 'cause I was good. I t'ink I nearly scared Scalp outa comin' here, I did 'em so often. So don' you say I'm good or I'll go back to dat Bible Camp an' prove I ain't all over again."

"Don' you t'ink we should keep 'im?" Lulu said to Joshua. "T' save d' Bible Camp, if nothin' else?"

"It's okay with me," he said. "They're people who need savin'."

"Now dat I'm here t' stay," Thomas said, "I'm goin' over t' watch 'em bring d' *mistik* in."

"What's that?" Joshua asked.

"It's jus' a tree," Thomas said.

But the scouts had already returned. A felled spruce tree needled the space in front of the nearest drum lodge. It reminded Joshua of the tall Christmas tree put up every year in the town hall for the school Program — it had that kind of promise in it. Coming-day walked solemnly out from the drum lodge, keeping almost in step with the drumbeat. He carried in both hands the skull of some dead thing. It was once dyed vermilion, ages ago it seemed by the weathering, though the blood flush of the animal seemed never to have died completely from its slate-dry bone.

Joshua stared at the T shaped shank, at its chipped and

136

flaking, yet still ghastly color.

"Is that really a buffalo skull?" he asked.

"I s'pose," Thomas said. "I ain't never seen one aroun' here. It wasn' Comin'-day dat shot it, dat's fer sure."

Walking Horse took the skull from Coming-day's hands. He placed a long spike in the eye socket and, using the flat end of a hatchet, he drove the nail into the spine of the tree. Joe Little-dog and others chopped the feathery branches away from the trunk. Somebody chipped off the pole above the skull. Quickly the tree was stripped down. Joshua was disappointed with it, its promise torn away with its green-black wrappings, except that the bone thing glared oddly from the truncated top. Now Coming-day seemed to be drawing with chalk a picture on the bark beneath the bone, a red-coloured spruce, so that it looked like the tree had taken the light of the rising sun, standing aflame between earth and sky. A very old man, his face shrunken inward through his mouth, stooped to fix a few pale-leaved poplar boughs beneath the sign, the last man to touch the tree where it lay on the earth. Walking Horse picked up one of several lines like leather reins which Joshua had not seen attached in the bark and, hauling with other men, pulled the tree into the lodge. It did not take long to stand it up in the centre of the circle. As the flaming skull stood at last in its place atop the tree like another sun placed in the heavens, a quiet sigh more felt than heard, like a breeze stirring in the leaves, went up from the throats of the people who stood all around the boy.

The drum beat deafeningly. Above the low palisade of branches twined about the foot of the lodge, Joshua could see into the other drum lodges where men pounded from their chairs as if in silence. The people in one of them seemed already to be dancing.

The noise made it impossible to talk. Now talk appeared anyway to be unnecessary. People moved about as if they knew what they were doing. Lulu walked away leading Joey by the hand. Thomas retired to the low wall of poplar branches behind them. Joshua sat down with him in the grass. He could see Lulu and the little boy sitting among the oldest women and children on the far side of the lodge. At the left edge of his vision, he glimpsed an old man, then another and another, leaning with their backs against the wall and their feet straight out before them. Just then two men carried in the litter with *Uskatik* making almost no sag in it. They placed her next to Night Traveller at the side of the drums. She could just look out over the poles of her litter.

The men and women who had stayed in the centre now danced in two facing horns, men on one side, women on the other. They did not dance, properly speaking. They simply bent their knees, bobbing up and down. Their eyes held the Sun Dance pole. They moved in the amplitude of the drums, wrapped in the rhythm, swallowed in the matrix of the sound. The thin, high wail of the drummers' chant jerked up with them and down. The morning sun cast splashes of light through the cone of the roof, drenching them all in brilliance. It was as if they had been transfigured and one's eyes were dazzled in sight of them. Joshua continued to look at them that way for a long time, he did not know how long, but it seemed as only a moment.

After a time the sameness of it thickened his senses. Sitting tight against the wall with the poles angling above him, he began to grow heavy-lidded. The heat pressed in like water all about him; he felt like he was sinking to its silent bottom. The drums grew faint in his ears. Then he started, and everything rose up clear again. He would stay that way as long as he could focus his attention and then, bit by bit, everything would slide away again. At last he didn't know whether or not he was dreaming.

In the late afternoon he seemed to be staring at the centre pole. Coming-day stepped through a haze to the tree and stood beneath the skull. Walking Horse came with the hatchet swinging in one hand. He had a peeled willow stick in his other hand. It was pointed sharply on one end. He came up to Coming-day from the side. Coming-day looked straight ahead at the bark on the tree. Then all of Joshua's senses rushed suddenly together.

Walking Horse pointed the stick into the muscle on the man's chest. He raised the hatchet. Then he struck the stick very hard with the flat end of the iron. The skin on Coming-day's chest turned white around the tight depression before the puncture came. Then the flesh closed round the skewer. The blunt axe beat five six times on the willow with a dull clap clap. Coming-day did not twitch a muscle on his face. He looked straight ahead at the tree. The red point came through on the other side by his right breast. The sweat stood out like dew on his chest. Then the blood came running out along both ends of the stick, piling up at the tips before it dripped on the ground. Walking Horse took two of the leather lines hanging from beneath the red skull. He tied them tightly in the notches at the stick's extremities. His hands were bloody when he came away. Coming-day backed out from the tree. The lines went from loops to tautness. The man raised his eyes to the skull. Then he leaned out fully from it, hanging his weight on the strips of leather. The willow stick bulged beneath his copper flesh. He stayed that way, alone with the tree.

Everyone but the drummers got up then and began to leave the lodge. Joshua looked once over his shoulder at Coming-day straining from the lines, his feet moving in a slow shuffle to the rhythm of the drums.

"What's he going to do?" Joshua asked Thomas once they were out in the open. "Someone should stop him before he bleeds to death."

"He'll be okay," Thomas said. "Le's get somet'ing to eat. I'm starvin' t' death."

Lulu was frying bologna in a smoke-scummed skillet when they came back to the tipi. Mr. Singletree was sitting on his sagging bench again, looking but not saying anything.

When they had eaten, Thomas said to Joshua, "C'mon. Le's go see what dose other guys are doin'." To Lulu he said, "Sorry we can't stick aroun' fer dishes."

"Dey didn' train you very good at dat Bible Camp," Lulu said. "You jus' make sure you don' get Scalp into no trouble."

"You'll stay outa trouble yerself," Thomas said, "if you keep yer hands in dat dishwater."

"Did it work that way for you Thomas," Joshua asked, "when you were at Camp?"

"Tell 'im again, Scalp," Lulu said. "By Jeez, tell 'im some more. Maybe he'll smarten up yet."

The western sky had turned a dark blue-black. It looked as if a blackboard had been smudged with puffs of coal and pure white chalk. Now and then the puffs blew up in light, then reappeared again.

Joshua saw Coming-day still slumped and shuffling from the pole as they passed the first drum lodge.

"Isn't one man doin' that enough?" he said. "Why is there more than one set of poles?"

"We got lotsa differen' Ind-yuns here," Thomas said. "Dere's

139

Salteaux an' Assiniboine an' Blackfeet besides us Cree. Dey all likes t' do t'ings deir own way. Excep' fer d' Salteaux. Dey're such stupid buggers, dey go along wid anybody."

As they came up on the far drum lodge, Joshua could see men and women still dancing. They were all quite young and they danced together, not apart. No one was suspended from the centre pole. There was not even a pole. Joshua stopped with Thomas outside the lodge. A group of young men who wore headbands holding back their long, straight hair were playing cards around an upturned washtub. Open bottles of beer sat on the ground beside most of them. Joshua watched without much interest for longer than he cared.

Suddenly Joe Little-dog was among them. He kicked over one of the bottles of beer. The beer foamed out onto the grass.

"Hey watch it!" one of the players said.

Joe Little-dog's face looked like chipped stone.

"Git up, you free-fuckin' Blackfoot."

Walking Horse was running past the first drum lodge. "Joe," he called. His mouth was moving but that was all they could hear.

"T'ink you c'n do it," Joe Little-dog was saying, 'wid my little daught-er an' not pay. Git up."

"Joe," Walking Horse was shouting.

"So you do pimp," the young man said, "for the little hoo-er. We'd lock you up out in Alberta."

Joe Little-dog kicked the washtub over. Cards and coins arched into the grass. Suddenly arms were swinging every which way. Walking Horse was in it now, punching at any face with a headband, and Joshua lost sight of Joe Little-dog in the swarm of limbs which closed over him. He could see figures bent with running on their way from all over camp. Then he felt a jar of bone on his knuckles, numbing all the way to his elbow. The salty taste of blood was in his mouth before he actually felt the fist slam into it. Thomas, he could see for an instant, had blood spurting in a bright arc from his nose. Then it grew too dark almost to see what he was hitting and, in turn, what was hitting him. He felt glass break on his shoulder and he kicked out in fear, his foot driving between a man's legs. He sensed, more than felt, the man double up and go down. Then something clubbed him in the back of the neck.

Thomas was holding up his head. The rain beat into his eyes, soaked through his clothes. Lightning blinded him for a moment like a flashbulb going off. Then the sky seemed to crack like an egg. Wave upon wave of thunder washed away the steady throb of the drums.

"Are you okay, Scalp," Thomas said. "Are you okay?"

There were spots dancing yet in front of his eyes. But he could see that there was no one left outside the lodge. The rain slanted into the grass, tumbling upward where it hit, then falling again in puddles.

"I think so," he said. "It feels like I was hit by lightning. How's Joe? Where'd everybody go?"

"Dey run fer d' cars. Why don' we find one ourselves?"

As he ran Joshua felt like he was drunk. They splashed through a puddle by a high-finned Dodge and tried the door handles before they saw the faces beneath the headbands. Finally they found an old hunchbacked Pontiac that was empty.

"Man," Thomas said, "dat was a good one. We almos'—"

"Good?" Joshua said, his voice quavering almost out of control. "Good? You call it good when—"

A head came up in the window of the car behind Thomas. Through the streaking rain Joshua saw her face clearly in the moment of a lightning flash. It was Lulu. Her blouse was all undone. They looked at one another through a frozen instant. Thomas had turned now too to catch what it was. Then Joshua was out of the car and gone.

"Scalp!" Thomas cried behind him. "Scalp, don' go!"

So she really ain't no different from all the rest of 'em, goddamn her goddamn her! She'd do it with anything that wore pants

Thomas found him sitting in the first drum lodge. He leaned for a long time over him. The rain leaked through the roof all over them.

"It'll be okay, Scalp," he was saying. "It'll be okay. Dey can't help it. Dey all got t' do it. It'll be okay."

Joshua sat looking only at the man who, dangling from the lines, looked only at the tree. The man's face glistened in the rain. It was fogging his glasses.

Sometime in the night, after the rain had stopped and the lightning passed over the hill, a crowd gathered again in the lodge. Someone lit a match to a piece of paper. Joshua saw Walking Horse's face above the flame. There was a long cut of drying blood on his swelling cheek. The flame caught in a bunch of twigs—someone had at least been careful to have dry wood — and then the fire moved in mounting shadows on the wall. Men and women were beginning to dance again in a broken ring. Joe Little-dog bobbed up and down, both his eyes swollen shut. Shadows moved on the walls in time to the drums, as if a ring of unseen dancers were come for the night. The buffalo skull glowed fiercely against the dark like some feeble midnight sun. The drums beat on and Joshua trembled with their pulse as much as he did with the damp night air.

In the dawn of a new day the dancing ceased though the drums beat, beat. The dancers withdrew. Now the man sagging from the taut long thongs began to dance, lifting his legs slowly at first. Coming-day was changed. Joshua would not have known him, met in the woods. There was something terrible in him, sounding in his voice. He was singing now in the low-high wail which was not like the call of souls in the church, crying singly for mercy. It was like no human cry at all, nothing to be understood by human ears, but something risen from the dirt to sing terribly the sun. And it wasn't in his voice alone that the terrible thing was. It was in his eyes. They caught, more than his eyeglasses did, the rising of the sun through the spread of poles and a light danced in them, wild and frenzied. It was as if there was something inside him straining to come out. Along the lines rising like a bridge to the pole the light leaped and glinted in the nail-eyes of the skull. Light filled the lodge, bathing the man and the tree.

Now Coming-day danced faster and faster, his feet way out in front of his body. His moccasins stirred the dust in the stamped-out grass. It rose like smoke. The drums grew wild and soaring. The man flung himself outward on the ropes, arching furiously backward in the empty space. He jerked on the lines at every step. The willow stick bulged like it was alive beneath his skin. His shoulders wrenched at it, straining from the tree, until at last the stick ripped loose the flesh burst apart and Coming-day, of his own momentum, almost fell. But with his arms swinging wildly he caught himself and stood. He stood still and straight and the light caught the first thick trickle of blood from his torn-out flesh. In the golden glow it looked like sap. It oozed out slowly for a moment, then stopped. On the skin it lay like resin.

Out of an eternity of stillness, a file of people began to move past the standing man to the tree. Each one seemed to be laying something, a bolt of cloth, a pair of gold-flashed earrings, a rifle, a wide-buckled belt, at the foot of the tree. The pile grew like a heap of opened Christmas presents. Joe Little-dog managed somehow with his bruised eyes to go forward to the tree. He took from his pocket a mickey with a red-starred label. The fluid streamed in a shaft of golden light down into the dirt. Walking Horse followed with a pickle jar that looked like it held water, except that foam sprang up as he poured. Then Joshua knew for certain he could not hold back. Taking from his wallet a scrap of paper, he wrote with a ballpoint he carried all year round in his shirt pocket:

I.O.U.

one trumpet
a bit dented on the horn end.
I played it two years. My uncle Joshua had it before me.

Joshua Cardiff
(Scalp-by-Manatoe)

He did not think yet what his father would say, who for two years now had driven willingly the sixteen miles a week for the sake of lessons to Nisooskan, or his Grandpa, who treasured the horn of his dead son almost as much as he did any one of his living sons. He simply carried the scribbled paper toward the tree, his heart beating with the drum, and feeling now the lifting sensation of being one with it all, separated no more.

As he met Coming-day on his way to the pole, the man looked at him. His eyes were soft now, flesh and blood behind the glasses once more. He reached toward the boy and placed a hornily knuckled hand upon his head. Then the old man's eyes lifted toward the top of the pole. Joshua felt his scalp glow like the painted bone in the sun.

For a moment, the buffalo appeared to him out of the tree. It wasn't just a skull at the top any more. Its nostrils were wet and blowing, almost at eye-level. Through the wood it watched him, the wind lifting its beard a little, its eyes fierce and red. Then it was wood again.

"Buffalo," Joshua said to Coming-day who still looked above. "I saw a buffalo watching me from inside the tree. It was there and then it was gone."

"Buffalo," Coming-day said slowly, looking out of the lodge

across the valley now. "Buffalo. Nobody here seen one like dat fer years. Not since my fad-der died. W'en we come fer his body, d' chapl'in tol' me it was d' las' t'ing he saw. He said he could see it inside of d' black hood."

Joshua didn't try to see what was real any more, it was all half-dream, half-nightmare to him, each minute of it since he'd left the Bible Camp. He wasn't sure if he would ever wake up.

When the dancing resumed in the heat of the forenoon, he sat finally at rest, feeling Thomas there beside him and an old man whose name he didn't even know. When he began to nod again in the pressing heat, he didn't care whether or not he was dreaming: he could still hear the drums beat   beating.

2. Buffalo Hunt

He was dreaming of what a hunt would accomplish. For three years, in fact, he had lived in the ongoing dream, awakening from it only in those moments when he wondered whether he (not the image) was the one being dreamed onward, then slipping—as though he had never ceased to be drifting—deep within its current again, his sinews flexed through its every motion, it was so real; except that he never reached the end of it: he always woke up before the last rise of ground was cleared, opening his eyes on bedroom walls white-grained like blowing snow or on classroom windows no more translucent than ice-blocks cut from the lake.

It was of bison. He was mounted with Thomas Singletree on horses they had stolen (while a dog barked somewhere far off) from a Blackfoot camp. This much too he remembered about that foray: they had crept from opposite directions into the enemy encampment and he heard a stallion neigh at once in the shadows, close by his end of the tipis. As he drew near, a man stumbled out through the flap of a tent into darkness, already discharging water on the grass as he walked. He himself squatted quickly then, pretending to be voiding on the ground. Dreamlike, the man watched him for so long that he felt constrained (even in the dream) to groan once or twice. The man went back at last into the tipi without saying anything and he was relieved, since he not only spoke no Blackfoot, he didn't speak any Cree. So he and Thomas rode with Coming-day and Joe Little-dog and the rest of the Reservation Crees across the plains, strung out from ridge to ridge against the sky. They rode in a land where no Reservations yet existed, where Lacjardin was only an abandoned hunting camp at the lake-end and no white man had yet strayed far enough from the River to discover what had no need of discovery: that men had for ages lived in motion with this ground-swell of earth. The fact that he himself was white no longer even occurred to him; he simply rode with the shirtless bronze men through the short dusty grass where grasshoppers leaped occasionally, startling a drowsing horse, and gophers stood on shallow dirt-hills at their approach, chattering, watching intently until, with a bark, they plunged down the throats of their burrows, drawing thin rivulets of clay behind them like grains of sand in an hourglass. They rode up high hills where the earth stretched away from them like a broad dish and they could see as many as three or four blue lakes at once, enclosed by bush, and in the hollows sometimes among the clumps of trees, buffalo would be grazing in the shade. But the dream ride always took off when, topping a green rise, they found the world turned suddenly brown beneath them, bison filling the foreground into what seemed infinity, a slow-moving river of animals leaving scattered islands of grass in their stream. Then the horsemen spread out, circling downwind for a start, and they approached slowly in a long concave line until the first animals began to raise their heads, the bearded bulls staring stupidly at first, then advancing a step or two as if to see more clearly what was blurred before them, before shouldering against the herd, hazing it into conspicuous motion.

That was the bravest moment of all, gripping with steady knees for a lifetime it seemed the flanks of a trembling horse, feeling the warm wind on the face, while Coming-day prayed that the buffalo would live forever. Then they were riding suddenly the horses reaching terrifically for distance bodies already blurred and elongated like greyhounds chasing deer in a meadow and it was closer than anything to flying, riders horses bison beating on soporific wings through the high dry air their close-ranked bodies blotting out the earth so as to be uninferant of progress except that the hooves beneath them jolted on the solid ground drumming in the grass and they were all one now fused with the dust and the motion. Down the line men were notching arrows each in turn sighting feather to flint the shaft consecrated to the chosen animal the chokecherry thill released in silence from the spreadeagled bow driving between brown woolen shoulders the beast stumbling going down bison dividing around it like water pouring around a rock and the linked man and animal vanished sucked backward in the noiseless wind of the rush then only the steady dip and rise of the horse beneath him the sound like rain on a barrel of the steady hooves and Thomas beside him riding in that same peaceful fury to the silence at the edge of the world. When the last ridge bulged above them, rimming the sky, the herd was changed already in direction flowing smoothly now as a snake around a post to follow the lowland of the valley. Only one old bull beside them went straight up the hill red-eyed with fury plunging at the slope soaring it seemed for a moment then out of sight like the cow jumped over the moon and the ridge came up hard beneath them mounting almost against their faces until the dream (not stopped) reverted suddenly went back to the beginning and the instant of the kill was never reached.

So he dreamed of what a hunt would accomplish. Although at first he did not even remember the dream, didn't know that he had had it. Later he would wonder whether it began at the Sun Dance or in the books he was reading: *A Tour of the Prairies, The Big Sky,* or maybe the story in *Strange Empire* of the half-breeds against the gun, great-Grandpa, and all of White Canada. Sometimes he liked to think it began on the closing Sunday of the Bible Camp, after he had sneaked back into the heat of the afternoon service in the tabernacle, hardly too soon to catch a ride home with his parents. That night he was to catch more than a ride. His father led him (though he was fifteen now, too old for this) out behind the outhouse where the moon was silvering familiar trees, and he wanted to say something while his father took off his belt only he couldn't say "It was like church there at the Sun Dance" because it was better than church had ever been, better even than the time an itinerant evangelist had preached revival, saying he was God himself come to cull out those bound for hell from those He was going to rapture. In the semi-darkness now they eyed one another, father and son, two figures almost the same height, the same rigid and unflagging will set upon the same stiff and unbending summits of two necks as though carved from one stump.

"Hold out your hands," his father said. The voice carried without heat, without righteousness, without anything.

"I didn't get in any trouble," he said in the same even voice. *At least before now. Because he doesn't know yet about the horn; when he finds out, that will be trouble sure enough*

"Hold them out anyway," his father said, holding up his Sunday pants with one hand.

He extended the left one first at arm's length, flat and open. As the first stroke welted across his wrist and palm, he was unexpectedly beyond all caring, counting now with the slow, methodical fall and slap of the belt until at twelve there was a pause and he exchanged the left hand for the right, counting now to thirteen and then only the silence beginning almost as complete and instant as the last dull clap of the belt ceasing: *six and a quarter wasted that makes two bits a hit not so much for the sneaking off with Thomas to the Reservation or even the not letting anybody know so that they would naturally assume at Camp I'd come home with someone from Lacjardin after the evening service but because the fee was paid from Sunday through to Sunday and I got only three days' worth of it. So now at least it's paid for*

Lying that night in the sloping darkness beneath the roof and holding his hands outside the covers, he thought of Coming-day tied by his chest to the Sun Dance tree, sap dripping from his skewered breast and sunlight glinting from his suddenly inhuman eyes. Then, entering by day once more into the routine of hauling hay from roadside ditches and trucking wheat from fields squared neatly into geometric swaths, he was vexed by the steady succession of yellow noons. The sun seemed different now from the time when men had danced to it. Sitting at last in the shrinking desks of the September classroom, he longed merely to breathe Indian air again.

One January morning, the dream entered abruptly into his conscious field of vision. The news reached Lacjardin that five Indians had been found dead in a shack down in the furthest corner of the Reservation. He heard the story in Goodman's store before school. The coroner in Melfort said it was from wood alcohol. They'd run out of anything more to drink on Sunday. He didn't hear the names. He was desperately afraid. Not until noon, back in the store again from school, pacing on the sway-backed board floor where four close walls were racked above him with tinned vegetables and jams, fruits, meats, nuts, nails, boots, rifles, ammunition, cans of paint, hunting caps and coveralls, placards for fire and crop insurance, and a coal-burning booker held the middle of the room where several men sat on wooden benches, did he find out listening to the conversation. The dead persons were only names to him, faces maybe seen without noticing on the town's one street or faces looked long upon, though not known, at the Sun Dance. He was relieved, though he now felt grief and outrage even for all the people who had ever — would ever — feel that there was no more left than that.

While he loitered still as long as he could before it would be schooltime again, a man sitting by the stove spit on the floor, then rubbed it with his boot into the black, oily boards. "They'd drink gasoline if it didn't taste so bad," he said.

"How do you know it tastes so bad?" said one of the men. "It sounds like you been trying to cheat the Liquor Board some yourself."

The first man rubbed his hands on his knees, grinning. "You know I don't drink," he said. "It's against my religion."

"He jist siphons our gas while the rest of us sits there in church," a third man said.

All the men laughed. The first man spit again.

"At least I got sense enough yet on a Sunday to get my jug filled at Rosy Briarmash's," he said. "If them damn Indians sent a squaw over, Rosy would of filled her jug too."

"They're bush Crees though, ain't they?" said a sour-looking man. "Maybe wood alcohol is their — what do you say — their house special."

Even as he listened, he was suddenly beyond all talking, beyond all listening. The dream had entered his waking life. It rode now against the grain of everything he had ever learned among farmers, among white men. It went deeper even than the Sun Dance had gone to uproot him and, swept along as he now was by its restless motion, he could do little more through two years and more than to ride it out: staying every chance he got on weekends with Thomas in the four-room government-built house on the Reservation.

So it came to pass at last, on a Friday evening in February, that he proposed his wild scheme.

"I mean a real buffalo hunt," Joshua said. "Not just stalking a deer through the trees on foot. We've all done that. But I mean a *real* buffalo hunt."

Thomas' father woke up. He was sitting on a wooden bench with his back against the wall of his kitchen. He spit a wad of tobacco at the slop pail in the corner. It was undershot and scudded across the board floor.

"Ain't no buffalo *left*," he said. "All of 'em went back in a hole in d' groun', *wayskut,* long time ago. My fad-der he showed me d' hole. West of Battleford."

"Excep' north of P.A.," Thomas said. "Some dere in a pound. But how in hell do we get us way up dere?"

"Well, okay then, I don't mean a *real* buffalo hunt," Joshua said. "Next best thing, though. You know those purebred Hereford bulls the government left in the Community Pasture for the tribe?"

"One of 'em got ate las' winter," Thomas said. "You wasn' here dat weeken'. Walkin' Horse wen' t' town fer d' mail an' he come home fer everyone t' sign d' cheques first. We spen' all d' guvermint's money on whisky. We din' get no food, you know, and we was all so hungry drinkin' dat we had t' butcher one smaller bull an' split d' meat. Wid a axe. His balls was too big. But he was really, really good."

"Jesus! But you see? You say you butchered him. That's too much like what they do in the stockyards. I mean hunt them on horses that we steal, like your ancestors did in the old days. You see what I mean, eh? You see the difference."

A bedroom door opened and Lulu came out. She smiled at Joshua.

"My little brud-der he is gettin' t' be a brat. Jus' like his big brud-der. He says he won' go t' sleep widdout sayin' good night t' you."

Joshua got up. He could see the dark outline of Lulu's breasts beneath her flannel nightgown. He followed her into the bedroom. Her black hair covered the white flannel to her waist. The light from the gas lamp above the kitchen table cut a swath through the doorway and up across one of the beds.

"We're going on a buffalo hunt, Joey," he said.

"What's a bufflo?" the child asked, squinting in the light. Joshua laughed.

"It's something like a cow," he said.

"Someday I will come."

"Someday. When you are older. Goodnight, Joey. Maybe you can dream that you're along."

Lulu's hand brushed his as they recrossed the room. She closed the door softly behind them and they joined Thomas under the white-hot mantle of light above the wooden table.

"Yer crazy," Thomas said laughing. "We'd get a year in jail."

"Ain't nobody left got horses 'cept d' Cree," the old man said juggling his belly on his knees. "All you white folks has tractors an' tourist cars. Ain't no horses left 'cepting our own. An' nobody's gonna steal his own horses to hunt bull."

It seemed to Joshua that now it was already accomplished.

"You all know Snorri Steerson's place, don't you? He's got horses. Twelve of them. Two wagon teams of Clydesdales. He shows them every winter at the Royal in Toronto."

"Ain't nobody here ever hunted on a horse," said Mr. Single-tree.

"A man's got to start sometime," Joshua said.

At midnight a band of twelve men set out on the frozen lake. Beside Joshua and Thomas, Walking Horse and Joe Little-dog walked in the thick of the group. Coming-day led them. There was whisky passed back and forth by thick leather mitts and it warmed the winter in the flesh. The crust was thick on the snow and it was rare that a foot broke through. But the dry powder squeaked loudly in the cold. It vibrated the toe-bones and set one's teeth on edge. Almost at once they passed the buildings of the Bible Camp, winter silent. Joshua saw the whiteness of the tabernacle. They crunched on, along the drifted surface of the snow. The trees walled in the valley on each dark shore. Long, quavering howls of coyotes came to them at times, amplified by the cold air. Twice, they saw one loping around them by the shore. The moon was already behind them when they turned the V-plow corner in the lake. It stretched their shadows out before them, life-size on the snow. They heard a different howl beyond the bend. It came from the trees, deeper, more assured.

"Timber wolf," Coming-day grunted.

"What's he say?" a young man asked.

"He say we is havin' trouble before dis day is out," Coming-day replied.

They watched the trees more closely after that. When they could read the painted letters "Lacjardin" on the four grain eleva-tors at the head of the lake, they angled across the ice to the south shore. The snow was deep in the woods. At times they were up to their waists. It felt warm on the legs.

They came out of the trees at the top of the hill, their breathing making brief clouds in the air. A road stretched away before them to the east across the flat land. Where it crossed the railroad tracks

151

it intersected another road, running companionably with the railway out of the town. The twelve of them paused to survey the roads. Against the moon to the west of them a file of dark pines stood in the empty fields, lining the driveway to a farmyard. It was Snorri Steerson's place.

The fence was hard to cross in the deep snow. They waded down through the ditch and up onto the solid surface of the road where they followed it to the west. Their boots clicked on gravel in the hard-packed snow. At Snorri's place they turned into the driveway.

The bulk of the men lingered in the shadows of the pines while Joshua, Thomas, and Coming-day crept on their knees through the trees toward the darkened house. The snow squeaked at times beneath their pinching bones. It didn't matter; when they'd reached the wall and pressed cold ears flat against it, they could hear nothing inside, nothing save the sound of blood pumping past their own eardrums. Coming-day motioned the other men to follow. They walked upright then on the moonlight track through the barnyard. The wide door of the big red barn squealed a little on its rollers. There was thick frost on the metal track. It was warm inside the barn with the smell of horseflesh. They tramped up the concrete runway between the stalls. One docked tail cleared the furrow of a bulging rump as they passed and there was a plop-plopping in the gutter. Coming-day fumbled among harnesses on several posts.

"Got six bridles," he said, distributing them. "Find hay bales fer makin' d' rest."

Joshua and Thomas went out the back door into the haystack. From a half-dozen square bales they took the twine. The sweet, dusty smell of hay was in their nostrils as the bales fell apart. Somebody closed the front door from the inside as they came in again, shutting out the moonlight. They left the back door open.

"We gonna hunt us some hottawa buffalo," Thomas chuckled.

The Clydes were impeccably trained. Not one resisted as each was backed from its stall. There was only the heavy stamping on the straw and the white flash of fetlocks. The runway rang with the plodding hooves of horses as they led them out the back door. Joshua opened the gate at the far end of the stackyard. The barbed hoop hugging the gate post ripped his mitt a little, letting in a bite of cold air. Eleven horses were led past him, stamping in

the hay. Most of the men grinned. When the yard was emptied of
life, he looked at the slack wire lying on the snow, securely stapled
to recumbent posts. It seemed that the whole farm — yard, barn,
house, haystack, granaries, the land — all of it — would pour like
a sack of timothy husk-light when the ear-twine had been gutted
out through the opening.

In the open pasture they tried to mount. The Clydes stood
patiently, each bare back almost six feet from the ground. A man
they called Johnny Get-ahead leaped up from one side and fell off
the other, face first in the frost. He would let no one help him up.
He swore at Joe Little-dog who offered him one hand as a
mounting stirrup. He made it, at last, by hanging from the
animal's neck, his right foot kicking in the mane. The bridle reins
fell off the horse's neck when he crabbed onto the broad back and
he had to crawl out on the branching neck to reach them. The
horse lowered his head just as the man closed one hand on leather
and he tumbled, buttocks over biceps, forward. He landed on his
back. Nobody laughed. He got up slowly, saying things in Cree to
the horse. He lay the reins this time over the animal's neck in the
direction of his assault. His new attempt was successful. The
others followed his example, enjoying the benefit of his experience. At the end of two minutes, all were mounted save for one
older man. This one clung like a hornet's nest under the arch of his
horse's neck. His name was Young-Man-Afraid-of-his-Horse.

"Hey," said Coming-day, "You should ride 'im dat way."

Everyone laughed. Young-Man got down, smiled sheepishly.
No one offered him any help. He walked around behind the mare
and looked at its rump. He nodded and walked six paces farther
back. With his hands outstretched, he came, pumping like a gym-
nast. Just as his palms met the rump of the mare, the animal
stepped ahead and he slammed into her, a half-foot beneath his
attempted seat. The mare farted loudly. They all laughed again,
loudly, heedless even of waking Snorri.

"I think she likes you," said Walking Horse. "You better do it
again."

Joe Little-dog slipped off his horse convulsed with joy.

Walking Horse said, "Joe wan's to try her now. You be careful,
Young-Man. You might lose yer horse."

But Joe stepped to the head of his own mount.

"I am only neckin' a horse. Never go behind."

He laughed louder than the rest as he remounted. They rode off across the field, then, toward the road. The snow crunched crisply, punctured by the grey rock hooves. Young-Man followed behind, leading his mare. When they reached the fence by the ditch, he parked his mount close to the wire and using the two strands as steps, he clambered up. Some of the men dismounted and booted over enough posts so that a stretch of the fence went down. They crossed it, the horses stepping primly over the wire, and they doubled back on the trackless road. Once on the solid surface, the horses grouped with their accustomed partners in instinctive traces. It was as if they were strutting in the Winter Royal. The procession high-stepped past Snorri's place like it was a judges' stand, two by two in a duet of teams wagonless, the riders looming darkly on the backs of their gigantic mounts.

The moon had gone down when they plowed down their former path to the lake, the horses' bellies leaving dragonstrails twisting through the trees, but the stars flamed unwaning in the frozen heavens. Riding hard across the lake, even on a lumbering Clyde, it was the nearest Joshua had ever been to freedom. His steed strode the wind wheeling like a hawk on the wing and lower, as a skater whirling on the wind-blown ice. Off to his left Thomas thundered by howling like a blizzard. He was bouncing high at every step. All around in wide dashing circles the Crees rode yipping. Far in the distance under the perforated snowcrust the singing ice gave out the odd report under stress.

When at last the group rebanded, Joshua looked northward through the trees. He could see his family's house set whitely on the bluff.

His father's face went white when he found out about the missing trumpet. There was no whipping now, only sudden despair, his head turning away, then unspeaking sorrow.

I don't care, Joshua said to himself, I don't, I don't.

After a day or two, when it evidently could not be hid from Grandpa, Richard Cardiff said, How are you going to tell him? Aren't you afraid it might kill him? To give away his golden-throated horn, to deny the very son whose name you bear, what would make you do a thing like that? Have you thought of what you're going to say? I guess there's nothing left to say—he was right about those Indians. I should never have hired that pair, trying to save a bit of money. It's my fault too.

But Grandpa, not surprisingly, had something left to say. With his eyes burning on the scalp until Joshua's whole head felt like a light bulb burning out, Grandpa said to him, Let the day perish wherein you were born, and the night in which it was said, There is a man child conceived. Let that day be darkness; let not God regard it from above, neither let the light shine upon it.

And that was all. Grandpa addressed him after that only as he would a perfect stranger. He was welcomed in the family house no more.

I was damned anyway. He said so himself. So what does it matter. It doesn't bother me.

Grandpa went to the Reserve by himself to get the trumpet back. Joel told about it, since Grandpa gave it afterwards to him.

The chief had it right in his house, Joel said. It was in a cupboard. He knew Grandpa was coming for it, so he didn't bother to put it in the hole back of the house, not like the rest of the offerings. I'm really glad, Joel went on, that you gave it up; I can play it pretty good now. Grandpa says I'll play it in time like Uncle Josh. I'll bring all heaven down to earth when I can sound like him.

A feeling of terrifying emptiness crept into him when Joel said that. It was like reality had vanished, leaving in its fast-dissolving wake one thin beam of light which lit up for a moment the world he seemed condemned to move in, like a drive-in movie glimpsed only, always, through a fog.

The horses were standing quietly amidst a haze of steam into which Joshua stared silently. Joe Little-dog broke the circle of silence which seemed to have crept in on all of them.

"Why'n't we do somet'ing really big, now dat we stole horses?"

"What do you figger is really big?" asked Coming-day.

"Makin' a surprise attack on d' army," said Joe Little-dog.

"A surprise attack?" said Coming-day slowly. "Eleven red men an' a white man ridin' a hun'erd an' fifty miles over open prairie on dese stolen jackasses wid every Mountie in d' province lookin' fer us an' you call dat a surprise?"

"We could steal trucks t' drive d' horses to Dundurn," Joe Little-dog said hopefully.

A man called Many-birds spoke in Cree.

"What's he say?" said Joshua.

Thomas snorted.

"He says he would like us all t' ride out to Mikey Betrofsky's

155

place an' take his scalp. I t'ink he has hot underwear fer Mrs. Betrofsky."

"Don' wear any," muttered Many-birds.

"Mrs. Betrofsky would kill you herself, a nice Ukrainian lady like dat," one of them said.

"How you gonna get her up on a horse? She's bigger dan a buffalo."

"He could tie her up behind wid a rope."

"*Numuwatsh*. It would kill d' horse if he had t' drag her."

"Dere is a way. We hunt her instead of d' buffalo."

"Or let him ride *her* to hunt d' buffalo. Den we can have his horse."

"Fuckyerselves," said Many-birds.

"Goddamn it," said Joshua. "Don't let them ride you. You can't let little things bother you. We're goin' on a buffalo hunt."

"Bull," said Many-birds.

Almost untroubled they rode away. When they arrived at last at the end of the lake where the frozen Stoney River spilled under ice out of the blackened reeds and cattails toward the scrub land north of Birch Hills, they turned up the hill into the trees. When they came to the fence of the Reservation they had to kick that down too to get the horses across. They split up then to ride home for their rifles, agreeing to meet again at the place where the fence was down.

"Are you worried any more?" Joshua asked on the way to the house. They were walking now because of the sculpting cold, asked by it only that life should be arrested momentarily long enough to carve on it features more real than life itself immobilized forever caught in one transfigured act, leading the frosted horses.

"You mean about bein' caught," said Thomas, "No, I'm not. If you wen' wid me one time away from d' Bible Camp, in spite of d' preacher an' yer fad-der, alone among yer people t' go to a Sun Dance, an' alone agains' yer people, I t'ink now wid my people aroun' me, I got t' go wid you, no matter what yer doin'."

"Never mind about me," Joshua said quickly. "Worry about yourself. Because we might get caught, I'm not making any promises. The horses aren't the real problem anyway. I mean Snorri's a friend of my father's or at least my father does his income tax every year for nothing and he won't press any charges as long as his red-ribbon Clydesdales come back in one piece. But if the farmers around here ever find out who shot their cattle, there might be holy hell to pay."

"Dere ain't dat many dere now, anyways, in d' winter. Hell, if you'se worried about 'em, we don' have t' shoot 'em. We can always hunt our bulls in d' paddock. Dey din' cost us nothin'."

"That doesn't seem enough," Joshua said. "Now it's got to be all or nothing."

It was still dark when they took their rifles from the house washed by sleep, the boot-clinging snow still creaking even on the painted plank stairway to the basement. In the landing they divided a box of lead-tipped cartridges, the brass shells clicking one by one into their parka pockets. Then blowing on their hands they tied their rime-rimmed hoods again and, stocking the old Lee Enfields, went out into the cold where the horses were tied. Carrying the rifles they could only mount one at a time, one on the ground with the guns, the other swinging on the trapeze of the equine nape, then reversed, except that the rider now mounted held both the guns.

They were shortly met by the other horsemen, straggling one by one out of the woods to the place where the fence was down. Little was said this time in the hour so dark before the dawn. It seemed that now, set as comfortably as they could be against the moving cold on the backs of the horses, twelve reddened faces slicing through the windless air, they had to fight the muffling hand of sleep that would shut even the darkness out. It had not been so difficult, Joshua thought, for a mere boy of fifteen to travel all of one short night to the centre of the drumming sound it seemed had slept with him all his life and to give up his sleep for it during another day and even another night until at last on the third day he had drifted off blanketed in the enduring rhythm. But now in the algid pallor of this arctic night it would be so easy to slide deep within the warmth of an enshrouding sleepdrift. For a moment he even welcomed the idea; then he fought against it stiffly, his thighs heaving with his horse's withers. They set the horses to the south, recrossing the lake but well below their former crossing. On the farther slope up from the lake again they struggled on foot in the bottomless snow, both to rest the animals and to heat their blood.

They rode that way across the rolling fields, down for a time to stamp their contracting lives into fullest circulation, then up again to ride proudly as hunters ought. Their future lives were far behind them now. As the first brown light of the dawn contended feebly in the eastsoutheast with the darkness at the rim of the world, lighter shades were cast on the fields until with the blackness all transmuted into brownness, it seemed to Joshua that they were riding into a browned and even yellowing snapshot from his great-Grandma's album of the old days when the settlers first came into the north.

At last it was morning and the new day was old the ancient of days. Over a road they rode and meeting another fence they kicked that down too to cross. The old new world lay before them.

So it's little wonder she this land has turned cold unyearning inviolate though ravished any woman would who is plowed for profit and that coldly without love as each man has her impounding her womb with title to it section township range and meridian for his private access and emission so that this vital earthy female worthy of at least an equal partnership more than willing for a bride's rhythmic bed is forced to prostitute stripped without even any pay.

He looked at the band of Crees around him and he thought again *that new world in all its heart-aching wildness and freedom like a woman abandoned to the wild delights of love. So then it must be right, she wants us too. We've got to do it.*

He caught Thomas' eye brown grave and wistful like woodsmoke in October as they crossed the dead fence and he needn't even say it struggling with words, the despairing and imperfect bridges between man and man. And then he was wrong because Thomas, it seemed, had entered into his very mind, speaking too, and bridges could be built.

"Dat is why we won' never become farmers," he said. "Dey," and the *they* swept the horizon as far even as Nisooskan's elevators on the grey-brown ridge by the southern sky, "don' understan' dat."

They moved without motion across the land progressing progressionless, stretching over the white infinity as prayers told on a rosary. So they were surprised when dropping over a rise they saw the long row of white-faced Herefords nuzzling through the fence in the feed-boxes. The red-boxed feed trucks were disappearing in the distance towards the town, catching for a moment the glint of the rising sun, bright glare on metal like sputniks arching through the freezing waste of space. Nels Pedersen owned them and his two hired men drove them. But they were a concession (everyone knew it) on the part of the federal government, a subsidy in return for bull-feed and for allowing the Reservation stock the run of the pasture. It would not have been good, Joshua thought, if the trucks had been a little later this morning. Because Pedersen's men were Norwegians too. Every Norseman for three towns around had a big investment, emotional and probably otherwise, in Snorri's Clydesdales. He had done something for their sense of nationality in this land without fjords. No, Joshua thought, it would not be sociable for Crees to see the Norwegians today.

They crossed their last road, hoofs rattling on stones, and this time they did not have to boot a fence down. Wide-swinging timbers opened back from the approach road just beyond the feed-troughs and they rode in on the snowplowed trail, closing the gate firmly behind them. There was little need to bring passing farmers in for a ringside seat at the hunt just because of an open gate.

When they had walked by the white-faced steers all shoving their faces deeper and deeper into the troughs and sometimes butting an infringing head out of the way, they rode to the top of the first ridge all in a row and looked westward to the long narrow bull-run which ran the depth of the pasture. Coming-day called a council along the line then, a proud chief sitting tall on his horse in a pasture.

"Since we ain't here fer nothin' but t' hunt buffalo," he said, "we should find d' closes' t'ing. Not d' friendly-faced ones down dere dey won' do. It ain't a real test fer a brave man to hunt dem. So why don' we hunt d' bulls, as it has always bin fer men t' do?"

There was no dissenting voice, not even from Joshua who wanted to shoot the cattle of farmers as well.

"Walkin' Horse, tell us how you'd go about it if you were d' leader here," the chief commanded quietly.

"I am fer d' balled-ones too if dey will have me."

"Bull," said Many-birds. "You don' soun' enough like a god-damn heifer in heat."

"But there are only six of them," Joshua said at last.

"Why don' we drive some of dose feeders up t' d' bull-pen," Thomas said deferentially. "Dat way we'll at leas' have a herd."

He was near one end of the line and it was hard to hear every word he said, even in the crisp air.

159

"What's he say?" Coming-day asked.

Walking Horse told him. Coming-day thought for a moment. The railroad ties in his brow tightened a little.

"It is a good idea," he said at last. "Wid d' bulls bein' part of it, it is still a manly t'ing. Dey will lend to us deir manhood. Dey will share it wid us, our brud-ders."

So they did it that way, fanning out around the reluctant Herefords, shooing them away from the last mouthfuls of breakfast.

"Git on," said Joe Little-dog as he kicked a backward-turning steer on the nose. "You ate enough to die on."

The cattle bawled crossing the first gully as if they hoped their half-brothers, the big bulls, would come to relieve their harassment. When the drivers reached the fence of the run (no longer winding wire strung on flimsy pickets but solid poles browned in creosote post-hole augured into the earth and notched and nailed too, parallel with the ground) they herded the Herefords running slightly now along the railing to the south. Some of the horsemen galloped their mounts foam-flecked at the mouth and stepping heavily too out around the stream of cattle down to where a gate opened chute-ward from the run. The cattle swept into the opening, outflanked in every quarter. The bulls came waddling curiously from the clumps of willows on the western perimeter, their distended bags swinging freely just above their hocks. The Clydesdales scented them, lumbered sideways. Two or three rumbled a nervous whinny.

"Take 'em to d' north," Coming-day shouted.

They all circled wide to the south then and trotted up, waving their rifles and yipping, towards the cattle being sniffed at by the bulls. The cattle shuffled off slowly, bulls in the rear, bunching at first, the bulls' noses running high upthrust over the steers' flanks their eyes rolling.

"Rabbits screwin' run faster," Thomas yelled, grinning across the space between the horsemen. The smoke of his breath came in short signal puffs.

"These bulls got only steers for their last chance," Joshua yelled back. "You'd run slow too for that, wouldn't you?" There was some laughter among the men. "Watch careful though when they get going. Bulls don't run like no rabbits."

Rifle barrels that had been pointed at the frozen ground came up suddenly, glinting like unsheathed swords in the sunlight.

Stragglers in the row of horsemen moved abreast in a straight line behind the moving herd.

So he dreamed of what a hunt would accomplish. And he should have known but that he always awakened out of the no-logic non-temporal sequence of the dream and he could not reach its conclusion, even though he fell asleep again within seconds. Always it went back to the beginning. He would dream often in the nights to follow, though, of every movement every gesture making the turn by the fence at the road processional the horses swinging on an axis like the musical ride and the running herd galloping now sliding down the gully up again and galloping squat necks bobbing woodenly hinged with the buttocks and Joe Little-dog humping his spent horse to stay with the run and the first bawls of surprise and then communal terror as the pot-pot of the three-ought-threes ripped through hocks and leaping shoulders and Thomas to the left of him unable to get an angle on the churning red bull shooting at last up the alley beneath the lifted tail and the pink muscle contracting ingorging the bull stumbling nose digging a furrow the blood from the mouth staining the snow and sweeping by the kicking carcasses Coming-day Walking Horse even Young-Man making their advancing shots on all sides his own clip emptied at last through the throat of a steer and Thomas hard on the tail of the last bull shouting *Whoooee* his rifle kicking once twice the bull still running carrying lead now and then even the mile was spent the rail fence rushing up turning to the outside away from the wounded animal but the beast wheeling suddenly charging sidelong the tired Clydesdale snorting with fright rearing the look of amazement on Thomas' face sliding slowly off the long broad back rope halter torn from his hands and the curved horns catching his ribs in the air well above the ground rolling him on his face skidding slamming into the crosspieces at the corner of the fence and no sound even the bull burrowing burrowing as if to reach the centre of the earth and it took seven eight shots at his straining rear away from Thomas lying on his face to even draw him off squatting at last on crippled haunches blinking until someone blasted his eye out and he toppled dizzily like a redwood in slow motion falling down forever. Joshua ran across the snow to where Thomas lay arms outstretched as in a long dive one of his mitts lost and his bluing fingers clutching through the fence at the ice and it was too late he knew it without even turning him over not alone from the bore holes in his back where the horn had blunted through his body and blood now oozed with the woollen clots of parka stuffing but his head was crushed against the solid post.

In the two days it took to thaw the earth for the grave Lulu did not shed a tear. The old man was silent when the band of hunters brought the body home. He said nothing when the people of the Reservation came to sit with him in the kitchen. The women brought food. But he did not eat. He sat on the wooden bench, his back against the wall, in silence. He looked very tired. The flesh hung heavily from his face of bronze. In the basement on a bed of cushions the women bathed the body. Lulu helped them clothe her brother in his deerskin jacket with the bright beads of the soaring eagle. They bound him with leather thongs so his forehead touched the tips of his knees. There was no more blood there. The women sat with Thomas. Sometimes Joey sat with them, his head resting in his sister's lap.

Behind the house, a little way into the woods, the men built a small shed of logs. Inside it they put oil drums open at the top. Into the drums they shoved brushwood and then stove wood and set it afire. The smoke seeped through the chinks of the logs. The men stayed there feeding the fires. Coming-day looked very sad. Joshua foraged frantically in the woods for brushwood and brought it to him.

In the nights he sat by Lulu in the basement with the body of Thomas. It was quiet in the house save for the breathing of the sleeping women and the men at times who would chant in the kitchen overhead. They could see the dark form of the body huddled on the cushions in the darkness.

"He sleeps now," the girl said.

"Goddamn," Joshua said. "Goddamn, it's no use. It's all gone now. I've lost him for us."

"In d' night he sleeps," the young woman said quietly, beyond refutation, as though it were only by daylight that her brother would be dead.

On the second day the ground was thawed. Walking Horse and Joe Little-dog dragged the drums out. They burned the shed to the ground. While the embers were still glowing, Joshua took a spade and began to dig. He worked furiously, scooping the earth in a brown arcing blur. Once his shovel rang on the steel of another spade. He had not even seen Many-birds digging at the other end of the grave.

In the second night he fell asleep on the basement floor. Lulu covered him with a blanket. He dreamed of Thomas on a horse and of a bull. None of it had happened yet.

On the third day it was warm. A chinook had gusted in from the west in the night. They buried Thomas that day, lowering him hunched forward into the matrix of earth. His skin was very dark. They planted his head to the north where Touching Spirit dwelt who would direct the wandering soul in its long journey. Then they covered him with earth. The sun blazed on the snow and there were standing pools of water in the clearing behind the house.

In the late afternoon when the mourners had gone home and the plunging sun sent its last streaking flames to the east, Lulu took Joshua by the hand. She was wrapped in the heavy hide of an old buffalo robe. He allowed himself to be led into the woods again until they were near the mound of earth. She let go his hand and sat down on the ground beside the grave. She looked at him and her eyes were brown like a doe in a thicket. Then she opened the robe. She was naked save for her boots. He felt the blood rushing in his loins. She did not even beckon. She lay down and her eyes drew him with her.

"Not here," he said quietly.

"D' buffalo are dere," she said, touching the dark mound beneath her belly, her eyes not even flesh and blood now, and less like twin clots of mud than two empty holes.

For a moment he was terrified, his conscious part wheeling already, set on the instant to dash pell-mell out through the bush and away though his body stood rigid and frozen before her—and the horror swelling now in the roaring silence, soul, reason, mind, whatever, gathering in furious recoil, flinching not alone from the dread of putrefying flesh nor from the thought that even thinking would be inhaled at last like a bubble exploding inward, snapped through the pinhole of a vacant skull: but from the uncreate feeling that it was Death herself, the Gorgon, Medusa-face, on which he had looked (and for another moment he would think that he was merely mad)—until somehow he missed knowing that he was already kneeling above her, the lung-crushing heaviness still aching in his chest, and then he was upon her flesh of woman

163

clay-coloured by the brown mound of earth the brown buffalo robe drawn in silence over his arching back and he ceased to exist there was only the motion ceaseless enduring the rhythm older than life and the tight gripping bond of living man woman earth the trees overhead like cathedral spires and Thomas in the belly of earth.

In the night the wind blew in the trees and it began to sprinkle before dawn, the rain drops perforating the snowcrust with many pin-points. It rained all that morning, rutting the earth, as if in promise of the coming spring. In the afternoon the rain turned to snow.

3. Stubble Burning

There were five months left to run in his probation. They weighed heavily on him in the cab of the truck in the chaff-dry heat of late September, smelling the synthetic fabric of the seat which stuck to his back and the familiar odor of his sweat coalesced with harvest dust, as he waited for his father's wave from the combine coming up the field. He could see his father clearly now, magisterially riding on the platform, raised above and ahead of the trailing column of dust as though he flew in the funnel of the stubble-licking whirlwind, ingorging digesting and voiding the endless swath in a spout of dirty straw.

(Once more he saw the awesome figure of the black-robed magistrate high on the elevated stage of the town hall in Nisooskan, unattended by flag or ceremony with only the glass-covered portraits of the Queen and Duke behind him on the bare plank walls, speaking from on high as though he too rode the whirlwind. Rosy Briarmash whose farm in the swampland out east would hardly grow fireweed had stood with his chin upthrust toward the bench which towered over him. He had pled guilty to the charge of manufacturing homebrew but as for selling it, he said, he had never done that and he wasn't aware that the making of it was a crime. The whirlwind had touched down on him then.

"Not a crime!" the voice had thundered out of the vortex. "Twice you've been taken in possession of untaxed liquor and you knew that was a crime by the fines I laid on you at the time and this time Albert Goodson has gone blind on your brew and your very still has been rooted out by your own hogs. On at least two counts you are in violation of the Criminal Code and you have admitted to one of them so let me be the judge of crime here. Rosenthal Briarmash, in view of your past record and your incorrigible character, I deem it necessary to the public good to sentence you to two years and a day in the federal penitentiary at Prince Albert."

They had led Rosy then, manacled to two Mountie constables and swearing feelingly at the magistrate, out the front door of the hall. In the stillness which ensued he heard his own name rushing from the vortex of the wind and he rose to stand beneath the bench. On the floor beside him he listened to the drone of the indictment being read by the Mounted Police corporal and then the voice above him asking for the plea. He fought for a time to keep his voice from fluttering with his stomach. When he pled guilty too he was asked if he had anything to say before sentence should be passed and he was prepared for the question since Rosy Briarmash had been asked the same one but he had not been able even to speak at home in the face of his father's furious bafflement and he had little expectation of outfacing the eye of this onrushing gale. So he shook his head. Like Rosy, he had no lawyer either. His father said counsel was a waste of money where one knew one's guilt.

"Then let me be certain that I understand the facts," said the magistrate. "You are admitting in this courtroom as you have already done to the arresting officer that it was your plan and your leadership that brought about this waste. You admit that you led a raiding party on Snorri Steerson's Clydesdales and a hunting party against the stock in the community pasture in the a.m. hours of February second. You say that you alone destroyed property of farmers in this district. Then you hereby publicly acknowledge that you alone are responsible in this matter?"

"I did and I am," Joshua had replied and his voice had echoed above him more than he had wished.

"Yet you will offer no explanation for your conduct?"

He shook his head again, feeling so abjectly naked, the back of his scalp and ears standing out like stigmata. He was no longer even certain now he understood it himself. And he could feel the need for understanding in the watchful eyes behind him, as though a simple explanation would save the whole community from the need of introspection, as if the simple chain of words in the reason could be repeated in the curling rink and the Post Office until men were linked tightly together again, united and unassailable for the very reason that there was no unknown within the circle of their emptiness. So there was silence behind and before him, a world-waiting silence rushing all around him as he braced himself against the storm that would send him to the pen.

"I cannot take lightly the death of so many cattle," the magistrate said at last. "Nor can I be reconciled to the instigation of lawlessness among Reservation Indians. These are rather grave offenses. Yet in view of the convict's age and the fact that this is a first offense, I am disposed to leniency. I will therefore bind you, Joshua Cardiff, over to the recognizance of your father for a term of one year, you are not to leave the jurisdiction of this court, and I charge you to hold no intercourse with Cree or other Indians for the duration of this term. Not least, you must also make restitution to the owners of the cattle for losses which shall be arbitrated by the court. In addition, your conduct shall be subject to the hearing of this court in its regular circuit. Richard Cardiff, do you agree to set your signature to this indenture when it shall be drawn?"

His father, out of the midst of his embarrassed presence in the room, quietly agreed.

Grandpa said he wouldn't come if it was the Last Judgment Day.

But an Indian boy was killed, Dad, Richard Cardiff said. This time it's us who must shoulder the blame, and he's suffering enough because they were so close.)

The combine turned the corner perfectly, still picking up the swath, and the dust billowed up above the machine in the slight following wind. It had eaten only a few yards into the width of the field when the wave came, a flick of the upright wrist, brief, peremptory, as if to say "Don't save any gas getting here." He started the truck and moved out quickly, the stubble popping on the rubber of the tires. He was in third gear and trailing his own cloud of dust by the time he reached the advancing harvester. He swung out to the right then and turned and as he came up behind the flying chaff, he leaned across to tighten his passenger window. The whirling straw beat on metal and glass, he could feel the dust itching on his neck and in his nostrils and then he was by it, edging up beneath the spout until his face was even with his father's boot. He held it steady then in bull-low, dancing by the side of the shaking machine in a metallic pairing. His father's hand came down onto the auger lever and he heard the first splash of the spouting wheat from the long, uptilted cylinder. He tensed himself to keep the truck from jerking as the box received the seed. A dozen rods from the upcoming corner the hopper emptied, clang of turning screw, and the hand came down to jerk the lever up. His father's dust-blackened face leaned down then and made a drinking motion in concert with one hand. He nodded and swung the truck away from the course of the machine. He stopped at the corner and fumbled beneath the seat among grease-gun cartridges and wrenches for the sealer full of Kool-Aid. The ice-cubes rattled as he ran to intercept the combine.

"Take it over," his father shouted in his ear as he came up the three-rung ladder. He steered while his father's teeth gleamed through the glass jar.

"I'm going back to check for spillage," Richard Cardiff shouted again above the snarl of the motor. "Just hold it steady."

He swung down then and was gone behind the moving machine. Joshua lifted the pick-up over a stone that would have caught the table. He knew it was there because the stubble was much taller where the swather table had climbed above it. The immense tablecloth of sky above him was so blue and hollowing back that the eyes ached to look into it. It was a good day for combining. Within a mile or two in every forward direction he could see other combines at work, creeping like red and orange beetles on the tilted land. His father appeared on the ladder again. He held up a husked head of wheat.

"We're getting every kernel," he said. "There's none going over on the ground."

He took the wheel and Joshua started to get down.

"You haven't seen Whisky Hosea?" his father shouted, grinning. He shook his head, smiling for the first time.

"Be careful going by the house. He may be fixing to dynamite the bridge."

He was down in the stubble again.

"You don't want this?" his father yelled, holding up the jar of orange liquid.

He shook his head and then the dirty chaff washed over him.

(Whisky Hosea was a teetotaller. And whatever else he was, it could be said for certain that he was not first and foremost a farmer. For, although he lived on his one quarter of land to the north of them for more than a generation before they became his landed neighbours, he had never made any money from it. He

168

was a man of ideas. Some said before he left England as a young man, he had been a student at Cambridge. That was why, they said, he never looked or spoke to anyone when he went to town. It was not that he was haughty; it was just that he was thinking thoughts above the heads of simple farm folk. Be that as it may, he was the ready lord of hospitality to all comers happening to set foot in the thick gravel of his driveway. The visitor who showed signs of a listening ear was led into his study off the kitchen where leather armchairs and a wall of books kept company with the cream separator and a washstand. There he would talk of the military strategy of Napoleon and the factors contributing to the French Revolution. He was beside himself when a listener contributed to the discussion and traces of Received Standard English revived on his tongue in those moments. Stacks of *Life* magazine and *Time* and *Newsweek* covered tables in his living room and he always asked God, in his prayer at mealtime, to bless President Kennedy before he petitioned the same benefit for Prime Minister Diefenbaker, then Pearson. Four of his sons remained at home, waiting around the oval wooden table for the prayer to end. They were all of school age. Three older boys had gone to B.C., giving up not so much their title to a share in the garden patch of patrimony as the hope of ever making a living from it, and the eldest had been killed on D-Day on the beaches of France. His remaining boys now ran the farm, making what they could from one hundred ten acres of feed grain, forty acres of pasture, and two hundred odd cattle. Every dollar spent was entered in the embossed ledger sitting closed on the dining room table.

Hosea had been given the name Whisky by some men who lived out east in the swamplands because on Sunday afternoons he drove his youngest sons up and down the roads of the district gathering empty beer bottles. The boys never saw the money like other youngsters did. The cent per bottle bought groceries for a missionary aunt in the south of France. And the name "Whisky" became part of the man. It was generally held by those who had never set foot in his house to be community revenge on a man who remained aloof from the circle of humanity.

This supposed aloofness turned to isolation in the spring; Joshua's father had been a quite unwitting catalyst. When they came to do the seeding, they found Whisky Hosea and his boys hard at work rebuilding their boundary fence two rods over onto

Cardiff land. His father had asked old Whisky what he thought he was doing; he called him Whisky though he too had never tasted a drop in his life. Whisky said he was fencing in his land and kept right on about his business. Cardiff found out from one of the boys that apparently, the week before, Whisky had made his own survey chain on his new forge and, starting at the municipal road, he had brought it end over end down the dirt road by the side of his property. Three hundred twenty lengths of the chain brought him onto the Cardiff land. Richard Cardiff walked around then until Whisky Hosea would have to turn away to avoid him.

"Why," he asked, "in fourteen years of neighbouring, did you pick this year to check your boundaries? If there was any doubt in your mind, you ought to have had it resurveyed when I first bought the land. And why, now that I think of it, were you satisfied with the border when old Bill Falkner owned this land before me?"

Whisky said then he only thought of a resurvey last week but he was going to be fair about it and not charge anything for fourteen years' use of the strip. Cardiff pointed in vain across the road to the stone cairn in the grass which established the boundaries at their former junctures.

"How is it, then," he said, "that the farmers across the way still have the old survey lines written into their land?"

That was rather obvious, Whisky said. Joe Howard didn't know yet that the survey lines were wrong. But he would tell him. He stopped his boys from playing catch with Joshua — they were throwing a hammer back and forth for want of a better football — and he went back to the work of stretching the wire from the corner-post. Cardiff asked him at last where the measurement had started.

Whisky said, "From the verge of the ditch, of course."

"That's why you're on my land," Cardiff said. "The section line runs down the centre of the municipal road or any road for that matter. You should be well enough read to know that."

Whisky said his land title mentioned nothing about buying half the road, that he had paid for one hundred sixty acres thirty-six years ago when Cardiff was just a schoolchild, and at long last he was going to claim the whole of his purchase. Cardiff swore at him then and Whisky turned his back on him, bending to the fence again. It was the first time Joshua had ever heard his father swear. He grinned at the thought of it.

They had taken the truck to town then to see the new preacher. Mr. Davidson was a pleasant, florid man with thick shoulders and a bull neck. He had once been a gold-miner in Northern Ontario and he was now a little fat from want of exercise. He was already at work on the next week's sermon when they entered his study. He hated to see trouble among the brethren, he said. He quoted the line from First Corinthians which censured brother going to law with brother and that before unbelievers. He was glad Richard had come to him first. But he wondered if the problem was not a deeper one than a quarrel between two men. He had often worried whether there was not something wrong with their spiritual lives the way Hosea Ely and he raced each other out of the church every Sunday.

"Could I ask you, Richard," he said kindly, "how your personal relationship is with God? Do you have daily fellowship with Him?"

"Yes I do!" Cardiff said, a little fervent now.

"Well, I didn't mean to pry," the pastor said. "I only felt it my duty to say something because twice now in prayer meeting, your wife has asked us to pray for you that you might lead your family in morning devotions."

Joshua felt his father come close to swearing for the second time in his life and then he said he hadn't come to town to talk about religion, he had come about his land. When Mr. Davidson said nothing for a time, he added, "I was saved at my mother's knee when I was six years old and my soul's been secure ever since. But my land's not. What are you going to do about old Whisky?"

Mr. Davidson said rather wearily that Hosea was a reasonable man, if a little bit eccentric, and God would work through the well-springs of his conscience if nothing else would move him. He prayed then, generously and tenderly, that God would move in this matter to restore amity among His children. He did not ask Cardiff to pray with him.

They went ahead with the seeding, leaving an open strip by the fence. Every day for a week Richard Cardiff drove over to see if the fence was still there. At the end of a week he brought a deep-tillage cultivator and plowed it down. It took two days working in leather mitts with new posts and galvanized coils of wire to

171

rebuild it in its old position. The three rods of late wheat never did catch up. Hosea Ely did not speak a word in town that summer and the doors of his house were opened to no one.)

When Joshua reached the truck again, the combine had already turned the corner a mile away and would soon be coming up the field. He sat on the runningboard on the north side in the shade. He watched a few grasshoppers leaping in the towering stubble. It was even too hot for the crickets to be at their dry buzzing in the grass. Northward he saw the last hayrack of barley sheaves jouncing across the field behind the dwarfed Ford tractor. It pulled up behind the rack where the spike-pitcher was already having to throw the sheaves up into the threshing machine's jaws. The long spout blew the straw in a blurring arc onto the mounting stack beside the Ely barn. There were some who said old Whisky still used a threshing machine out of sheer cursedness, wanting to be further distinguished from other men. Others said it was an idea he had about resisting new technology and that was the reason he had been the last threshing outfit these last fifteen years. One man in the elevator office in Lacjardin had said quite bluntly that Whisky was just too short on funds to update his equipment. Yet here all the rest of them were still at work, Joshua thought, while Mr. Ely would be done with harvest in an hour or two and he needn't even bale the straw for his cattle. And there was something about the way his crew of boys all worked together that kept alive the spirit of an older time.

He got up on the fender to see how the combine was coming and he could see his father waving harshly, both arms crossing frenetically over his head. The self-propelled came on unerringly. So he drove quickly then and took the first half of the hopper on the move. His father's hand waved at his window in a braking motion and they came to a spasmodic halt, the combine starting briefly in a final drive-belt lunge. He scrambled with his scoop shovel up into the truck box and levelled the grain to the four corners. A red-backed ladybug was crawling at the base of the splashing stream of wheat. It would almost crawl free of the buffeting flood and then a sudden rush from the auger would bury it again. The aluminum scoop slicing through the kernels revealed it once more, the brown arms still climbing, kernel over kernel, to keep itself from being lost in all that crush of grain.

"Try to get back in time if you can," his father said, and the

172

otor throttled up again.

The loaded truck whined in bull-low, laboring in the soft dirt of
e field. Out on the dirt with the grass strip brushing like a scalp-
ck beneath the centre of the truck he got it into second, then into
ird gear. The plank bridge rattled as he crossed the creek near
ly's house and then he was turning westward towards home. The
ad was a straightaway, running over sloping hill and gully
rough the open land, the three miles home. He pushed it hard,
e footfeed floored, and the truck bounced springless on the gra-
lled road. He shifted coming over the railway crossing and
gan the mile-long climb up the gentle hill. At the brow of the
ll he met two figures walking on the road's shoulder. In that
eting instant rushing by he glimpsed the brown-skinned faces
oking straight ahead and walking, nameless, faceless even save
the light about the eyes, and the arms not swinging like it is the
rth in motion past them turning slowly and not their feet that
es the moving.

They are already to where they are going they have always been
re maybe and they always shall be it is in their eyes the world
ught into them by sight. Though now I sit in darkness, going
where, bringing death and misery, I, who am every dead thing.

Then they were gone and he was wheeling in the driveway
hing through the yard and backing into the auger by the gra-
ies and the auger engine backfired but still went right on run-
g with one spin of the rope. The empty screw clanged loudly
il he opened the slide at the back of the truck and the first nia-
a-rush of kernels silenced its clamoring maw. He tilted the box
raulically and watched the grain then and saw the ladybug,
protesting, ride the stream down into the hopper. It went right
struggling, its red back clambering to break away from the
ping maelstrom of wheat sucked into the auger but the tum-
g wall slid conically down and it was whisked away at last in
vanishing point at the bottom. His mother came running
ss the yard with a plastic bag and another sealer of Kool-Aid
e truck box settled noiselessly on the oil-pressured cylinder.
You'll be needing this one," she said handing him first the
er. "It's so awful hot. And I made some sandwiches to get you
ugh the afternoon."

I'm ready for supper already," he said, grinning weakly.

le was on the road again and the Indians were by the crossing

now, still walking like they hadn't moved. He passed the
headed east where they would be turning south, and he thought
Thomas walking with him in the woods and there was a rushi
feeling in his stomach, high under the point of his breastbone.
felt like he wished he could be dead so he could find out where
it was Thomas had gone. His foot grew impatient and the tru
rushed on over the land, nearing sixty now and leaving a torna
long column of dust above the road.

When he reached the field again the combine was waiting
the truck, unwilling to spill its seed on the ground. It squatted
the straw-littered field, swollen, gargantuan, sputtering v
impatience until the truck box came under its spout, and then
jerk of flesh on metal released its pent-up load.

As he waited for the second hopper-load to fill, he noticed
cattle feeding into the barley field freshly threshed by the F
They came in a long streaming line from the pasture along
creek, running now past the fenced-in haystack, out of the sh
cropped grass and dust into a promised land of barley leavi
From a distance they appeared like buffalo. He saw Tho
again lying beneath the fence.

Then his load was full and he was rushing over the land a
the dust curling up like smoke. When he turned the truck
into the field once more, the cattle were everywhere. T
tramped in the swaths still squaring round the field, they ra
the chewed-over stubble and they trampled the three rods o
wheat standing by the fence. The combine was immobile at th
end of the field and he could see his father running alon
swath. He drove to meet him. Richard Cardiff was in a rage.

"I've been waiting for something like this all summer long
shouted. "I knew Hosea Ely was biding his time all this wl
knew he would be up to something before the snow came
look at those cattle — what they're doing to my crop! Ohhh,
the gun was here, I wish I had a gun." He was howling
"Joshua, bring the gun. On your next load home bring the gu

"I'd go to jail," he said, "or have you forgot? I'd go to jail."

"Get Mom to bring it then. And bring some bullets."

The truck came to where the cattle were.

"Wouldn't it be faster to chase them off?" Joshua said.
can't combine over dead carcasses."

"Then bring the gun for old Whisky, I don't care — he

weigh as much as steers — but just make sure you bring the gun."

They were running now, outflanking the straying cattle and urning them back through the stretch of sagging fence. Some ran ar to the south and Cardiff chased them with the truck through he field, driving in a cloud of dust over his own swaths. Turning he truck sharply once, he bumped a steer on the hip. The steer ran rokenly. Joshua stayed behind to guard the gap until the gasping attle ran head-on at him, pursued by this ferocious honking dog. he truck stopped as the last steers poured back onto Ely land and en Cardiff was down and after them, reaching for clods of dirt fling at their flicking heels.

"Stay off my land," he yelled as though the steers could under- and. "Don't ever come back again, you hear?" He was running the barley stubble when he called back over one shoulder, Don't just stand there. Help me!"

Joshua caught up with him and they stampeded the trespassers rthward. The steers ran far ahead. There was no sign of move- ent around the Ely barn or the house. The threshing machine d been drawn up into the yard by the garage and stood silent w. They walked back through the thin stubble. They could feel e ball-bearing roll of the wheat in their boots.

"Whisky Hosea hasn't looked on the end of this day by a hind- ht," Cardiff muttered.

"You don't think he did this deliberately, do you?"

"You suppose a hundred head of cattle just happened into my eat field? They didn't plan it themselves, you know."

"But the fence wasn't cut. Just one post was butted over like an ery steer had done it."

"Then you tell me why they all were in my field."

"I can't say. Maybe they were hungry. You were here all the e. Did you see anybody down at this end?"

"What are you — a lawyer? It was deliberate. I tell you that. d Whisky has gone too far this time."

This spurning to offer proof persuaded him. Joshua pondered. Nothing should surprise him now.

The standing wheat was badly trampled. The empty truck d in the midst of it like a dusty hailstone remnant from the m. They took what tools they could find from the cab and king in the no-man's-land between the fields, they shored the ging wire. The space was thick with thistles nettling on their shins like the dry bite of cactus. Cardiff hammered as if he swung a mace. On the walk back to the truck he stepped unseeing into softness. He kicked the clinging mass wildly before him into the wind. Some of it blew back in his face. He didn't bother to wipe it from his cheeks. On the ride back to the combine he did not speak. His hands worked like a wringer. The air was angry with his presence. And then as load after heaping load poured like sunshine from his land to his bins, he seemed to forget. The smell dried on his boot.

All that afternoon the truck shuttled over the silent land. It grew late and on the way to the yard Joshua heard the wheels humming bits of a hymn. The gravel-crunch sang the refrain Work for the night is coming. The "coming" was long drawn out teetering on the verge of a precipice. Then he was swinging out of the yard again with the sun reddening behind him. The truck which bore him still was rushing, racing even to get into the shadow which fled before it.

In the evening, the headlights tunneled into the mouth of the blackness. The dim lamps of the combine winked in the flying dust as a miner's light wavering far away through a tunnel. The truck now seemed to race on iron rails beneath the bulk of star-strung roof. Then there was but one more hopper-load. He was on the road returning to the field when he saw the fire. It crept low along the dim horizon. When he turned down the dirt road and rumbled across the wooden bridge he could see the combine also on the road. All its running lights were on. The fire was behind and to its right. The flames were higher now.

He waited on the road at the field approach. The combine slowly drew up to him. The light beams bounced with the rocking table. He ran to meet it.

"What're you doing?" he shouted above the engine.

"Burning off my stubble," his father said, his lips shaping the words larger than shovels. "It was a good yield. I figger it went near forty bushels an acre."

They manoeuvered the machinery in the road so the truck could take the last dump. While the spout of wheat was falling through the arc of light and shadow, a wind sprang up in the south. It gusted over them, spattering the wheat against the wooden walls of the box. They watched as it licked at the fire and the red tongues shot out before the creeping face. New fi started in advance of the parent and came scudding down the field bellying like sails before the wind. Suddenly they could hear it, the voice of the fire, speaking with a host of roaring tongues. It was as if the world was set on fire and the firmament was rolled away in smoke. They stood together, the father and son, trembling on the road as the fire swept past them twenty feet away like a herd of bawling cattle. The heat scorched the dirt on their staring faces. Then it was gone, the wind harrying it like a wolf pack, and it leaped the fence like a stag.

Cardiff ran after it then in the blackened field rimmed with embers. Joshua followed him.

"Not so far," Cardiff was yelling, "not so far, Lord! I only meant to threaten him."

The fire ran on breathlessly until it leaped in the strawstack like a boy leaping from the barn loft. Then they could see the barn too, skeletoned in fire, before the wind died down.

Cardiff knelt on the smoking ground. His knees pressed a little shower of sparks up into the blackness.

"O help me, Lord!" he cried. "I've gone too far this time. O save me, Lord, for I am black with sin."

4. Migrating Moon

All day long above the half-built barn the ducks scudded downwind beneath a low ceiling of cloud. The wind blew so stiffly out of the northwest that, at times, the great V's sideslipped across the sky like winged half-moons. Their infrequent calls dropped down quick and wild, sometimes blown away before they were quite heard. Now and then a lone duck's wings would whistle overhead, the bird driving silent and intent to regain whatever flock that had gone on.

The air was damp and miserable. It seemed to crowd through clothing, seeking nothing but itself. Joshua wished, standing in the V of rafters to be nailed together, that the afternoon would end. For a time he had wished that he was using a hammer, not to warm himself (that was impossible) but simply to make a little noise that he could control. Then even that desire passed as the afternoon grew colder, though behind him the Ely boys still were sheeting in a wall of the barn, and his father continued to drive nail after nail beneath his vibrating fingers.

A car came up the gravel lane between the trees. It was Mr. Ely. He drove in to the red garage. Soon after, Joshua saw him walking on the dirt slope toward the house. He held some papers — they looked like envelopes — in one hand.

"There," Richard Cardiff said, "that's what I call a brace. Wild horses couldn't pull those rafters apart."

"Perhaps you were expecting some to run over this roof?" Joshua said. "Maybe we should warn Whisky to take out wild horse insurance."

"I wouldn't bother," Cardiff said. "Just look out for yourself. I expect a wild horse down from the house any minute now," He was putting his hammer into his carpenter's apron. "How many of these things have we got left to do?"

178

"Four," Joshua said. "I mean two ."

"Let's do them quick and maybe we can call it a day. Then this blame wind will have been good for something. I don't want even to think about swinging those rafters as long as it's blowing like this. A man would fly away up there like a flock of ducks."

"I think you'd be shot down quick enough," Joshua said. "You-know-who wouldn't let you fly off with his rafters."

They both laughed. Joshua picked up the second last pair of two-by-fours.

"The last pair look to be cut wrong," he said. "They angle the same way."

"Now how did we do that?" Cardiff said. "I suppose," and then in spite of the staccato hammering along the wall he spoke softly, "old Whisky will threaten to take us to court for that too."

Joshua fit the angled edges together on the sawhorses. He did not respond.

His father said, "Don't think I meant it that way. There won't be anyone going to court. Anyway, it's me, not you, who might be worried. If at all. Whisky can just as well try to prosecute the wind. All he can prove is that I was mad at him. But I'll admit that. And there's no evidence of negligence, much less of intent. He's getting what he wants right now: a new barn built for free. That's all there'll be to it, no matter what sort of show he makes."

They were sawing the extra two-by-four when Mr. Ely appeared beside them. He waited until the handsaw had completed its last gasp.

"You're wasting good timber there, aren't you?" His whole face seemed to follow his words.

"Nope," Cardiff said. "Not unless you're going to do without mangers."

Joshua brought the wide-spreading arms together on the top rafter cut. He could smell the sawdust, fresh and faintly yellow, like being in the woods in the fall.

"I spoke with the insurance adjustor," Mr. Ely said. The words carried a slight English accent. "I went to Nisooskan."

Cardiff was taking nails out of his apron. "Did you ask him for mileage?" he said.

"My policy didn't cover the strawstack you burnt down."

"I'm surprised it covered the barn," Cardiff said, winking at Joshua. "An old rat-bin like that, are they going to give you

179

enough to replace all the little fellows?"

"You're a blessed lucky man, Cardiff," Mr. Ely said. "First that the cattle weren't burnt with the barn, second that I updated its replacement value this spring. I've decided to drop my suit for it."

"I'm surprised," Cardiff said. "I thought for sure you'd want a spare barn around. One for rats you know—"

"I know there have been more rats," Mr. Ely said, "than I would like on this farm. They come in the oddest guises. What I'm hunting right now is a rat in a strawstack, a pack rat, I guess you would call it, that can pack the whole business over here. You're blessed lucky, Cardiff, that the insurance covered my new barn. It's paying for everything but that one strawstack."

"What about for labour?" Cardiff asked.

"There isn't any. You volunteered your services."

"My boy's working for nothing, though. You'd better count on paying him something, hadn't you?"

"He's working for you."

"I don't want anything," Joshua said.

"I want some straw," Mr. Ely said. "Plus the thirty-seven dollars for the premium."

"You volunteered to pay that thirty-seven dollars," Cardiff said. "Call it a blessed good thing that you did. Because now you're nothing out of pocket for a winterized barn, something your boys won't be freezing their fingers off in, milking those excuses you keep for cows. And if it's straw you need to pack them in, why, I've got a whole stack of bales you can have. They're worth a whole lot more than loose straw. Pick them up if you like. They're down the hill on my north quarter. You won't be able to get to them after the snow flies."

"You can unload them at the back of the barn," Mr. Ely said. "Just as soon as you finish it."

Cardiff rammed the nail down with three hammer blows.

When the last clap whipped away on the wind, Mr. Ely said, "When do you plan to move the fence line?"

"I'll take you to court," Cardiff said, "if you so much as look at it. And I'll ask for compensation for that new fence I put up. I can prove that you deliberately moved the old one. It didn't blow there."

"I'll add surveyor's charges, then, to what you'll have to pay in court costs."

"Before you do," Cardiff said, "go to the Municipality next time you're in Nisooskan. Find out what the law says about road allowances. You'll save yourself surveyor's *and* court costs."

Mr. Ely walked around the barn. When he came back, they had just finished the cross-brace. He stood there, watching, yet not watching them pack up the tools, laying the handsaw on its back teeth-up in the box, wedging in the square, wrapping the hammer in an apron, and all the while the hand going on his face, like it was milking his mouth and jaw. His fingers and wrist were long and slender, like a typist's or a violinist's hand. Finally, when they looked right at him, his face came at them again, his words riding up quick and hard like outriders.

"I'll let the fence stand where it is, but only if Bran sells me lumber at cost for a new paddock and a self-feeder. Then it won't cost you anything, you won't be out a cent. Though I don't know why you didn't arrange with him sooner to buy a sawmill; then I could have hired a decent carpenter and you might have stayed at home."

"That's a shame, all right, a crying shame," Cardiff said. "Even though I don't know what you're talking about."

"Indians," Mr. Ely said. "It's a wise son who knows his own father. They were all talking about it this noon in Nisooskan."

"Talking about what?" Cardiff said. "You come at things just like a woman, the wrong end about. What was everybody in Nisooskan talking about?"

The last two words sounded mock-English.

"Your father bought a sawmill, didn't you know, for the Reservation? The Indians were with him at the bank this morning to sign papers on the loan."

"You're joking," Cardiff said. "You should go on T.V. Your jokes are every bit as feeble."

"Ha," Mr. Ely said, "we'll see who's laughing if I take you to court."

"Let's go," Joshua said quickly, before any more could be said. "We've got to get over there."

The hammering on the barn wall paused and they could hear the quick, high whistle of wings borne on the wind.

"It won't do any good," his father said before they came to the corner which led southward to Grandpa's house. They were

181

driving in silence, the right front fender rattling over the wheel-ruts. "You'd do just as well to stay away from there."

Joshua glanced at his father's face looking straight above the steering wheel, and beyond his silhouette the fields passing, white stubble running into summerfallow, the only color now the railway red and orange of the elevators in Lacjardin rising out of the gentle valley.

"I've probably—" he said, and then started over. "I know I've made mistakes, some bad ones, and I'm sorry all the way round. I haven't wanted to hurt you, or Grandpa either. But I can't stand by and watch him hurt those Indians I've already hurt. Three wrongs don't make a right."

"Does a sawmill really seem that bad? Grandpa's just as liable to lose an arm and a leg as the Indians are. What we should find out is why, all of a sudden, he's willing to do so much as loan them the money. Business makes strange bedfellows, as the saying goes, but does he have to do business with them?"

"I don't think it's business," Joshua said. "I think he's after more than that."

His father slowed for the corner in silence. The grove of maples with the elms behind stood like castle turrets in the middleground.

"I suppose you're right. But if so, then what the — then what *is* he doing, tell me that?"

Uncle Glen was in the living room with Grandpa when they came. They were watching the World Series on T.V. Grandma had gone with Auntie Carolyn to Mission Circle. Grandpa leaned forward when they came in, his face readied with greeting, as if he had been waiting for someone. When he looked at Joshua, his eyes included even him for a moment, before absenting themselves. Richard and Joshua pulled up chairs from the folded dining room table, sat down alongside the chesterfield.

"Well, how do you like working for Whisky Hosea?" Uncle Glen said, grinning at Joshua. "Has he kept you warm with whisky, or just by breathing down your neck?"

Grandpa was looking straight ahead at the T.V. but his eyes weren't moving with the play.

"He's after us right now," Joshua's father said, "to get him lumber for next to nothing from the Cardiff sawmill. Dad, do you know what he's talking about?"

Grandpa's face held the same power it always had.

riding with him in the truck at combining time his voice soaring the moon through the sky and living together the World Series game, the trumpet lessons and Uncle Josh before Joshua fell asleep on the jacket which smelled like grass and ivory soap

Grandpa said, "What's the score? I must have been way off somewhere..."

"The Dodgers are still ahead," Uncle Glen said. "The Yankees have had it."

"The Dodgers don't have the Babe, though, they can never keep him down."

"The Yankees don't have him either, Dad," Uncle Glen said. "And I imagine they will keep him down. You know he's been working the graveyard shift quite a few seasons now."

The inning ended; a talking parrot came on the screen with razor blades.

"Grandpa," Joshua said, "don't you know how completely the Reserve will be ruined? If you cut down their timber, it will look just like here? And they won't farm it either, I know they won't. Thomas, before he died, told me they wouldn't. Ever. So I ask you not to punish them because of me. I'll go away if that's what you demand, but let them be, please don't take it out on them."

Grandpa's face was as dead as a block of wood, a wooden cigar-store Indian.

The parrot went away and the dwarfed figures of men on the grey diamond came back. The announcer was reviewing the batting order, then the color man was chatting brightly.

Uncle Glen looked sideways at Grandpa on the chesterfield, then back at the T.V. set.

"Why have you gone out to them after all these years, Dad?" Joshua's father said. "What was the point all this time of your 'Be ye separate'?"

After a time, Grandpa's mouth worked. But his eyes were like wooden nickels.

"I didn't go out there. They came here to me."

"Who came?" Joshua's father said. "And why would they? It was clear how you felt. That time I got Indians out to pick roots, they wouldn't even have come unless I told Quinn it was all right."

Grandpa was silent for awhile. He seemed to be watching the game.

183

"Dad?"

"It was Johnny Get-ahead," Grandpa said flatly. "A couple more of his friends."

"But why would you do business with them?" Joshua said sharply. "Why you?"

Grandpa's face was still like a stick. The crowd noise up over a hit carried the living room into the ballpark.

"They wanted to sell their trees," Grandpa said, after the runner stopped at second. "There's nothing wrong with that." His voice sounded like he wasn't in the room.

"But they'll ruin the Reserve," Joshua said again. "Even if guys like Johnny G. don't care at all. I'm amazed that Coming-day will go along with it."

Grandpa looked at him fleetingly.

"If your Christian principles really meant anything," Joshua went on, feeling like he was now on solid ground, "I don't see how you could help a people divided against themselves to head for wrack and ruin."

"I'm not," Grandpa said in the same far-away voice. "The band council voted for it. I'm only helping them out."

"Buy why should you care now? You didn't have anything to do with them all those years."

running there again and again though laying waste the bush they had once hunted in

"Maybe," Joshua said, "he wasn't so bad after all. Great-grandpa, I mean. At least if he was cutting down their bush, he was still consorting — wasn't that how you put it? — with them. We've got to give him full marks at least for his blissful familiarity."

Grandpa's eyes almost ignited for a second with an old flame.

"That's why I'm loaning them the money," he said brusquely. "To keep them there, so they won't go familiarizing everywhere. Haven't you seen how their kids for years have been leaving the Reserve? They want to put a stop to it too. If we just bring in a little income to hold them — before familiarity can breed more contempt . . ." His voice trailed off, tired, it seemed.

Joshua said it without thinking, "*You bastard. You bastard. At least if he was taking them to wrack and ruin, he was doing his best to go along with them.*"

Grandpa's face looked only at the T.V. set. It was grey as the

184

bark in winter.

"You better leave," he said flatly, though not so far-away now. "From someone who has no part left in this family, I don't need to hear anything like that. You'd better go. Just go on."

Uncle Glen looked hurt, embarrassed, kind, but seated where he belonged.

"I'm sorry," Joshua said. "I didn't mean to call you that."

Grandpa looked only at the T.V. set.

"You should never have called him that," his father said on the way home. His face was set in the moment of his flinch.

"I know," Joshua said. "Don't I know I shouldn't have? But he doesn't give a damn — I'm sorry. But he doesn't, not at all about them. Not one damn."

"He's helping them do what they want to do, isn't he?" His father looked at him, long- and heavy-faced.

"Sure, but for what reason?"

They rode in silence up the hill.

"I've got to go out there," Joshua said suddenly. "Do you mind?"

"You mean drive you? No, if that's what you think you've got to do. But what about your parole?"

"I'm going to ask to go to school or something in Saskatoon. Will you back me in that? Good, then I'd better go alone. I don't want you helping me to break parole. No one needs to know I've gone out there."

"Don't do anything foolish," his father said, before the car door closed. "I don't know what your mother and I would do if there was to be more trouble over them."

The road lay silent as a dead thing. Crusts of mud festered on its surface. Joshua walked through a hollow where a creek must long ago have run down to the lake. He couldn't see the lake now for the land rising on both sides of the draw, or for the trees ranked close along the slope of the north shore. The trees stuck up dark and barren as old bones uncovered from the dirt. The evening was coming on as surely as the ducks now settling in their flight for skim landings on the lake. The wind was dying away, though leaden-bellied clouds still dragged out of the west toward him. Most of the light came up from the stubble field on his right. Days of rain had washed it white and thin like rotting hair. Far out across it, he saw something move in brown bounds . . . deer

. . . toward a blackened grove. It seemed the only warm thing left on the face of the earth.

Rain was beginning to mist all around him when he heard the four-beat pant of a John Deere engine. He turned about. Row-crop wheels, pressed tight together on the front of the tractor, looked in the distance like landing gear. A wagon box swung from side to side on the greasy road. It was Ole Johanneson.

The driver throttled the tractor back as it came alongside of him.

"Want to ride?" the man said out of a tiny squirrel face.

The rain was falling more heavily.

"Okay," Joshua said. " 'Preciate it."

He came toward the hitch of the trailer.

"Hop in th' wag-on," the man said, his voice hopping along in rising inflections.

Joshua clambered up the wooden wall and over. Ole Johanneson pushed in the hand clutch lever and they jolted over the road. Joshua felt as if his ribs and teeth were shaking down through his legs. The wagon had iron-rimmed wooden wheels like Indian wagons.

Ole lived almost, though not quite, among the Indians. He came from Carnegie, a general store with a Post Office and gas pump, just beyond the western border of the Reservation. His house was a log shack set in a hollow some way down from the store, a hollow so abrupt that the shack lay like a tree trunk in the ditch below the road. He had never married; he lived out his nights alone (unless there had been an occasional squaw — no one ever said) in the one-room hut. He made his living cutting wood and hauling trailer after trailer of it to towns around.

Ole looked back over his shoulder and grinned. He looked forward just in time to swerve away from the shoulder of the road. The trailer zig-zagged. He put his feet up over the steering wheel and drove with his arms wrapped beneath his thighs. He looked round, had to swerve again. Ole unwrapped himself and stood up, and Joshua lost sight of him in a sudden gust of rain, then saw him briefly again. He seemed to slide in and out of the mist like a lost thing — like some Flying Dutchman (Norwegian, Swede, what did it matter?) of the continent.

They passed the turn-off to the Bible Camp and then the tall white house of the Indian Agent loomed ahead out of the wet and the cold. The house was dark as a granary. Quinn had died over the summer, died in his sleep of a heart attack. The coroner said he was pretty much boozed up. The house was empty now, though the school was still being used. A young girl just out of Normal School drove out everyday from Carnegie. She boarded with the people at the general store.

They passed between the thick gate posts of the Reservation fence.

Jericho, old Jerky-yo. He shut them up so maybe it would look like their own walls, nothing more, did them in, they just tumbled down on top of them.

He shouted to Ole as they slowed at the ford, water swirling away through the spokes of the wheels, and then he got down on the first rise of ground. Ole waved before the tractor ferried him off through the rain and the mist. Joshua walked beneath the dripping trees until he saw, amidst their bones, glimpses of light from Joe Little-dog's house. Then he ran.

When he came into the kitchen, Joe was sitting across from Walking Horse at a linoleum-top table. Empty beer bottles clustered between them. Coming-day sat off to one side on a chair by the window. He wasn't looking anywhere, his eyes just meeting and holding the gloom without. Joe Little-dog set down a half-drained bottle.

"Hey," he said, "if it isn't d' guy who tried t' kill us off."

"Joe, I won't argue with you," Joshua said. "Maybe you're even right, for all I know. I won't come here no more after this one time. But I have to say something first."

Walking Horse turned around.

"Scalp," he said. "Fer Chrissake. We was hopin' you might come. Dey said you'd have t' go t' jail. Hey Joe, get Scalp a beer."

Joe looked at the table-top.

"Lorna," Walking Horse said, "bring a beer from my case. Hey, it's real good t' see you Scalp. Dere's nobody here really figgered you'd make it."

"I had to come," Joshua said. "The minute I found out. What's the matter with Coming-day? Did you all let him down?"

Walking Horse looked at him swiftly, then down at the table.

"You din' really hear, den," he said.

"What didn't I hear? I'm not sure who all did it, but at least I know there's going to be a sawmill."

"*Uskatik* is dead," Walking Horse said. "He's takin' it so awful hard."

"For Chrissake," Joshua said softly. "I wasn't even aware . . . I was thinking . . . I'm awful sorry."

"It's not yer fault," Walking Horse said. "Maybe he'll talk t' you, now dat yer here. He ain't said a word t' nobody since she died day b'fore yesterday."

Joshua walked over toward the window. Coming-day didn't look at him. Joshua stood beside him for a time. Coming-day's eyes behind the lenses looked like wooden slugs. Joshua let his hand rest on Coming-day's shoulder. His face was carved and cracked like wood.

"I'm sorry," Joshua said quietly. "Even though I saw her only later, I could see she was a beautiful woman. She must have been a real good woman too — really really good like Thomas used to say — for you to care . . . ."

Lorna had appeared from another room. Joshua remembered her chasing the dogs from the tent. She brought a beer from the porch. It had the bright Sicks label with a picture on it of Indians looking across a river at a steam locomotive. A yellow bi-plane flew somewhere above the Indian tipis.

"Dis is my sister," Walking Horse said. "She's married t' ol' Joe here, but she ain't as sour as him."

Lorna smiled. She was almost as heavyset as Walking Horse.

"Hi Scalp," she said. "I seen you a few times."

"Hi Lorna," he said. "I didn't know you then, but at my first Sun Dance I seen you hit your husband on the shins with a kettle. You were goin' after some dogs."

"She was alluz after little dogs," Walking Horse said.

Joe drank from his bottle of beer. Joshua took the cap from his own and swallowed.

After a time he said, "I heard somethin' about Johnny Get-ahead and some other ones going to my Grandpa for a loan. Is it true that you all voted for the sawmill?"

Walking Horse didn't answer.

"Yuh," Joe Little-dog said. "Yer goddamn drinkin' our profits up."

"It ain't so, Joe," Walking Horse said. "We ain't even started it yet."

"How come?" Joshua said. "How come you would sell the last

thing you had that was really yours?"

" 'Cause it was d' las' t'ing we really had," Joe Little-dog said. "If you don't like it you c'n gimme d' rest of dat beer."

"At least what about Coming-day?" Joshua said to Walking Horse. "Has he said a word of how he feels about this?"

"No," Walking Horse said. "He ain't said a word since Tuesday. D' council voted We'nsday fer d' sawmill right after d' funeral. He wasn' dere is why. D' las' time, he put a stop t' it."

Joe Little-dog looked up at once from his bottle of beer.

"It wasn' our fault." He talked above Joshua's face toward some spot on the wall. "Dere wasn' a damn t'ing left t' do. All our kids was goin' t' Sas-katoon. Some wen' as far as Edmon-tun t' make some money. My daughters all took off one after d' other."

Walking Horse said, "Las' time Comin'-day got it stopped. But dis time he wasn' even dere."

"Last time," Joshua said. "So they've tried before."

Walking Horse didn't answer.

After a time Joshua said quietly, "Were you for it too, Walking Horse?"

"No. No, I wasn'." Walking Horse looked a long time at him.

"He din' have no kids t' lose," Joe Little-dog said. "Johnny Get-ahead got my vote 'cause we din' have nothin' lef' t' do."

"Walking Horse," Joshua said, "can it be stopped? Can we end it now? Because if we can't, you might as well get off this Reserve. There won't be nothing left. When all the trees are gone, what are you going to do then? You won't farm, will you? I couldn't imagine it. Then what'll be left but an empty plain, all your houses sitting in the open behind that damn fence? You won't have even shade, much less a place to hunt in or to make home-brew. There won't be an acre like it was when your fathers first came. There won't be a single hidden place. Don't you see? It's exactly what my Grandpa wants. Can't we put a stop to it yet?"

"Who knows?" Walking Horse said, looking down the neck of his beer. Then he looked steadily at Joshua. "Why don' you move out here? Comin'-day said once'r twice how he hoped you might. He never had no sons, you know. He had hoped a lot fer Thomas."

Joshua looked swiftly at the statue of the man by the window. Coming-day didn't even seem to be breathing.

"No," he said. "You don' unnerstand. I can't. Joe's right, it's all

189

been my fault, Thomas and all the loss of hope in him, and now my Grandpa's wanting to get even, something he didn't want to do even after his own father's death. Maybe I can't explain it to you, but I always tried to be one of you and it can't be done. Don't you see, I wasn't born Indian and my tryin' to be one is going to wreck everything. I got to get away from here before I kill us all. And if you don't stop that sawmill, you might as well all be coming with me."

"Does Lulu know," Walking Horse said, "what you jus' said."

"I'm going from here to tell her," Joshua said finally.

"I used t' know yer great-grandfad-der," said the voice from the window. It was firm and deep and filled the room. Joshua looked around. Coming-day was turned halfway in his chair, his shoulders wide and burly, his hand holding onto the post on the back of the chair. "I figgered it was him, he was d' reason I had t' leave here fer good."

Joshua sat up from his chair.

"We were almost afraid you were going to do it again," he said. Then, hearing the sound of his voice, kind of high and fluting, he wished he'd not had to speak. Only when his tongue began to say the words, some of that wanted utterance, did he feel less keenly how his voice was occupying the space between them. "I'm sorry, sorrier than I can say about *Uskatik,* Coming-day. I'll always remember her, the way she looked at me when we first met at the Sun Dance. I —" He wanted to say that he knew what it meant to care for her, he had been filled with the sense of it too, but he couldn't find the words in the face of that suddenly bared pain. "I'm really sorry, I —. I'm sorry about too much, it seems. About Thomas. About not coming out here sooner, jail be fucked. About my Grandpa and my going away just now. But goddamn it, don't you see how —"

Coming-day's eyes were welling, though his voice was full and steady. "Once," he said, "she loved anot'er guy b'sides me. I never tol' dat to anyone b'fore. But after it was over an' my fad-der was hung, I figgered I had t' git away. I wen' like yer gonna do and I tol' her, an' I wouldn' let nothin' she said hol' me back. I wen' t' Sas-katoon an' I worked dere in d' stockyards herdin' cattle t' d' slaughterhouse. Den I got a job inside rippin' out d' guts. I din' come back fer two years. You know why I finally come back?"

Joshua shook his head. He was shaking inside and he couldn't stop it.

"*Uskatik,*" Coming-day said, and he was silent. Joshua could hear Walking Horse breathe in quickly and Joe Little-dog pick up his beer bottle and chug on it. His legs were trembling now and they wouldn't stop.

"She come after me," he said, and he traced a finger down the leather front of his brow. "Dat's how I got dis mark. Because she couldn' find me, an' w'en 'er money run out an' she still couldn' look me up, she had t' take a job. I run into her b'fore she did me. I smashed t'rough a glass door in 'er place of biziness."

"You don't have to say the rest," Joshua said quietly. "I can guess."

" 'Course you can," Joe Little-dog said savagely. "She was in a hoo-er house. What ot'er line a work could she be in?'"

Coming-day was looking out the window again. Joshua felt like a leaf on a bough in the wind. Suddenly Coming-day stood up.

"C'mon wid me over to my place," he said.

Walking Horse was standing too.

"Jus' d' boy," Coming-day said in the voice which filled the room. "You bot' stay here."

Lorna appeared from the other room.

"Come back afterwards fer somet'ing to eat," she said. "You got to have somet'ing to eat. You too, Scalp, if you wan'."

Coming-day only nodded, didn't look back.

"Thank you for the beer," Joshua said to Walking Horse, including Joe too. The trembling would not stop.

Coming-day walked upright before him through the porch, down the steps. He turned into the woods. The drizzle was ended, and though it was cold, the air smelled rainy fresh. There was a break in the clouds to the west. The sun was still hid but there was a glare along the fringes of grey through the trees.

Coming-day did not look back. He walked remarkably swiftly for an old man. Joshua had to hurry to keep up. The unlimbering of his legs kept his knees from shaking so badly.

A house showed through the trees, a shack built of logs. Coming-day turned off the path before they got to it. He was making for the edge of the clearing. Joshua could make out a platform set high in the trees, a floor almost like a child's tree-house.

"C'mon up," Coming-day said, looking over his shoulder at

191

Joshua, and then he was pulling himself up by the first branch. The bark was black and slippery.

When the man had clambered onto the floor, Joshua swung his feet up into the tree. Coming-day was sitting cross-legged on the boards.

"Sit down here wid me," he said.

After a moment, Joshua sat down at the edge of the boards.

"Now," Coming-day said, "what made you t'ink you c'n really get away from here?"

"That's not what I'm looking for," Joshua said quickly. "Not anything like that at all." He searched then for words, spoke them haltingly. "It's—. It's so it will be like it was before, like it always was, before we ever came here, if only I go away. It's so you can keep this land as if we'd never been, or never will be, because I'm the one at fault, my family, we're evil, and if we can just take that away—"

Coming-day looked in surprise at him.

"You don' figger dis place here is d' happy huntin' grounds, or even dat it use' t' be, do you?"

Joshua didn't understand, though Coming-day's eyes were holding him accountable. He tried to say it again as before, only better this time, though even as he spoke, he saw that Coming-day wasn't listening any more. He stopped then, uncertainly silent.

Coming-day looked out over the tree-tops.

"Do you s'pose you can bring Thomas back by doin' dis?"

Joshua looked dumbly at him.

Coming-day said, "I figger all dat matters is what *can* be. But I know you can't be nothin' by runnin' away. You won' be away from even yerself. I know fer sure, 'cause I tried. So what're you gonna do w'en it catches up wid you? You tell me dat, eh? How're you ever gonna get away from dat buffalo you seen? Even my fad'der had t' take it wid him. You see w'at I'm gettin' at?"

The old man waited, turned toward him. His face would not go away. But the scar in that skin was as much as Joshua could see. After a time, he could feel the old man regather his thoughts.

"Don' you see, at leas', w'at I mean, about yer tryin' t' be like you was never here? How could you be any diff'rent dan yer grandfad'der? D' minute t'ings wen' bad, or somebody died, an' you pulled out, what would be d' diff'rence? I know you say it's gonna save us. But from what or who? Don' we all need savin'

192

from ourselves, not somet'ing outside? Isn' dat d' way it really is?"

Joshua looked directly into the strange old eyes, down into bottomless wells of sorrow.

"What else can I do?" he said. "I don't know any other way."

Coming-day didn't speak. From his windbreaker pocket, he took out a clasp-handled knife. It looked like a barber's razor.

"I'm old," he said. "Dere's a lot of t'ings I would like t' do over again. I made mistakes. One of 'em was a terr'ble one. I was a young fella, filled wid d' madness of young guys. I wish I hadn' done it. I don' wan' you t' make a mistake like dat one. I wan' you t' know, so you won' do somet'ing jus' as bad. So will you do somet'ing fer me, t' help me try an' make it up t' myself?"

The trees were beginning to spin.

"I don't see how, I can't—" *the great-grandfather*

"I thought it was him, but it wasn'," Coming-day said, taking no notice. He was unclasping the steel razor. "She wouldn' tell me who it was. Someone had been wid her. I run across him soon af- *Cf. 74* terwards shinin' up t' my mud'der. I was already so mad, I hightailed it fer my fad'der. We come back fast, him luggin' dat axe—"

d'father "Don't," Joshua said, "you've told enough."

A whistle, short high quick, of ducks' wings passed over them.

"It's okay," Coming-day said, "all I wan' you t' do is help me so I c'n make it up myself."

"No," Joshua said, all of it going now in wide, ever wider, circles. "I won't, I won't do it!"

"You know, since d' time I firs' seen you, you been holdin' back," Coming-day said. His eyes were deep, reflecting, as well water. "At d' Sun Dance, you gave up d' wrong t'ing, not yerself but a way you was s'posed t' behave, din' you? You hurt yer grandfad-der worse because of it."

"No," Joshua said, "that's—"

Coming-day seemed to look right inside him.

"I thought maybe because you was bald, it was harder, it would take you longer, but it was still a good sign, you was gonna give up yerself, be jus' like him. But instead I see you tryin' t' stay like yer grandfad-der, always fightin' t'ings off, tryin' t' keep a distance b'tween . I thought maybe if I could give you a chance t' do dis fer me, it would take away dose t'ings in d' way—"

"I won't do it, I tell you," Joshua said, "I won't!"

Coming-day's face was as steady as a tree trunk.

193

"Okay," he said softly. He raised the blade right behind his ear. It looked like a whittling knife against his thick neck.

"For God's sake don't!" Joshua cried, and then he was grabbing for the razor. Coming-day's left arm surprised him, caught him like a vise on the wrist. His hand drew with iron strength the fingers down onto his razor hand. Joshua could feel the veins standing out and beating strongly on the back of Coming-day's knife-hand.

"I'm an ol' man already," Coming-day said. "Dere's nothin' lef' here fer me. I don' wan't t' wait aroun' no more. You c'n be d'one one dat helps me t' fin' Touchin' Spirit."

"I can't," Joshua said. He could hear himself crying, "I don't want to take your life."

Coming-day's hands jerked abruptly on his and Joshua felt the knife slice deep across flesh.

"Den take it jus' as a loan," Coming-day was saying, "help yerself out as much as me."

His voice still filled the tree-top, although Joshua knew there was no hope for any of them now. Blood gushed, soaked over Joshua's arm. It felt so very hot in the cold.

Then Coming-day lay back on the boards and there was a howling sound going on away at the back of Joshua's head. The trembling was over now. His muscles were relaxed. There was only the steady, hideous howling.

"Come here," Coming-day said, his cheek resting on the boards. The blood was washing out in surges beneath his neck. His voice sounded hardly any smaller.

Joshua crawled over beside him. And then Coming-day told him something he had never wanted to hear.

The sun was just going down when he reached the ground. Everything was quiet on the platform overhead. There was only the sound, growing slower and thinner, of the drops drop-dropping in a pool on the leaves underneath the boards. The sun looked like a ball of blood between the trees. For an instant the poplars seemed to take fire in their tops before the ball oozed completely from sight.

It was full dark, but the moon shone yet on Lulu's face.

"I felt so bad w'en I heard dat she was dead," she said. "An' now he's gone so quick right after her. He jus' didn' wan' t' live any longer, I guess. He really loved her. He was a good man. I'm glad at leas' dey brought you back t' me."

Joshua didn't answer. The howling had finally died away; there was only the creeping worry, clear as moonlight, of whether he would be discovered. He looked long at Lulu's face turned pocked and leprous in the moonlight. And then she surprised him, shocked him really. In the frosty air she raised her dress with one tug over her head. Her body glistened in the silence like a yellow birch.

"Come close t' me," she said.

"No," he said at once, "it's no good. Not at a time like this."

"Come on," she said. "Hold me close."

"No," he said. "It didn't do any good before. It can't undo what's already been done."

"What?" she said, frozen in the first instant of unbelief, and then she was turned around, pulling on the dress again. When she had slipped it over her hips she said, "Fuck yerself den. See if dat does any good."

"I'm leaving, Lulu," he said brusquely, trying to shut off the ache that was opening out.

the bundle lying in perfect quiet on the shelf among the trees and Walking Horse, after some time saying, I guess d' only way now is t' clear out fer awhile. Don' worry none. I'll say it was me dat was wid him up dere.

"I'm going away to Saskatoon for awhile. I can't stay here, Lulu, you don't know."

He could see the ducks now in the pre-dawn moonlight of the western sky.

"You bastard," she said. "I see yer no diff'rent dan any other man. Bugger off den. See how far you get. T'ink even you can stay away. But you'll come back yet to dis lake." She let out all her breath in a burst, was quiet for a time, then said absently, "Fer Chrissake. Well fer Chrissake."

He didn't speak again, watching the long, waving line of birds against the moon.

5. Trees

He came into consciousness slowly, climbing back up from some-where deep, and then he just lay there sweating in the semi-dark-ness, listening to her steady breathing beside him. There had been a dream *running* or something, but he couldn't make it out any better than he could those shapes of cardboard boxes old mat-tresses and things cluttered about in the basement. Those he had seen in the light, knew them for what they were, so no glimmer of doubt came off them as they huddled in obscurity. Well then, okay, leave it alone. Remember it maybe in daylight. Though he never did. He remembered only, always now, the clench of fear upon awakening. Funny, the closest thing to it, he suddenly recalled, was just last night before they fell asleep, when he got up to go outside for a leak. For a second there, he thought it was maybe because he hadn't slept in the basement since Thomas died. But it had started, really, on the stairs. As he climbed them he seemed to meet a face which loomed up into his very mounting. He couldn't make out any features at all, it was just there, and it produced the kind of effect he imagined jumping into ice water might. Then when he reached the landing, opened the door, turned the corner of the house, each time it was like something — no, someone, Thomas, Coming-day, his Grandpa (that was strange) — was waiting for him in the shadows, just standing there waiting to look at him. Look into him — maybe that was it. Though nothing more. It was all right again, going downstairs. He slipped into the sack beside Lulu, it was warm and drowsy and dark, she lay one sleepy hand up against his belly, and then he was going gone, down and away.

There had been something like it, vaguely similar, so very long ago. Though where? Grandpa's house. Of course. The winter Grandpa and Grandma had gone to Florida and Janie was just a baby. They spent November through to March in the empty house, keeping both it and the baby warm. That was shortly before the new house on the hill was built, while they lived summers yet in the shack at the bottom. Everything was glorious that winter — imagine, living right in Grandpa's house, eating every day at his table, sleeping in the bed his dad and uncles slept in as boys — no, that wasn't so glorious, everything but the falling asleep, that part was a nightmare. His parents were downstairs there in the bedroom off the kitchen — Grandpa and Grandma's room — with Janie alongside in the crib. But he had to spend the night alone, mustering every ounce of his five-year-old courage, just to lie in the west room upstairs. Though it was all right when the wind was blowing, he could fall asleep then. The wind charger hummed and whirled outside his window, turning and turning above the snow drifts creeping out from the trees, and it kept away the thing in the darkness — the presence which (he could feel it) was driven farther and farther back into the recess of the closet running along the eaves towards the bathroom. Grandpa had erected the wind charger. It was bright and friendly, like the light it could make even from the black, huge batteries down cellar. But when it was still, the thing in the closet crept to the little door (just his own height) in the wall and opened it up a crack to look. He would lie rigid with terror under the covers, his heart going colder than the frost on the nailheads overhead, though not wanting to cry out, and then it would float out through the darkness to hover bodiless above him, and he couldn't help himself any more, he would be yelling, hearing it from far away then suddenly up close as he went under the covers, until the light out in the stairway would snap on, steps starting on the stairs, and then his mother or father would come into the room, his mother saying even before she got there, "There, there, Joshua, everything will be all right," though his father when he came would just be clearing his throat. But either way it did the trick, the thing would have to clear out. His mother or his father would lie with him then and before he knew it he would be gone, awakening to sunlight and the cold biting his nose, otherwise toasty and nice beneath the covers.

Funny how he hadn't thought of that in years. Probably because you were taught to be a man and not to be ascaired — the word they used for sissies? — of the dark, nosiree noway. Though even then, it had just been while he was falling asleep. Could that be why they called it falling, perhaps? Only now, as a man, it was reversed, it happened mostly as he came awake. It couldn't be falling exactly.

running among the trees

Almost. Then gone, not a trace of it. Could there be anything to it, then? Now that it was the other way about? Though why should it make a difference? Older, perhaps. Sure, and still with the fears of a kid. Grow up, Joshua, think like the man you'll have to be, taking on a wife and all now, who knows, with maybe a kid already, it's getting late enough.

And there was jesusly lots to do yet. Even if they were getting married in the Melfort courthouse. He would have to be certain his father and mother weren't badly hurt, at least not vitally. Grandpa.

running toward the sun-dazzling

There it came again. Gone as fast. With just a touch of terror, nothing unmanageable in it. Because of Grandpa? He would have to go out there today as well, should let him know right off — try to make things up if he could. No better time than the present. He hoped it wouldn't be a bad scene . . . Awful, how you began to think even in their language, the cliches they all used up on the Avenue A campus, once you realized you had to counter the others — the heavy, dull, lifeless ones — that the people teaching you how to teach were always using. For instance: self-identification of the child with a given educational experience; or socialized discussion procedure, there was a good one; or the phenomenon of association; or normal probability curves: what the hell could any of them matter? It was crap, all crap, it never ever lived and breathed.

Lulu, he realized of a sudden, was watching, had been watching him. He could see her in the dim light, even before he turned, slightly raised on one arm, one breast free of the covers, just looking and looking at him.

"Hey," he said, "what d' you think yer doin'?"

"Keepin'," her voice was throaty with sleep, "one eye on what I brung home."

"Balls you did, so you really think so, eh?"

She caught him by surprise.

"Ho! don't you know you're not supposed to drag a man around that way? Go easier, woman."

She rested her head on his shoulder, still owning it.

"Why?" she said. "It works every time fer me."

"Whoo, it might not work at all, not after that sort of treatment "

"You smell like a fuck," she said after a time. "Why don' you do somet'ing wid dose pits so you won' give a girl dat sorta treatmen'?" She didn't make any move to pull away.

He turned fully toward her.

"How would you like to show me your normal probability curves?" he said. "Or would you rather start right in on the phenomenon of association?"

Both her hands ran lightly, lightly, over his scalp.

Just as they were ready, she said, "How'd you like t' go doggin'? I feel anyways like a real bitch t'day."

"You won't miss a teeny weeny thing?" he said, not able to hold back the laughter.

"Hell no, all I can t'ink is down deep. I wan' you t' be t'inkin' deep too, Josh, real deep."

They knelt on the bed like at a prayer meeting, single-file. She was warm and so damn good. As they worked and worked together, oh so slow now, so gently, holding her rib cage so completely vulnerable in his two hands, he was astounded to feel the face loom up at him out of the middle of her bent, working back. It was just there, the face really faceless, then quickening at last triggering his rush and it seemed to go out on the flood with him. Still he could feel her tremoring about him, and as he came back back he could hear her yet from far away going and going in broken cries that she held just enough for they two alone to hear.

Afterwards she lay on his shoulder once more.

"I wan' yer baby," she said. "Christ, I wan' it, Josh, I wan' it so bad."

He held her; they held together.

Just before they moved to get up, she said, "You won' change yer mind, once you get out dere? Yer grandpa won' keep you from comin' back?"

running toward a wood which seemed lit from within

"Not if it means hellfire," he said steadily. He was looking right at her, at that face which he had not really wanted to love.

" 'Cause I sure know what dey'll say. I'm jus' Ind-yun. Dey might make it so you won' want me at all."

199

"I will," he said, trying to sound cheerfully confident. "You don't have a thing to worry about."

Janie said, "I heard of white guys at school before, going out with squaws. But none of them ever married one."

His mother was punching down the risen bread for the last time into the pans. Tears were slopping off her hands onto the speckled brown dough.

"I really didn't want you to take it like this, Mom," Joshua said.

"I always hoped," her voice was jerking inward at each syllable, "that you would marry a Christian girl." Her hands were shaping blindly the loaves.

running toward the brightness beginning to sense now something else among the spines of trees

The loaves were placed in the big black oven, into the darkness where they would be changed, as it were, in the twinkling of an eye. That wasn't true; the electric stove had a glass window in the door. He was thinking of the old wood-burning range, the one he used to burrow behind when he was small. It was safe back there, cozy and warm from the cold, and hidden from those eyes which trailed him even from school.

"I guess if you love someone," he said — the confession still embarrassing him a little, it was so new it left him vulnerable too — "you've got to take her the way she is."

His mother nodded dumbly, reaching the pans into the heated oven.

The way she was taking it pained him badly, but he knew she would change, she knew she would have to.

"I'm sorry, Mom," he said. "I never wanted to hurt you. It'll be all right." He wanted to say "There there" as if the saying of it could make it all right.

"What I want to know," his father said, "is how you're going to live. Have you even thought of that? Or are you going to end up on social aid like the rest of them?"

"Couldn't you have faith at least in your own example, Dad?" Then he stopped, ashamed. "I didn't mean to be so un-generous. I really do feel you taught me something. A lot, in fact. We'll make out okay because of you."

His father looked at him openly, though still asking.

"You even made a teacher out of me — I don't know — where

200

they couldn't at Normal School."

"Do you mean to say you are going to teach? It sounds to me like you wasted a year, year and a half, in that Normal School."

"No, I do have a job coming out of it, if I want it. It's teaching school out on the Reserve. The poor girl at Carnegie has had it; she's through after two years. I hear she's quitting the profession, going into nursing or something. I guess nobody could have prepared her to make those kids want to learn out of books. Nor me either, if I'm going to be fair. I just happen to want to be there, is all."

His father's Adam's apple swelled up. "Then I'll say something else you might not like. This girl — ah, you say you love — if you marry her, aren't you going to live just like the Indians? I want to know, then, how you're going to make a better go of it than they have, how you won't be just escaping into the same poverty and viciousness they live in. I want to be sure that my grandchildren, your mother's grandchildren, aren't left to burn up in a shack, that our son won't be stabbed in a drunken fight, or God knows whatever else still goes on out there."

"Well, for a start, the DNR has said we can live in Quinn's house. And I'm going to be trying to teach their kids, things that might help them. I don't know, it seems —"

"Did anyone tell you, though, that that can't last very long? There's talk the Indians are going to be bused to Nisooskan."

"I've heard that, for sure. But I've got my application in already to Nisooskan. Chances will be good when I've taught those kids already. Even with just the one year's training. It'll mean going back for years, I guess, to Summer School. But we can afford it if I drive the school bus. I might as well, since I'll be going in every day. We'll be all right, just as long as Grandpa doesn't put his monkey wrench into the business of the School Unit."

"I think he's letting go," his father said.

"That's a relief," he said, though a little more uncertain now, not really sure why. "I don't know how he'll feel about me showing Walking Horse how to tractor a little. There's a bunch of them figure they can make enough from grain to keep the sawmill away from every last stand of timber."

"Well," his father said, looking him up and down carefully, but mostly like his equal, "it seems like you've thought of just about everything. I guess you've even got my blessing, Joshua. Try not to abuse it, eh?"

"I'm really grateful," he said, smiling for the first time. "That means a lot to me. I just wish I had Grandpa's now to go along with it."

"Isn't that asking for everything?" his father said quietly. "There are some things you probably will have to lose. You might as well start accepting that."

running into the reddened sun and starting to notice squinting against the light's winking the face among the columns of bark

There was that sudden touch, thrill, of fear again.

"I still need to go over there," he said. "I'd prefer, if I could, to face him myself."

" 'How have I hated instruction'," Grandpa's voice was saying, " 'and my heart despised reproof, and have not obeyed the voice of my teachers, nor inclined mine ear to them that instructed me'."

It went on and on, as steady as the sound of the milk sawing into the pail, but also inappreciable, like the sound of frogs going in the creek.

" 'For the lips of a strange woman drop as an honeycomb, and her mouth is smoother than oil: but her end is bitter as wormwood, sharp as a twoedged sword. Her feet go down to death, her steps take hold on hell'."

How long have I yearned for thee, how often I have longed just to come home. The Lord judge between me and thee, and the Lord avenge me of thee: but mine hand shall not be upon thee.

There was nothing he could do or say but to hear it out.

" 'Lest thou shouldest ponder the path of life, her ways are moveable, that thou canst not know them. Hear me now therefore, O ye children, and depart not from the words of my mouth'."

The pity of it was that Grandpa sounded so tired, like it or nothing mattered any more.

"Grandpa, you don't really believe it, do you?" Joshua said softly. "You don't think she's any worse or better than her grandmother before her, or even her grandmother's sister who married Coming-day?"

Something stirred in Grandpa's eyes.

"You don't know," he said, the sorrow welling up in his voice, but his face giving no sign any more of holding it back. "There's something you've got to hear me say, there's something horrible nobody knows —"

"I already know it," Joshua said in a voice quite as still as the air before the thunderstorm closes over.

Grandpa looked sharply at him.

"I killed Coming-day," Joshua could hear himself telling it. "He forced me to take his life. A loan, he called it. It was so horrible to me. But it's all right now."

running coming very near at last being nearly able to make out that face of old

Something in Grandpa's eyes broke. He looked into his pail.

"It's the silence has been so horrible," he said. "So horrible, horrible."

"It's all right, Grandpa. We've been forgiven, haven't we? Don't you believe he meant something of that?"

Grandpa's eyes were reaching out now to him.

Joshua said, "Will you forgive me for the trumpet? Can you believe I know how wrong I was?"

Grandpa was nodding, though his lids were covering his eyes.

"I gave up you, my family, my heritage," Joshua said. "But not myself."

"Yes," Grandpa said. "You're more of a man this minute than I was all those years."

"Don't, Grandpa. Don't think of it that way, I'm no better, no worse, than you or anyone. I tried to run away for so long, I was always running. I'm just not going to any more."

He was absolutely certain it was true, though now he couldn't stop the other from coming.

the face floating out to meet him coming through the trees so dark there in front but flaming behind

Milking was finished. Grandpa undid the chain on the cow's neck, turned her out through the back of the barn. Coming back for the milk pail, though, he surprised him.

"I still can't help myself, my very soul revolts at your going to live like them. Couldn't you just go there, Joshua, as your uncle would have done, had I only let him?"

"I thought—" he said. "What I always wanted was your soul's blessing."

He was trying to see Grandpa's face, but that other one was beginning now to blot it out.

"I can't," Grandpa said. "Even if I can't stop myself from loving you again, I can't condone it, I'm just not able."

He could just see Grandpa's eyes. They were not looking into his own, but wandering all over his scalp.

Grandpa said, "It's not my blessing, anyway, that you want."

They turned the corner of the barn, stepping into the warm red light. The sun was just going down behind the grove of maples. They walked together on the path back toward the house.

running now on the needled floor of the forest covering the ground although the place stays yet with him her dim shape just before him the shadows advancing and his feet drumming drumming down through loam down into clay his headway mattering no longer and then only his heart beating wildly as the bark creeps up his ribs

foon 127 - 131, 143
Groot 163-64

Munro 15-16

Chapt. 2 - 145

Owes a bit to D. Thomas 25

Drums 32

Example of flashback 42-45 The Burning Wood

Owes a bit to Twain & ~~Huck F.~~ 50, 91, 92, 155

Given his Indian name 64

Grandfather on his father & Indians 72

Thomas Singletree & "I know your real name" 82-3
                                                    85

On his coldness 106 to Leah

Thomas & Joshua on the Northern Lights 121

Joshua's "heart's ease" 124

Coming-day and the Sun dance 139, 142

Owes a bit to Hopkins? 154

Preparing Thomas' body for burial 162

Lulu and Joshua at Thomas' grave 163-64